HARLOT

Tracie Podger

Vicky

Look after
Charlotte

Tracie x

Cover designed by Margreet Asslebergs
Rebel Edit & Design
Formatting by Irish Ink — Formatting & Graphics

ACKNOWLEDGEMENTS

My heartfelt thanks to the best beta readers a girl could want, Karen Shenton. Alison Parkins, and Joanne Thompson - your input is invaluable.

Thank you to Margreet Asslebergs from Rebel Edit & Design for yet another wonderful cover. I've lost count how many covers we've done together.

I'd also like to give a huge thank you to my editor, Karen Hrdlicka, and proofreader, Joanne Thompson.

A big hug goes to the ladies in my team. These ladies give up their time to support and promote my books. Alison 'Awesome' Parkins, Karen Shenton, Karen Atkinson-Lingham, Marina Marinova, Ann Batty, Fran Brisland, Elaine Turner, Kerry-Ann Bell and Louise White – otherwise known as the Twisted Angels.

To all the wonderful bloggers that have been involved in promoting my books and joining tours, thank you and I appreciate your support. There are too many to name individually – you know who you are.

If you wish to keep up to date with information on this series and future releases - and have the chance to enter monthly competitions, feel free to sign up for my newsletter. You can find the details on my web site:

www.TraciePodger.com

CHAPTER 1

I couldn't breathe. I knew my mouth was open, I felt my heart beating, but for some reason, I couldn't get my lungs to function and take in the breath of air I needed. Maybe it was a good thing. Had I taken in that lungful of air, I'm sure it would have been exhaled as a scream.

I looked around the bedroom. Blood splattered up the wall in an arc, in another world it could have been mistaken for a piece of abstract art. I didn't want to look at him sitting naked. A hole, a bloody, dark red hole, had appeared in the center of his forehead.

I pulled the towel tight around my body. Only a half-hour ago he'd been alive, sleeping. The shower water that dripped down my body chilled me to the core. I grabbed my clothes, which had been strewn around the room, and pulled them on as quickly as possible. I stumbled as one foot tangled in the leg of my jeans. I screeched as I reached out to stabilize myself and touched his leg.

"Oh, fuck," I whispered, over and over.

Panic started to well up inside me. My hands shook as I buttoned up my shirt and looked around the room for my shoes. I spotted one but not the other. I grabbed my purse, the one shoe, and headed for the door. Then I froze.

I rushed back into the room and grabbed the plastic bag from the wastebasket; it contained evidence of our recent encounter. I picked up the towel I'd left lying on the floor and used it to cover my hand before I opened the bedroom door.

Moonlight streamed in through a small window in the hallway, illuminating the stairs and giving me enough light to navigate them. I crept down, pausing on treads that creaked under my weight and listened. I could hear my blood rushing past my ears to feed a brain that was firing off electrical impulses at a rate I wasn't sure my body could keep up with. Muscles jerked as if preparing themselves for the flight option my body was desperate to take.

I should have called the police. I should have checked for signs of life. I should have done a lot of things, other than the one I did—I opened the front door and ran.

———

I slumped into my broken and grubby sofa, wincing at the soreness of my bare feet. I didn't have the energy to clean them. Instead, I poured myself a glass of cheap wine and gulped it down. My hand shook so much it was hard to hold the glass to my lips. The wine burned its way down my throat, mixing with the bile that was churning in my stomach. I pulled my dirty feet up onto the sofa and curled up. Finally, the tears fell.

I hugged myself, trying to get some warmth into my bones. The trailer I lived in was freezing with just a small gas heater that gave off enough of a smell for me not to want to use it. I pulled a quilt around my shoulders and then cried harder. My grandmother had made that quilt; it was the only item I had that reminded me of her.

I missed her bitterly. I had since she'd died but more so then.

She would have hugged me; she would have known what to do. I would never have found myself in the situation I was had she been around. I cried out her name, praying she could hear and guide me. Not that I thought I could sleep, but I closed my eyes, hoping that dawn would arrive quickly and I'd have a clearer mind.

A sweep of car headlights across the room disturbed me. I sat up, pulling the quilt tight around me and held my breath. The lights came to a stop outside my trailer. I quietly slipped from the sofa, and in a crouch, I crept to the window. I sat on the floor, my back to the door, knowing if someone looked in, they wouldn't see me.

My blood froze in my veins when I heard my name being called, more so, when I recognized the voice. If he wanted to get in, one kick would have the front door fly off its hinges. I covered my mouth to stifle the sob when the door rattled.

"I know where you've been, whore," he slurred, before laughing. "You won't be going back there."

"Please, go away," I whispered, hoping for divine intervention. That came in the form of a dog.

Barking echoed around outside, becoming more frantic. I heard his heavy footsteps clomp down the wooden steps, away from the door, and then the headlights swept across the room again. I sat, straining my ears to listen for the engine of his car and breathed a sigh of relief when that sound became faint.

I knew at that point I couldn't stay there. I had to leave. I scrambled to my feet and rushed into my bedroom. I gathered what few belongings I had, and crammed them into a battered backpack. The last thing I picked up was the quilt. I pulled on some socks and my sneakers, still aware of how dirty my feet were, and headed for the kitchenette. Hidden in a cupboard, in a small tin, were my meager earnings, well, the portion of earnings I was allowed to keep. In addition, there was my 'gift' of a hundred dollars. At the thought of that 'gift' and the person who gave it, tears welled in my eyes again. I would call the police, but I would have to do it anonymously. There was no way I could go forward and publicly report what I'd seen.

I was scared, I was trailer park trash, and I was a prostitute. No one was going to believe I hadn't killed Philip myself.

CHAPTER 2

The night air was crisp as I locked the trailer door behind me, not that I needed to bother. There was absolutely nothing worth stealing left inside. It should have been a temporary place to stay; I'd ended up living there for a year. The dog, which I saw tied to a piece of rope in a neighboring yard, started barking again. A light went on and the front door, of what could only be described as a shack, opened. A man stood, illuminated by the light behind him, and shouted obscenities to his dog. It quieted.

I slipped into the shadow created by my trailer, followed the length and rounded the corner. Behind was a wooded area. I knew my way through that blind so had no hesitation in hoisting the backpack high on my shoulder and making my way forward. Rustling leaves, branches that creaked as they swayed in the gentle breeze had my heart racing fast. I knew I had about an hour before the sun rose and he would be back.

I wondered why he'd arrived in the middle of the night; normally he'd visit in the morning after I'd been at 'work.' He would grill me for details; jerking off like the sick fuck he was, then taking my money, giving me back a small allowance for food and to make sure his bottle of home distilled *moonshine* was always full.

He, my cousin, and the person who was supposed to be my guardian after our grandmother died, was also my pimp—not by choice, though. I'd been forced to *earn my keep,* when he'd taken everything our grandmother had left me, gambled away the house she'd owned, and left us destitute. Well, me destitute. Somehow he always had money for drugs or beer.

As I walked, I reminisced. The first time I'd been forced to have sex, I'd been a virgin and Damien had sat and watched his friend force my legs apart and rape me. I'd screamed, cried, pleaded even. All I received was a punch to my mouth to silence it and a kick to my ribs to remind me to keep still. Damien had never touched me himself; I thought he was incapable of sex. All he could manage was to jerk off to what he saw, or what he heard. Most of what I told him was lies. He'd want to know every detail of every hour I spent with his clients. It wasn't as exciting as I'd tell him, but I wanted to make each minute I spoke as raunchy as possible, so he'd come quickly and then fuck off. Bile rose to coat my mouth with acid at the thought of him. I wished, as hard as it was possible to do so, that it had been Damien lying on that bed, and not the gentle Philip.

I was so distracted that I didn't see the thin branch as it whipped into my face. My skin was cold enough for the sting I felt to have me cry out. I picked up the pace, hoping to make it through the wooded area and to the only road in and out of the shithole town I called home, before sun up. I was Damien's cash cow; I needed to be as far away as possible when he realized I'd finally run.

I had my suspicion that Damien might be responsible for what happened to Philip. I'd been so careful to keep Philip a secret, to only meet up on the couple of nights off I got in a month. I'd use my monthlies as an excuse to not service his friends. I'd seen Damien slit the throat of a dog once, he'd done it to scare me enough to never attempt to leave, and I hadn't. He was more than capable of killing.

I kept to the tree line instead of openly walking along the road. I didn't want to be seen, not that I would expect a truck to pass. The occupants of the trailer park were all either drugged or drunk most nights, and days. There'd be no activity until at least midday when greasy haired and dirty-bodied men would surface, followed by bleached blonde women with smeared makeup and chipped nail polish. Clothes would be optional. They would congregate around the cookout area, hoping someone would prepare some food, usually that was me.

My feet were sore from running barefoot and then squashed into sneakers a size too small. I trudged on, switching the backpack from one shoulder to the other. I'd thought about running away many times, I'd tried it, not getting too far, obviously. This time I was determined. I'd saved some money and sweet Philip had given me some. My heart ached at the thought of his name.

He was an older man, lonely after the death of his wife. He'd wanted a companion at first, someone to sit and chat to. I'd met him in a bar, I was sure that he was there to pick up a woman, and of course, I wasn't supposed to be there myself, I was underage. I was just delivering a package on behalf of Damien. We chatted outside and he seemed so genuine. I hadn't told him my age; I guessed he assumed I was old enough when he invited me to join him at his house. I accepted, needing the warmth of a real house and the company of someone other than the trailer park trash. He'd said that all he wanted to do was to talk.

That was all we did for the first few months that we met. We talked about anything and everything. He'd traveled the world, it seemed. He told me tales of foreign countries I'd never heard of. He described animals I'd only ever seen on the small black and white TV that barely worked, and sat in the corner of the trailer.

He was a lovely old man, and now he was dead. In my gut I knew his death had something to do with me.

———————

I guessed it to be midday by the position of the sun. Although late fall, it was warm. Sweat rolled down my back, my t-shirt was wet, and my shoulder sore under the strap of the backpack. A couple of cars had passed and I'd ducked into the scrub that lined the roadside. I wasn't sure how many miles I'd covered but I was still too close to not get caught. By then, Damien would know I wasn't home. I'd never stayed out all night before, not even when I'd been taken to a 'party' and passed around by his friends like a fucking blow up doll.

I lost count how many men had fucked me, how many women had laughed, watched, joined in, and how many times Damien had pulled on his dick. They sickened me to the point I was able to shut down. I didn't feel anymore, I didn't cry, or hurt, or laugh. I didn't talk much, even. Other than to Philip.

Philip had been my saving grace and it had cost him his life.

I wasn't sure where I was; I'd never ventured that far from town before. In front of me was a long stretch of road, woodland to one side and bare farmland to the other. I didn't own a watch so had no idea of the time. My stomach grumbled and I struggled to remember when I'd last eaten. I gathered my hair from my sweaty neck, cursing myself that I hadn't thought to tie it up. Maybe, when I got to wherever I was heading, I'd cut it short. I'd need to transform myself somehow, but I had no real idea what I would do.

I decided I needed to take a break and headed into the woodland slightly. I found a fallen tree and settled on the ground, resting against it. I had to make a decision to head inland or stick to the road. At some point, the woodland would run out and I'd be exposed. I rifled around in the backpack for the small packet of chips I'd grabbed when I'd packed. I ate slowly; hoping to trick my brain into thinking my stomach was getting a larger meal than the chips. I wasn't sure when my next meal was going to be. Feeling alone was something I was used to, but feeling alone and on the run caused a wave of anxiety to flow over me. Again, I prayed to my grandmother to keep me safe.

I curled up, I hadn't gotten a lot of sleep the previous evening and my limbs were beginning to ache. I thought of my grandmother. She'd brought me up from birth. I knew the bare facts about my mother, her daughter, even less about my father. She'd been a godly Southern woman, kind and loving. My life would have been very different if cancer hadn't taken her earlier than she should have left me.

The court had appointed Damien as my guardian, despite me never having met him before. He'd crawled from the woodwork, knowing there was a house that I'd been left, I imagined. We'd been evicted, if that was even the right word. I remembered two guys coming for him in the middle of the night, dragging me out by my hair, and throwing me to the ground in the front yard. It was a neighbor who had loaned me the use of the rat-infested trailer, and although dilapidated, I was grateful. I managed to get some clothes from the charity box at the church, and the quilt from a pile of rubbish in the yard after the new 'owners' started to decorate the house. I didn't see Damien for a month, initially. He'd turned up, however, beaten and drunk, and put me to work.

I closed my eyes and let the small rays of sun that filtered through the branches of a nearby tree warm my face. It was only when I slept, or dozed, that I lived a wonderful life, that I had dreams and hopes. There were times I wished I could keep my eyes closed forever and escape into my make-believe world. In that world I was at school, I had friends that didn't mock me, and clothes that fit. My body and my hair were always clean and smelled of fresh meadows. I was loved, and I felt secure.

I guessed I must have dozed off. I woke to raindrops and a darkening sky, a sense of foreboding washed over me. I didn't have a jacket, just a couple of thin t-shirts and one woolen sweater. I could layer, but then I wouldn't have any dry clothes. I sat and pulled my knees to my chest, deciding whether to sit where I was, partly sheltered, or continue on. I doubted Damien would be out in the rain to look for me, but I didn't want to take the risk. The last time I had tried to run from him, I'd ended up with broken ribs and a split lip.

I shuffled closer to the tree, hoping its leafy branches would give me some protection. I rested my head back on the trunk and looked up. The dark clouds rolled across the sky, obliterating the sun. I decided the semi-darkness would give me good cover so I rose, grabbed the backpack, and started out toward the road again. My feet slipped on the mud and the rain came down heavier. A river of water ran down the road, I sloshed through it. I was immediately soaked through and hugged the backpack close to my chest, hoping to give it some protection and keep the contents watertight.

The rumble of a vehicle engine caused me to dart back under the cover of the trees. I held still, waiting for it to pass. There was a part of me desperate to call out for help, a ride to the next town, even. I peered around the tree when the vehicle got closer and spotted a black truck. I couldn't see through the rain clear enough to identify the driver. The truck slowed as it got close and I held my breath. I scanned the woodland in front of me, hoping for a way to dart through the trees undetected.

"Are you okay?" I heard. I stayed quiet, but relief washed over me that it wasn't Damien.

"I can see you, your hiding skills are shit." It was a man who had spoken, but I held still and closed my eyes.

"Do you need help?" I heard, close enough to have me open my eyes and squeal.

Standing in front of me was a brown-haired guy, older than me, for sure. His hair was plastered to his head; rainwater ran in rivulets down his face. He had startling light hazel eyes, framed by long lashes that caught the drips and that any girl would die for. Yet there was hardness to his features that contradicted his kind eyes.

"Well?"

I shook my head, not able to find my voice. "So you're happy to stand out here, in the middle of nowhere in the pouring rain?"

I nodded, hoping that he'd give up and leave. He shrugged his shoulders and turned to walk away. I hadn't realized how tight I'd held my body until my shoulders relaxed, and I slumped against the tree. I dropped the backpack at my feet and before I could reach down, he'd returned and picked it up. I reached forward to grab it from him.

"If you don't want my help, that's fine. I don't have time for this, really. But at least sit in the truck until the rain passes." He walked away, carrying all my worldly goods.

15

I ran after him and as I reached out, he opened the passenger door and threw in my backpack. He took a step back and beckoned with his arm for me to join it. My mind was in a whirl, turmoil, and yet again, anxiety flowed through me.

"I..."

"Just get in until the rain passes," he said, a little softer than he'd spoken before.

He left the door open and walked around to the driver's side. I watched the rain begin to soak the soft leather tan seat, and it was more guilt for ruining his vehicle than need, that had me climb in. I closed the door behind me and was immediately thankful for the heated air warming my feet.

"What are you doing out here?" he asked, reaching behind to something on the rear seat.

Before I could answer, he'd handed me a small hand towel. I watched as he rubbed one over his head and face, and then he turned up the heat. Immediately the windows started to steam. Part of me was thankful, I couldn't be seen from outside, part of me was terrified as I felt closed in. I bought myself some time by wiping my face, running the towel over my head and down my hair.

"I'm heading into town," I said, quietly.

"What town?"

I stared at him. His lips twitched and creases formed around his eyes in amusement at my statement.

"The next one."

"The next one, huh? Then it's lucky for you, that's where I'm headed to."

"I don't need a ride, thank you." I didn't want to sound rude, but I didn't want to be in a stranger's truck, either.

"Then you have a fucking long walk. The next town is about sixty-odd miles from here."

I wanted to cry. Perhaps the anguish on my face had been evident. The guy put the truck into gear and pulled out on the road without waiting for my consent. I kept as close to the door as possible, with one hand on the handle and the other on my backpack. For a while we sat in silence, it was only when I saw a beat up car approaching us that I let out a sound, involuntarily. I slid down in the seat until it passed, not entirely sure whether it was Damien or not. I knew nothing about cars other than Damien drove a beat up vehicle of the same color.

I saw him glance at me quickly before focusing on the road ahead.

"Thank you, I guess I need help," I said. Without looking at me, he smiled.

"I don't generally pick up women standing in the rain, but you don't look like you dressed for this weather."

"The rain caught me off guard, for sure."

He didn't ask why I was hiding beside the road, and I appreciated that.

"Are you warm enough?" he asked.

"I'm getting there, thank you."

He took one hand from the steering wheel and reached behind him again. He fumbled around until he drew forward a hooded sweatshirt.

"Here, put this on," he said. "Although you'll have to let go of the door handle first. Perhaps you should know, you can't open the door while the vehicle is moving anyway."

I felt the blush at having been caught, creep up my cheeks.

"I'm sorry, I'm..."

"I don't need an explanation, you're running from something, or someone, and you're soaked through. So, just put the sweatshirt on." He hadn't looked at me while he spoke.

I pulled the gray hoodie over my head, immediately welcoming the soft fleece inside warming my skin. Whether it was the gentle rumble of the truck as we drove down the road, the warmth of the heater, or the sweatshirt, but I found myself drifting into sleep. I welcomed the dreams of a brighter future.

CHAPTER 3

A gentle tap to my arm woke me. The rain has eased into a gentle drizzle and it took a moment for me to get my bearings. My mind was foggy, as if I'd woken from the deepest, longest sleep, yet it could have only been an hour at most.

I straightened myself in the seat and looked around. We had parked on a main street, typical of a small town, I guessed. Beside me was a gun store; behind the barred window I saw rifles and handguns.

"We're here," he said. I slowly nodded and started to remove his hoodie.

"Keep it."

"Thank you, I appreciate that. And thank you for the ride. I don't have much but can I..." I started to open my backpack to find my money tin.

"I don't want anything. Can't say you've been riveting company, but it was my pleasure." His lips curled into a smirk.

I wasn't sure if he was kidding or serious. "I'm sorry, and...thank you, again."

I opened the door and climbed from the truck. Immediately the sneakers that had dried on the journey were immersed in a puddle of water. I sighed as I closed the door. He gave me a nod before the truck rolled forward and he drove away. I hadn't asked him his name.

I looked up and down the main street. On the opposite side was a small diner, that might be a good start. I could sit with a coffee; maybe get something to eat while I decided what on earth I was going to do next. I needed somewhere to sleep, perhaps a job to build a little money before I moved on again. I knew enough about surviving to be sure I couldn't stay in one place too long. Before I did anything, I had a call to make.

I entered the diner and immediately headed for the telephone I'd spotted from outside. I'd never used a public telephone before, in fact, I'd only ever used a cell a handful of times. I picked up the handset and held it to the side of my face. My finger hesitated over the number nine. I owed it to Philip I silently told myself. I dialed nine-one-one.

"Nine-one-one, what is your emergency?"

"A man has been murdered," I then rattled off the address.

"Okay, can you give me your name?"

"No, did you get that address?"

"I did, ma'am, but I need a little more information."

"His name was Philip," I said, giving the address again before replacing the handset.

Because I hadn't given my name, I wasn't sure how seriously they would have taken me, but I prayed they'd at least be curious enough to visit Philip's house. He had a large house, surrounded by a high wall and metal gates. I'd been impressed when I'd first visited, enamored, in awe even. He hadn't bragged about any wealth, nor shared his surname even. I knew nothing about him, other than his address and his first name.

I wiped my hand down the front of my jeans, not entirely sure why I felt the need to clean my palm as if I'd done, or touched, something dirty. I looked around and although the diner was fairly empty, I took the booth the furthest from the door. A waitress immediately approached, she was an older woman. She smiled then licked the end of a pencil.

"What can I get for you?" she said, holding the pencil poised above her pad.

"A coffee, with cream, would be great, thank you."

"Did you get caught in the rain?" she asked, as she scribbled on her pad.

"I did. I imagine I look a real mess." I ran my fingers through my hair.

She chuckled, "Sweetie, you look lovely, just a little...tousled."

I wanted to laugh. I'd spoken the most in the past couple of hours than I had in months, but I wasn't sure I could extend the face muscles into a laugh. I did smile, though.

She left a menu on the table then went to fetch my coffee. Using the sleeve of the hoodie I wiped some steam from the window and looked out onto the street. I wanted to find something that would tell me exactly where I was. I'd buy a map so I could plot a route to wherever I was going after I'd drunk my coffee and had a bite to eat. I was conscious of the little money I had, so scanned the menu for the cheapest item.

My mouth watered at the description of a burger, the T-bone steak and fries. Instead, I settled for an omelet. A plain cheese omelet was soon placed in front of me with a steaming mug of hot coffee. I hadn't had proper coffee for a long time. Once Damien had taken his 'fee' from my earnings, there wasn't much left for luxuries like fresh coffee.

Just the thought of his name had me slink in my seat a little. I know he'd often said that if I ran, he'd not only find me, but I'd be wishing I were dead instead of the alternative. I never asked what the alternative was, and knowing how sadistic he could be, I didn't want to know. It was just after he'd made that threat, that he'd killed the stray dog. I shuddered at the memory.

I sipped on my coffee and ate every mouthful as slowly as I could. I watched people come and go, some sat and ordered, some just wanted a coffee to go. I overheard the woman being called by her name, Rose. I smiled, it was a pretty name and so far her nature seemed to match. She greeted most by name and always with a broad smile. She reminded me of my grandmother and a pang of hurt jolted me back to my reality.

I'd finished my omelet and Rose came to clear the plate.

"Another coffee, on the house?" she asked. I nodded grateful for anything free and hot.

"Do you know of any places to stay locally, cheap if possible?" I asked.

She thought for a moment. "There's a motel but I think for cheap, you might want to check out Cecelia Mercier, she rents out rooms. Lives in the big white house on Grace Street. If you take a left out of here, you'll find Grace Street across the road, three corners down."

"That's great, thank you."

"You might want to get there early, lots of people passing by call on her in the evening when the motel is booked up."

"I will, as soon as I've drunk this wonderful coffee I'll wander down there."

She smiled and left the bill for the one cup of coffee and the omelet. I counted out my money and left it on the table. I drained my cup and with another 'Thank you,' I left the diner.

I found the big white house on Grace Street easily enough. *Big* seemed to be an understatement. The house was as large as Philip's but not necessarily as well kept. The front yard could have done with a mow, a little weeding, and the fencing needed some repair. My nerves kicked in as I walked the stone path to a sun deck and an imposing black front door. Before I'd reached out to knock, it was opened. A small elderly woman smiled at me.

"Rose sent you, yes?" she said, with an accent I couldn't place.

"She did, how did you know?"

"She just called, told me to look out for you. Come in." She stepped to one side and held open the door for me.

I walked into a wide hallway, its walls were lined with portraits, old and, I guessed, of family members.

"My father," she explained, pointing to a gentleman in military uniform and with a back so stiff he must have been in pain for that sitting.

"He looks..."

"Uncomfortable?" She laughed when she spoke, and for the first time in a long while, I laughed with her.

"I was going to say, very formal."

"So, how long?" she asked.

At first I didn't understand what she meant. "How long would you like a room for?"

"Oh, I'm sorry, erm, how much are they? I only need a real basic room."

"For you, ten dollars a night and you share a bathroom."

I had no idea if ten dollars was a good deal or not, but I needed somewhere to stay until I could plan.

"Thank you, I have the money here." I reached for the backpack.

"A cup of tea first, then we do the paperwork," she said, striding off.

I stood where I was, not sure if she wanted me to follow until she stopped in a doorway and beckoned me.

Her rustic styled kitchen was large with a wooden table set in the middle. She waved her arm, indicating toward a chair. I placed my bag on the floor and sat, mindful not to drag the chair across the tiled floor. The kitchen, although way larger, reminded me of my grandmother's. She'd loved to bake, everything from bread to cakes, every day. It looked like Cecelia did as well. On the side were jars of ingredients, scales, and utensils hung from a rack above the stove. Cecelia busied herself with making tea; I'd never drunk tea before.

"Where are you from, originally?" I asked, wondering if that was a rude question.

"France. My parents brought me here when I was a young woman. Not here, exactly, a couple of towns over. How do you take your tea?"

"I've never had it," I said, trying to look apologetic.

"See, Americans, and the French to be fair, drink too much coffee. Leave it to me."

It was a few minutes later that she placed a cup and saucer on the table, a pot, and a jug of milk. She poured the milk first, stirred the contents of the pot, and then used a small sieve to catch the tealeaves when she poured.

I took a sip. "Mmm, I like it," I said.

"I have that flown in from England. It's my favorite tea, and since it's nearly three in the afternoon, the perfect time for a cup."

I hadn't realized the time. As much as I tried to stifle it, I yawned, covering my mouth and then apologizing immediately after.

"Why don't you bring your tea and I'll show you the room. I think you'll find it quite comfortable. Before we do, I need to know your name, the rest we can do later."

I swallowed, unsure whether to be honest. I decided to be.

"My name is Charlotte."

The nickname that usually followed whenever Damien used my name nearly slipped off my tongue.

"Well, Charlotte, come with me."

I followed her to a wide wooden staircase and then along a corridor. She opened a white painted door into a small room and I fell in love. The walls were painted a soft cream, a bed slightly larger than the single I'd had in the trailer was against one wall. A large picture window looked out over a yard and then onto fields. It was the comforter that had me feeling nostalgic. It was similar to the quilt I had bunched up in the backpack. I ran my hand over the soft cotton.

"This is perfect," I said, as I placed my teacup on the small cabinet beside the bed.

"The bathroom is just next door, be sure to lock the door when you use it. I only have a couple of guests, so hopefully you won't be disturbed. Why not get some rest? And I'd like it if you joined me for dinner, shall I give you call if you've not come back down?"

"I... Thank you, I'd love to." I hadn't thought about dinner, assuming I'd have to find a store and buy something ready-made.

Cecelia closed the door behind her and I placed my bag on the bed. I unpacked the few items I had, smoothing out the quilt over the comforter. I hadn't thought about toiletries, nor did I have a towel, but I made my way to the bathroom in need of a warm shower.

On a shelf was a bottle of body wash. I hoped whomever it belonged to wouldn't mind if I used just a drop to wash my hair and myself. Hanging over a rail were a selection of towels for guest use, I hoped. I locked the door and stripped off my clothing while the shower heated up. I stood for ages letting the warm water run over my body, washing away the miserable day, and life. I wanted to emerge a new person. Perhaps I should have given Cecelia a fake name, start completely afresh with a new identity.

I thought up surnames, trying hard to remember any family names I'd heard my grandmother use. Nothing came to mind. I didn't have any friends so couldn't use theirs. Instead, I stared at the bottle of body wash and decided Johnson would have to do. While I dried myself and then cursed because I hadn't brought fresh clothes into the bathroom with me, I thought of a reason why I'd ended up in this town. I didn't want an elaborate lie, just something I could easily remember. I'd also have to adjust my age. I looked much older than my nineteen years but I didn't want to stretch it too far. I knew I should be in college, and I had attended school for a while until Damien decided *'school was for idiots.'*

I pulled on the worn t-shirt and jeans and opened the bathroom door. I was thankful that the bedroom was just next door; I didn't want to meet anyone in the hallway. I surveyed my range of pitiful clothing, deciding which ones looked less like the charity box finds they were. I'd left the slutty work clothes back in the trailer; those were the only new clothes I owned, and of course, bought by Damien. Why he thought the black, fake leather mini-skirt and the low cut, Gypsy tops were attractive to men was beyond me.

Dressed in a relatively clean pair of jeans and a slightly crumpled black t-shirt, I lay down on top of the bed. I sighed as my head sank into feather pillows and I turned on my side to look out the window. The view soothed me, for miles it was just farmland, trees, and in my mind, it represented freedom. I lay and just daydreamed, creating my fantasy life and feeling hopeful that it might not be a fantasy anymore.

I slipped on my sneakers and headed downstairs. It felt awkward to walk around someone else's house, and I did my best not to let curiosity overcome me. I avoided all the rooms with closed doors and followed the smell of food to the kitchen.

"Did you sleep well?" Cecelia asked.

"I showered, and then had a nap. The view from that bedroom is amazing."

"That was my father's farm, he had a dream to create a vineyard here but the soil wasn't right. I rent all the land out now, it's way too much for me to cope with."

I sat at the kitchen table and accepted the coffee that Cecelia offered. She joined me with her cup of tea and folder. I guessed we were coming to the part I was dreading.

"Okay, let's get some paperwork done. I do like to know a little about my guests," she said, with a smile.

She opened the folder and picked up a pen. "Full name?"

"Charlotte Johnson," I said, surprised how easy the surname fell from my tongue.

"Previous address?"

I stumbled for a moment before giving my grandmother's. Cecelia stared at me for a few seconds before writing it down.

"Date of birth?"

I gave her my real day and month, but added two years. I hoped I could pull off being a twenty-one-year-old.

"Do you have any ID?"

There she had me stumped. "Err, I don't drive. I guess I just never bothered to learn."

"Okay, we'll leave that for a moment." She laid the pen down and closed the folder. I tried not to have my sigh of relief obvious.

I sipped on my coffee to avoid her stare and the mounting tension I began to feel.

"So, Charlotte, are you just passing through?" It was asked as if in general conversation but my alert level went up a notch.

"My grandmother, who brought me up, died. I thought I'd take some time out to travel, see a little of the country before I decide what to do next."

"Oh, I'm sorry to hear about your grandmother."

"I never knew my birth mother, so I thought I might do a little research. I just feel I need to discover who I really am before I can settle down."

Although it had started as a lie, I was surprised to feel a pang of excitement wash over me. Maybe I would see if I could track down my mother. I knew her name, that was all, and no idea how hard it would be. I hadn't been given the chance to take anything from my grandmother's, as far as I knew everything had been either burned or thrown.

"I will need to look for a job, though," I added.

"I'm sure you'll have no trouble, although you might want to think about getting some ID."

Cecelia had finished her tea and stood to prepare the evening meal.

"Is there anything I can do to help?" I asked.

"No, I prefer to cook alone. I know where everything is," she said, with a chuckle.

"Well, how about I mow the front yard? I noticed the grass was a little overgrown."

She turned and raised her eyebrows. I wondered if I'd offended.

"I'm sorry, I just…"

"I think that would be a great idea. My nephew usually tends to the maintenance but he's been a little distracted lately. Let's go find a mower, I'm sure I have one somewhere." She wiped her hands on a towel and I followed her out the back door.

To one side of the house was a collection of small outbuildings. Cecelia opened the door and waved her arms to make a path through the cobwebs. I assumed the nephew must have brought his own mower. The building was a treasure trove of old-fashioned farm equipment, boxes and boxes of a lifetime of living in the same property without throwing anything away, and, I imagined, years of memories.

"Wow," I said, laughing and coughing because of the dust that was floating around.

"Yes, wow. Maybe we don't have a mower."

"Here, let me." I pushed past her and climbed over some sort of workbench with a saw attached.

"Ouch," I said, catching my jeans on the rusty saw and nicking my skin.

"Be careful, Charlotte."

Just as she spoke, I tripped and a pile of cardboard boxes collapsed on top of me.

"Charlotte! Oh, dear, are you okay?"

I was covered in dust and books. I hadn't hurt myself at all but was most definitely stuck. I started to laugh just as a hand that certainly did not belong to Cecelia, reached through the boxes and grabbed my arm. I was pulled to my feet and stumbled straight into the rock hard chest of the guy who had given me a ride.

"Oh." I cringed at my lack of vocabulary.

"A *thank you* might be better than, 'Oh'," he said.

"Thank you." I wanted to add the word 'jerk' to the end of the sentence.

"Charlotte, meet my nephew, Beau." She turned her attention to the guy still holding on to my arm. "We're looking for a mower."

"You don't have a mower, Cecelia," he said. I hadn't noticed the very slight accent when he'd picked me up earlier.

"Charlotte is staying with me for a couple of days. Help her out, will you? Don't just stand there."

Beau helped me climb back over the boxes and the workbench. I dusted down my jeans and shook out my hair. I shuddered, thinking of the creepy crawlies I might have on me. Before I could thank Beau, he'd turned on his heel and left.

Cecelia chuckled as we heard the putter of a mower engine starting; we followed the sound to the front yard. Beau stood in front of the mower with one eyebrow cocked and a smirk on his face.

"All yours," he said, leaving the mower running and walking into the house.

I mumbled under my breath, hoping Cecelia didn't hear how rude I thought her nephew was as I walked toward it. I used to mow the lawn at my grandmother's, so it didn't take me long to figure out how to use the machine. Cecelia gave me a smile as she returned to the house.

The sun was beginning to lower just as I finished the second round of mowing. I emptied the collection bag and turned off the mower, leaving it by the gate for Beau. I pulled off my sneakers, wincing at the stains and shaking off the grass. I sat on the steps of the porch and breathed in deep. Fresh cut grass was one of my favorite scents. I raised my face to the sinking sun and closed my eyes.

"Apparently you're joining us for dinner," I heard.

I replaced my sneakers before I stood. "I am, if that's not a problem."

Beau smirked again. He shrugged his shoulders. "Not a problem for me."

"Have I offended you? You were kind to me earlier, but you seem annoyed now."

"No, not at all. Just looking out for my aunt, that's all."

"Why do you need to look out for your aunt? I'm not a threat, I'm paying to stay here."

"You're running from something, Charlotte, if that is your name. As I said, I'm looking out for my aunt. In my experience, no matter how fast your run, trouble always catches up."

I bit down on my lower lip to stop the expletive from escaping. I couldn't afford to alienate Beau or Cecelia. Not until I had a job and could afford different accommodation. His comment stung, though.

"It is my name," I said quietly, and pushed past him into the hallway.

My earlier bright mood had been dampened. Beau was right, I guessed. It would only be a matter of time before Damien caught up with me. I had no doubt that he would come looking for me; I was his only source of income.

HARLOT

Despite Cecelia's chatter through dinner, I stayed mostly quiet. I didn't have a great appetite normally, even less when I was being scrutinized by Beau. He seemed to study everything I did, from the way I ate, to how I shifted in my seat. He made me feel extremely uncomfortable, and I began to resent him.

I finished my meal and chose to clear the table and stack the dishwasher. Cecelia offered me a coffee but I used tiredness as an excuse to escape. Without a word to Beau, I left the room and climbed the stairs to the bedroom. I kicked off my sneakers and lay on the bed, watching the sun set beyond the fields. A lone tear ran down my cheek and I angrily brushed it away. I needed to toughen up, for sure. I couldn't blame Beau, if I was in his position I would be cautious.

With a sigh, I rose and undressed, careful not to shake out any remaining dust and grass from my clothes on the carpet. I'd need to hand wash my t-shirt at some point, the jeans could go another day.

CHAPTER 4

I had a restless night, tossing and turning, waking periodically in a cold sweat. The image of Philip kept playing through my mind. I felt like a coward for running, guilt had started to consume me. I lay as the sun began to rise thinking of him. All he'd wanted was a companion, at first. He hadn't wanted to fuck me, just chat and have someone listen to him. He missed his wife, he had no contact with his son after a family feud, and I think he saw something in me that made him feel comfortable to open up.

I'd told him I was older, of course. I'd told him a whole bunch of lies and I regretted that. We'd only had sex that once and I guess even that was out of loneliness. He'd had a particularly rough day and I did what I thought would help. I seduced him. He was reluctant at first, in fact, as he came, he cried with guilt, apologizing to his dead wife over and over. I guessed that should have made me feel bad, but I wasn't with him for my own satisfaction. That day, he had needed me, and he had needed a distraction from his grief.

He hadn't deserved his end and I began to think about that. I had been in the shower; anyone in that bedroom would have heard me. Why hadn't they come for me as well? I thought about it, nothing had been disturbed, and I'd unlocked the front door when I ran. I hoped the police had found him; the thought that he'd be there for days before anyone reported him missing worried me. I could hardly call the police again, though.

I decided to shower and dress. Laying in bed thinking wasn't helping. Cecelia had told me that I was welcome to help myself to coffee. I grabbed a cup and poured from the pot before heading out to the backyard. It was a bright morning and already warm. I sat on the steps of the deck and sipped from my mug. Movement caught my eye; to one side of the yard was a wooded area. I watched a topless man, with tattoos down one arm and across his chest, and wearing low-slung jeans, swing an axe and chop a log. He reached down to pick up another and placed it upright before swinging the axe again. Beau was obviously an early riser, and judging by the muscles that rippled over his back, a fit man.

He stopped and stood upright, swiping his arm over his forehead. I hoped that I'd turned my head away from him quickly enough when I saw him glance over. I didn't want him to know I had been staring at him.

I kept my gaze on the ground in front of me with the mug raised to my lips, as I blew gently to cool my coffee. In my peripheral vision, I could see tan, lace up work boots, the bottom of his jeans were scrunched around the top. He didn't speak, so eventually I looked up.

"Good morning," I said, hoping for a polite response and making sure I kept eye contact. I didn't want the taut chest and the six-pack to distract me.

"Are you drinking that?" he asked.

I looked at my mug. "Yes." I raised my eyebrows in response to his strange question.

"My boots are muddy, can you fetch me a coffee?"

I stared at him. "Please?" I encouraged, hoping to remind him of any manners he might have.

"Please," he grunted out the word.

I rose and headed to the kitchen. I didn't ask how he took his coffee but poured and left it black. When I returned to the deck, I handed it to him. He looked in the mug at first, and then took a gentle sip as if tasting to check whether I'd spat in it. If I'd have thought about it, or if I was that way inclined, I might have.

He took a couple of large gulps then threw the remainder on the ground. Without a word he handed the mug back to me, I kept my hands around my own mug. After a moment, he reached down and placed it on the deck.

"Do you think I'm rude?" he asked, surprising me.

"Very much so."

He laughed. "I guess I should work on my social skills. Thanks for the coffee." With that, he turned and walked back toward his pile of logs.

Beau certainly baffled me. He was the guy that had stopped to help me, insisting I got in his truck then offering to drive me, yet he looked at me with disdain. He acted as if I wasn't welcome, someone to be wary of. Was I giving off vibes to justify that?

"Oh, Rose is hiring, if you're interested," he shouted over his shoulder.

I scrambled to my feet. I could work in a diner; it couldn't be that hard. I collected Beau's mug and took both inside to wash up. Cecelia was puttering around the kitchen.

"I helped myself to coffee, I hope that was okay," I said.

"Of course it was, I told you to," she said with a smile.

"Beau said that Rose was hiring, I'm going to head over to see if I can get an interview."

"That's a great idea, she's a good woman."

I rushed upstairs to brush my hair and teeth, and made myself as presentable as possible. I'd never been to an interview before; I didn't have a resume and no time to invent one. I ran through the story I'd told Cecelia the previous evening as I left the house and headed to the diner. I had to make sure I didn't slip up, those two were friends, I was sure.

The diner wasn't busy when I entered; I guessed it was still a little early.

"Good morning," I heard from behind the counter. Rose stood having been bending down to retrieve something, I imagined.

"Hi, err, good morning to you," I stammered, nerves kicking in.

"Coffee?"

"I was actually here to see if you were hiring staff. I can wait on tables, clean, in fact, I'm pretty good at most things, except cooking. I haven't done much of that, but I'm a quick learner, I can make coffee and maybe sandwiches, and..."

She held up her hand to stop my rambling.

"Coffee?" she asked again, I nodded as she poured, not really waiting for my answer.

She indicated toward a booth and I picked up the mug and sat. Rose joined me.

"Now, have you ever waited tables before?" she asked.

I felt my shoulders slump a little. I didn't really want to lie to her.

"I haven't, but I'm pretty quick to learn. I just need a job, Rose. I don't mind what it is, I'll clean the restrooms quite happily."

"How old are you?"

"Twenty-one. I know, I look younger, and that has been a pain, I can tell you."

I didn't think she believed me, but she nodded her head slowly.

"You can read and write, I take it."

I blinked a couple of times. "Of course I can."

"Just wanted to check you'd been to school, Charlotte."

I wondered how she knew my name, I was pretty sure I hadn't told her when I'd sat for a meal the previous day.

"I have. I'm taking some time to find myself, if the truth were known. My grandmother died, I don't know my birth mother, and I'm a little lost right now. I want to earn some money so that I can save, and then decide on my future."

She leaned back in her seat. "Mmm, I don't know what it is about you, Charlotte, but something in me wants to help you. I think you need help, and I'm sure you'll tell me why one day. For now, be back here at midday for a trial. I need some help for the lunch rush."

I could have hugged her, kissed her cheeks even. I felt my smile broaden to the point those muscles that only seemed to have woken up recently, ached.

"Oh, thank you. I won't let you down, I promise."

Rose stood and picked up my empty coffee mug. "I might be an old woman, Charlotte, but I know a tale when I hear one. It's okay, though. You have your reasons, for now. But I will be keeping an eye on you." She finished her sentence with a smile, but she clearly hadn't been fooled by my story. I suspected it was the age I'd given.

"I..."

"Nothing to say right now. Just promise me one thing, at some point you'll be honest, I need to be able to trust you. I can't until then."

I nodded, having no answer to that.

––––––––

"How did you get on?" Cecelia asked once I'd returned to her house.

"I have to go back at lunchtime, for a trial," I replied.

"That's great news," she said, smiling at me.

"I guess I ought to sort out some better clothes. Is there a store nearby?"

"Ellie's should have the basics but for anything fancy, next town over, I'm afraid. Maybe Beau could drive you?"

"That's fine, I'm sure I can find what I need here."

I didn't want Beau to drive me anywhere. I took some money from my tin and then left the house and made my way back to the main street. I only needed some toiletries, a couple of fresh t-shirts, some underwear, and a new pair of jeans if I could find some. I hadn't wanted to dip into my money but hoped to earn it back in tips as quickly as possible.

Ellie's had most of what I needed. I piled some panties, socks, two t-shirts, and toiletries on the counter. I stood for ages in front of a display of hair dye, deciding if I should. I wondered if it might cause suspicion if I just went from blonde to brown without having the 'wanting a change' conversation first. I picked up a box and added it to my purchases. I counted out the money inwardly wincing that I'd spent more than I intended and was handed a bag. I took a slow walk back to the house.

I kicked my heels in my bedroom for an hour or two until it was time to head back to the diner. My palms sweated a little the closer I got. I fiddled with some strands of hair that had come loose from the bun I'd tied at the nape of my neck. I assumed I'd have to tie my hair back and wanted to arrive looking prepared.

The windows were steamed up as I pushed open the door. The diner was full and I soon realized it was 'special's day.'

"Charlotte, I really need some clean plates, we're getting low. Head on behind the counter, Kieran will look after you," Rose called out from the other end of the diner. I waved to let her know I'd heard.

"Hello?" I said as I rounded the counter and into the kitchen area.

"Charlotte?" an older man asked. I nodded.

"Thank God, girl. We're sinking here." He pointed to a counter, which was piled high with dirty dishes.

"I'm on it," I said, with a smile. I didn't care what work I was given, I'd do anything.

I filled a sink and started to wash the plates. I was sure they had a dishwasher but for speed, I wanted to clear as many as were needed for the lunchtime rush. I washed, rinsed, dried, and stacked. My hands were sore from the hot water but I found myself humming along to the tunes played on the radio.

"Phew, that was a rush," Rose said, when she entered the kitchen.

"I think I have enough clean for now, shall I put the rest in the dishwasher?" I asked.

She nodded and pulled open the door of a large stainless steel appliance. I stacked and watched as she set it.

"What would you like me to do now?"

"There are some tables to clean," Rose said.

I grabbed a cloth and a bottle of disinfectant spray. I smiled and greeted customers who came or left. I scrubbed tables, some chairs, and mopped the floor to clean up spilled food. My shoulders and back ached, but I was enjoying myself. I was legitimately earning money that I could keep for myself; I didn't have to prostitute myself for a portion of it.

"Charlotte, you can stop now. I don't think the diner has ever been so clean," Rose said.

I stood and stretched my back; strands of hair had stuck to the beads of sweat on my forehead. I blew at them. Rose handed me a cup of coffee and I slid into a booth. She joined me.

"Well, you've definitely got the job," she said, looking around. But then she sighed. "I love this place, but it's too much for me now, to be honest. I'd appreciate your help. Shame you're only passing through."

"I don't know how long I'll be around. I don't have plans, Rose, I'm just trying to find someplace I fit in." That was the first truth I'd told her.

————

Two days later I was waiting tables when my fears came to life.

"Refill?" I asked two guys sitting at a table.

I held the coffee pot above one mug. I wasn't sure what it was that had me look at the TV in the corner, but an image of Philip filled the screen. The sound was low but scrolling across the bottom of the screen were words that had my blood run cold.

Ex-mayor, Philip Stanton, was found murdered in his home yesterday morning. Sources have confirmed evidence, and we believe it to be a woman's shoe, was found in the ex-mayor's bedroom. So far there have been no arrests but our source tells us the police are following substantial leads.

"Hey!"

I turned from the TV to see the mug overflowing and a river of hot coffee spilling into the guy's lap. He'd jumped from his seat, pulling his pants away from his crotch. Rose ran over, holding a wad of tissues in her hand. I was frozen to the spot.

"Ex-mayor?" I whispered.

"Charlotte?" Rose's word cut through the fog in my head.

"Shit, I'm so sorry," I said, placing the coffee pot on the table and taking the towels from her. I mopped at the coffee as best I could.

"Go get a cloth," she replied.

I rushed behind the counter, but all I could think of was that Philip was an ex-mayor, and the police were following leads. I was glad he'd been found but terrified at the same time. I grabbed a cloth and by the time I'd returned to the table, it was cleaned and empty.

"They've left, I guess the poor guy had to go cool off his balls," Rose said.

I tried hard to swallow down the panic and blink away the tears. "I'm so sorry, I got distracted."

"I noticed."

"It won't happen again, I promise. I'll pay for the spilled coffee." Even I noticed the level of desperation in my voice. I needed the job.

"There's no need for that. You've got an hour left of your shift, maybe go help Kieran since we've quieted down out here."

I walked to the kitchen and quietly began to stack dishes in the washer and wash down countertops.

"Knew him, did you?" Kieran asked.

I wasn't sure what to say, or whether he was referring to the guy I'd poured the coffee over or Philip.

"Your face went white when you saw that TV report," he added.

"My grandmother knew him. I was a little shocked, that's all."

Shit! I shouldn't have said that, I thought. I might have to come up with a story in case I'm asked to expand on what I'd said.

I spent the rest of my shift in the kitchen, and then headed to the restroom to wash up before joining Rose at the cash register. She handed me my day's tips, a little less than the previous. I imagined the guy with scalded balls hadn't left a tip.

"I'm sorry about earlier. My grandmother knew him, I was a little shocked," I said, having to keep my story straight in case Kieran said anything.

"I'm sorry to hear that, did she know him well?"

"I'm not sure to be honest, I only met him a couple of times."

I crossed my fingers, hoping she wouldn't ask much more. "Shall I see you tomorrow?" I asked.

Rose smiled and nodded. Hopefully the matter was dealt with.

The first thing I did, when I left the diner, was to head to the convenience store and buy a newspaper. Philip's murder was front page news. I scanned the the article looking for any references to a suspect and my missing shoe. The more I read about Philip, the faster my heart beat. His son, the one who hadn't bothered with him for years, had made a statement stating how heartbroken the family was, how they were determined to do whatever was necessary to bring their father's murderer to court. My hands began to shake as I continued to read.

I folded the newspaper and placed it in a trashcan. I knew nothing about forensics but was pretty sure the police were, somehow, going to discover I was the owner of the shoe.

I should have stayed. I should have called the police immediately. There were a lot of things I 'should' have done, but was it too late? If I went to the police would I be a suspect because I'd run? So many questions ran through my mind, muddling my thoughts to the point I just couldn't think anymore.

————————

I found some scissors in a kitchen drawer and took them to the bathroom with me. As I stood in front of the mirror, I held my hair to one side and chopped. It wasn't the neatest cut, but then I wasn't thinking straight. I opened the hair dye and read the instructions. It all seemed easy enough. Within an hour I'd gone from having long, blonde hair to short, choppy brown. The style aged me, which I guessed, was a benefit. I cleaned the bathroom, being sure to bag up all the excess hair and took it out to the trash.

"Charlotte!" I heard, when I walked back into the kitchen.

"What do you think? New me," I said, startled by Cecelia.

"I could have cut it, if you'd asked. But it does make you look a little more mature," she said.

The smile I gave was forced. "I thought it might be easier for working at the diner. I'm forever having to retie my hair, and I'd hate for a customer to find some in their meal."

"Makes you look like you want to disguise yourself," I heard from the back door.

"Beau, that's not a nice comment," Cecelia said.

Beau strode through the kitchen and poured himself a coffee, he didn't offer anyone else one. I wondered, again, what had happened to make him so arrogant. Was he as rude to all the guests, or just me?

"Maybe I do, maybe I want to shed the old me and start afresh," I said, raising my chin in challenge.

He didn't reply, but stared at me over the rim of his mug while he took sips.

"I have to head to the store," Cecelia said, gathering up her purse.

I made my way to my bedroom to collect some money, not wanting to share the same space as Beau. I was desperate to watch the news, but all I was doing was renting a bedroom. I hadn't been shown the living room. I decided I'd find a coffee shop, or perhaps see if the town had a library and I could reread the newspapers.

I found the town library easily enough, it was the largest and most impressive looking building in a courtyard tucked behind the main street. I found a small table with unoccupied chairs in a corner, near the children's section, and opened one of the three newspapers I'd taken from the stand by the librarian. I read. The article was a repeat of what I already knew. I picked up a second newspaper. I scanned through until I saw a bunch of words that had me hold my breath.

It is believed police have a man, name not released, helping with their investigation.

A man? Who? *Helping with their investigation.* Didn't that generally mean they had arrested someone? I wasn't sure whether to breathe a sigh of relief or up my anxiety levels. The press had already mentioned a shoe, a woman's shoe. The police would still want to know who it belonged to, wouldn't they? I wished I had someone I trusted to ask the many questions that ran through my mind. I had been witness to many crimes in my trailer park. It was a nightly occurrence for the police to arrive, lights, and sometimes guns, blazing, and then take someone away. I'd never really known what happened after, though. Sometimes those people would come back and regale Damien, while I overheard, with horror stories of their time in the cells. Sometimes I never saw them again.

I looked up, my eyes stung from staring at the small text for so long. I watched a group of girls, probably about my age, laugh and quietly chat as they sat at a long table with piles of books in the middle. I guessed they were there to research their homework questions and I envied them. One glanced over and then quickly looked away before I could offer a smile. I watched as she bent her head low to her friend and whispered. The other tried to glance my way before her friend grabbed her arm.

Being laughed at by my peers wasn't new. I guessed it was the only thing I didn't miss about the small school Damien had yanked me from, when he'd decided the only education I needed was how to please a man. A thought occurred. Maybe I could take myself back to school. I'd loved to learn, I wasn't dumb, often top of my class, which added to the ridicule I'd received. First, I needed to deal with the Philip situation.

———

It was getting late when I headed back to the house. As I walked, I wondered if I'd ever be able to call somewhere home. I was hoping that, in time, I'd be able to work enough shifts to afford my own place. That might have been a 'pie in the sky' dream, but dreams were all I had.

I stopped by a store to pick up something to eat and kill a little more time. I browsed a used bookshelf. Reading had been a guilty pleasure of mine. I'd hidden books in the trailer for fear of Damien discarding, or selling, them if he could. Again, it was always about controlling my level of learning to what he thought I ought to know. I picked up a romance with a cracked spine and dog-eared pages. I loved books that looked read, that looked like someone had really enjoyed the words on the pages. Somehow it connected me with the previous owner. We had something in common, despite never having met. I bought the book because it had been so 'loved' rather than for the content. It was also to give me something to take my mind off my situation in the hours I spent alone in the bedroom.

Beau was standing on the sun deck with a can of paint and cleaning off a brush. One side of the railing looked fresh. I hesitated on the path but took a deep breath and walked to the front door. As I passed him he grabbed the book from my hand.

"Romance," he said with disdain.

"I don't know, I haven't read the back. I liked the cover."

"You know this crap isn't even close to real, Charlotte. There are no happy endings in life."

I stared at him. "I read to escape my *crap*, Beau. And as for happy endings...what did she do to you, to make you such a cynic?"

Silence ensued, a flash of anger crossed his face, and his usually light hazel eyes darkened. He slammed the book into my chest, causing me to stumble back a couple of steps. I'd spoken so far out of line I wasn't sure I'd be able to make it back. I wanted to apologize, I opened my mouth to, but he held up his hand to silence me. He then turned and walked down the path to his truck. His wheels spun on the road as he roared away.

"Was that Beau?" I heard, Cecelia stood at the front door.

"Yes, I think he was late for something."

I saw her brow furrow, in worry I assumed. I should have kept my mouth shut. Damien would often tell me I had a smart mouth, I was way too articulate—not that he'd used that word—for my age. It upset me to know I might have caused her to worry. I'd apologize, whether he wanted to listen or not, in the morning.

I took my book and the snacks I'd bought to my bedroom. I curled up, draped the quilt around me and opened the book. I soon fell into a world I could only dream about.

I heard the front door slam shut, I'd been so absorbed in the book I hadn't realized the time. The small clock on the wall showed it past midnight. For those few hours, I'd managed to immerse myself in a world of fantasy, of a hero and selfless love. I sighed. One day I'd have that. I changed out of my clothes and climbed into bed.

Thoughts of Philip, lost shoes, and a broken Beau, merged, giving me a restless sleep. I woke in the early hours. My head was pounding and my throat dry from thirst. I climbed from the bed and pulled on a t-shirt. I needed a glass of water but hesitated by the bedroom door. I listened for any sounds of life before gently opening it and creeping downstairs. Feeling my way along the wall, I reached the kitchen. By then, my eyes had adjusted to the dark. I stood at the sink and let the water run for a little while until it was ice-cold. I held a glass under it.

"What are you doing?" I heard. Beau's voice startled me and I dropped the glass into the sink.

"Shit, you scared me," I said, picking it up and inspecting for any cracks.

"Jumpy, huh?"

Maybe it was the headache, or the embarrassment that I was standing in just a t-shirt and panties, but his comment made me pissed.

"It's the middle of the fucking night and you scared me, nothing more," I snapped.

I refilled the glass and turned off the water. Beau was standing in the doorway, but I wasn't going to let his arrogant ass stop me from going back to bed. I walked tall toward him. I saw his eyes scan me from my ankles up to my breasts.

"Excuse me," I said, as I got close.

He stepped very slightly to one side, causing me to squeeze past him, as I did, the smell of alcohol hit me. I wrinkled my nose in disgust.

"You don't like me, do you?" he said.

"I think it's the other way round, not that I really care."

With that, I climbed the stairs and went back to bed. His laughter followed me. As much as I liked being at Cecelia's, and it was within my budget, I made a decision to find somewhere else to stay. For whatever reason, Beau didn't like or trust me. I understood, he was astute enough to know a woman walking in the rain wasn't out for a casual stroll. I just didn't need his probing comments, or his fucking rudeness.

———

I woke later than I would have liked to. I rushed around the bedroom, dressing in the previous day's clothes and ran down the stairs.

"Good morning. Sorry, I'm late for work," I said, as I passed Cecelia in the hallway.

I didn't wait for her answer but ran through the open front door and up the road. I arrived at the diner with minutes to spare. Usually I was at least ten minutes early; lateness was a pet peeve of mine.

"I'm sorry, I overslept," I said, reaching behind the counter for my apron.

"You're not late, bang on time, actually. You changed your hair," Rose said.

"I decided, new start, new me." I said, forcing a smile. "What would you like me to do?"

"You can wait on section one, I'll take a coffee break," she said.

There were only two sections in the diner and it had amused me, initially, to hear the seating area had been divided up. Section one was the row of booths lining the window. It was usually filled with truckers, or people passing through, those were the ones who tended to tip better. I liked section one.

I stood beside a family waiting on orders. At first they ignored me, continuing with their conversation while scanning the menu.

"They've arrested someone," he said.

"Have they? That's good, Mayor Stanton was such a lovely man. The reporter said they were looking for a woman, though," she said.

I should have interrupted them, asked them if they'd chosen their meal but I wanted to hear more. Unfortunately, their two children diverted their conversation to food.

I took their order and placed it on the counter for Kieran. I decided to wash down a neighboring table in the hope I'd be able to overhear them pick up the subject, sadly they didn't.

They've arrested someone. They're looking for a woman.

Who had they arrested? The TV was set to an old football game and I was anxious to listen to the news. When the lunchtime rush was over, I set about to clean down the tables and mop the floor. It was the first time I wished my shift was over, so I could head back to the library to see if there was any news.

"Would you like something to eat?" Kieran called over to me as I stacked the dishwasher.

Although my stomach grumbled, I thanked him and told him I wasn't hungry. I wanted to leave as soon as I could. When the clock showed three p.m., I pulled off my apron and left it under the counter.

"I'm off now," I said.

"Okay, would you like a double shift tomorrow? I know it's short notice, but my usual evening girl just called in, she can't make it," Rose asked.

"Of course, I'll take everything you have available."

She gave me a smile and a small envelope with that day's earnings. It was handy being paid daily; I could watch my little stash of savings grow quicker. I wanted to ask her about alternative accommodation but that meant taking the risk of her speaking with Cecelia, and I didn't want to upset either. I decided, once I'd checked out the newspapers at the library, I'd walk down to the motel and see what the room rental was.

The library was empty and I smiled at the librarian as I passed to the newspaper stand. I picked up a local and national then settled at a table. I flicked through the pages, becoming frustrated at the lack of news. Neither had reported on any developments on Philip's murder. In one corner of the library was a bank of computers. It had been a while since I'd last used one, and the ancient machines we'd had in school bore no resemblance to the sleek silver machines that sat side by side on the counter.

"Ma'am, I'd like to use one of the computers but it's been a while. Do you think you could help me?" I asked the librarian. She had to be as old as Cecelia and Rose combined, so I hoped she'd know what to do.

"Of course, you'll need to pay. We make a charge by the hour," she said.

I wasn't sure what I was paying for, air time or something, I guessed, but I handed over the required dollar for one hour and followed her.

We sat side by side on stools at the bench. She showed me the on button, that I could figure out, and then how to access the Internet. I told her I was doing some research to find my birth mother, so we typed in a fictitious name. I thanked her in the hopes she'd then leave me to carry on.

"If you need anything else, just give me a wave," she said, finally leaving me alone.

I deleted the name and retyped Philip Stanton. A list appeared, the first was a biography. I decided to take a look. Apparently, Philip had been the mayor of my old town for many years, most of it before I was old enough to know what, or who, a mayor was. It seemed he was loved by the townsfolk, hence the outpouring of grief I was beginning to witness in articles. I was pleased that he was so loved, but disheartened at the same time. The outpouring cemented my belief that if I were accused of his murder, I'd be destroyed.

I scrolled through various articles until I came to one from the previous day. It confirmed what I already knew, that someone was helping with the investigation, but there was no mention of an actual arrest. It stated that a female's shoe had been found under the bed, and the police were asking for the owner of that shoe to come forward for elimination purposes. I wasn't dumb enough to know 'elimination purposes' meant questioning. It was as I was about to finish my research when a photograph caught my eye. I opened the article to see the back of a man being led into the police station. I couldn't be sure, but wondered if Damien was the man 'helping with the investigation.' He certainly had the same long, straggly hair tied at the nape of his neck. I wasn't sure whether to let out a sigh of relief or hold my breath in fear.

Damien wasn't the most intelligent, if he had killed Philip, he would have been likely to shoot his mouth off when he was either drunk or drugged. He often bragged about his criminal lifestyle. Most of it went over my head; I didn't believe half of what he said. He was dumb enough to give my name to the police, though, even if that meant implicating himself in more crimes. I closed down the computer and just sat for a while. There was a small part of me that wanted to go to the police, explain what had happened, but I was scared. The idea of checking the motel was pushed to one side, whether Beau liked me or not, at least I wasn't alone at the house.

CHAPTER 5

I was up and at the diner an hour earlier than my shift. Having not eaten much the previous day, I was ravenous. I ordered the burger and fries, a soda, and followed with a scoop of ice cream. I sat in peace; it was the lull that occurred after breakfast and before lunch. Saturday, so Rose told me, was a mixed day, a hit and miss depending on the weather. We could be steadily busy all day, or it could come in fits and starts. However, the early evening was always a rush.

"You look tired, girl," Kieran said, as he sat beside me in the booth.

I had noticed dark circles start to frame my eyes. I wasn't getting much sleep; there was just too much going through my mind. I gave him a smile.

"You look like a young woman with the weight of the world on her shoulders," he added.

I opened my mouth to speak but it seemed the words didn't want to come. I could open up to him, I could ask advice; he seemed like a worldly man. Instead I just smiled. He patted my hand as he finished up the cup of coffee he held and then rose.

"Well, best get my groove on," he said, giving me a wink. I laughed.

"Groove? You haven't had *groove* since the nineteen-sixties," Rose said, taking his seat.

I loved to listen to the banter they had going on and wondered if they were actually partners. No one had mentioned a relationship, but there seemed to be a vibe that went beyond friends.

"Silly old man," she grumbled, staring after him.

"How old is he?" I asked.

"Sixty-eight this year. Won't slow down, though. He was in the army for God knows how many years. Turned up here one day, oh, fifteen years ago, I guess, and has stayed. Well, in between jetting off wherever for the army."

"She was a fine woman back then. She fell instantly back in love with me," Kieran shouted from the kitchen.

Rose shook her head and laughed at his comment.

"Are you two...?"

"Companions, or friends, or whatever you youngsters call it," she said.

"That must be nice, to be close to someone," I said.

"You really are feeling a little lost, aren't you?" she said, gently.

I willed the tears not to well in my eyes. I nodded instead of speaking.

"I'm..." I didn't finish my sentence. I wanted to tell her I was in trouble, that I needed help. Instead, I closed my mouth and squeezed her hand.

"Another time," she said.

———

Lunch time was a steady stream of people in for a quick bite to eat, or just to sit with a coffee. I tried to usher the coffee drinkers to the stools at the counter, leaving the booths free for those who wanted to eat. It seemed a waste to take up that space, to me. I had a half-hour break before my next shift and decided to sit in the kitchen, watching Kieran wiggle his ass to whatever song was playing while cooking steaks. He sang along to all the tunes, whether he knew the words or not. I would never have guessed at his age, he looked at least ten years younger.

"Here you go, girl, have a taste of this," he handed me a steak wrap.

"Mmm, lovely," I replied between mouthfuls.

"That's my secret sauce."

"What's in it?" I asked, wiping my mouth with a napkin.

"If I told you, it wouldn't be a secret now, would it?"

He laughed as he prepared more wraps. I looked at the clock and slid from the counter I'd been sitting on, then headed to the restroom. I washed my hands and splashed some cold water over my face. I gently slapped my cheeks, trying to bring some color to my skin. The image that stared back at me in the bathroom mirror had a haunted look about her. With the darker hair, my skin looked so pale. Maybe I needed to invest in some makeup.

Early evening diners and people grabbing a bite to eat before heading to the town's movie theater, started to arrive. There was a buzz that was different from the day. A large group of friends slid into two booths, chatting excitedly about their planned evening.

"Where's Kacy?" one asked, as I waited to take their order.

"Can't make her shift tonight," I replied, smiling as I did.

I recognized the girl from the library. "Shame, we like her," she said, looking me up and down.

I stood, still waiting to take their order, until a family came in. "How about I give you a little more time to decide which soda you want? I'll be back in a minute."

How fucking hard was it to choose between three different sodas. I settled the family in the last remaining booth and smiled at the children as they recalled the movie they'd just seen. Their faces became animated as they played out the scenes. It took more than a minute for their mom to get them to decide on what they wanted to eat.

Watching families together, having fun and laughing, hurt way more than the group of stuck up girls.

I enjoyed the evening shift; I liked the tips more. I could see my little jar filling up nicely and secretly wished Kacy, whoever she was, would stay off work. If I could get just another week of double shifts, I'd triple my savings. That thought spurred me on. I smiled, laughed, and was as helpful as I could be, knowing that soon enough I'd be on my way.

It was almost ten o'clock when we locked up the diner and Kieran insisted on walking me back to the house.

"Enjoy yourself, did you?" he asked.

"I did. I know this is mean, but I hope Kacy is sick and that's why she can't come in. Not, like, really sick, just mildly enough to give me some extra shifts," I laughed as I spoke.

He chuckled along with me. "She's on her way out, the poor girl. I think she's been off sick more than she's been at work. Rose is a sucker for a girl in need, though."

I hoped that was just an off the cuff comment and he wasn't referring to me.

"So, girl, how long are you staying around for?" he asked.

"I don't know. I was honest with Rose from the beginning. I do like it here, though."

I did, in just the week I'd been in town, I'd grown to like the people, the job, but it was just too close to Philip and Damien to safely stay.

"How are you finding it, staying at Cecelia's?" he asked as we neared the house.

"I really like her and the bedroom is comfortable."

"Getting on with Beau?"

His question startled me. "I'm not sure he likes me very much," I said.

"He's a good man, been through a hard time, though."

"I'm sure he is," I replied, not wanting to say too much more.

"Well, here we are. We'll see you tomorrow."

"Thank you for walking me home, I appreciate that."

He gave me a nod and turned back to walk the way we came. I decided to sit on the sun deck for a little while. My brain was still buzzing from my shift and all the coffee I'd drunk. I wanted to wind down a little. I could hear voices from the room I was sitting outside.

"But you don't know a thing about her," Beau said.

"I don't need to. I wish you'd just trust my judgement. The girl needs help, we all know that. When she's ready, she'll tell us."

"And if she doesn't? Whatever trouble she's in, it might find itself on your doorstep."

Beau sounded angry and I had no doubt they were talking about me. I also heard footsteps, and before I could move, the front door opened. I was sitting in the shadow and watched Beau sigh heavily. He lit a cigarette before pulling the door gently closed, then sat on the top step.

"Yes, I'm in trouble. And no, I don't anticipate that trouble affecting your, or Cecelia's life," I said, aware of the bitterness in my voice. I had startled him.

"How can you be sure?" he asked, turning to face me.

"Because I'll be gone soon. It's obviously a problem, me being here, and that's something I didn't want to happen."

"She is the only family I have. I don't want her anxious over a stranger."

His words stung a little.

"I understand that, and if I was in the same position, I'd feel the same. I don't want to cause trouble, Beau. I'll move on as quickly as possible."

I left him to finish his cigarette and walked into the house. I avoided the kitchen and climbed the stairs to the bedroom. The sanctuary that I'd found had soured somewhat.

I didn't bother to undress but sat on the bed, pulled my knees to my chest, and wrapped the quilt around my shoulders. I rested my forehead on my knees. I'd never felt so alone before.

There was a tap on the bedroom door. I ignored it at first, assuming it was Cecelia and not wanting her to see my tears. A second tap came and before I could make a decision on whether to get up and answer it, the door opened.

"I think you've said all you need," I said, looking at Beau standing in the doorway. The light from outside framed him.

"What trouble are you in?"

"It has nothing to do with you, and I wouldn't burden anyone with my problems, anyway."

He walked into the room and closed the door behind him. The room was lit only by the moonlight. He crossed the beam of light that blazed into the room and sat on the end of the bed.

"Charlotte, what trouble are you in?" he repeated.

"Why do you want to know, Beau? So you can mock me some more? So you can tell Cecelia that *you told her so*?" My hushed tones rose in anger.

"Because, for some reason, my aunt likes you. Rose and Kieran like you. They want me to help you."

"They want *you* to help me? What are you, Beau, the police?" I laughed bitterly.

"No, not the police."

"Have you all had a discussion about me?"

His lack of an answer was all I needed to hear. I let my head rest back on my knees and for a moment we sat in silence.

"My grandmother died, I never knew my mother, or my father. She left me her house but the court awarded a guardian. A cousin I'd never met before turned up and took over my life. He's a drunk, a drug addict. I don't know what happened, but one night I was dragged from my bed and thrown out into the yard. He'd lost my house and I was being evicted."

"And that's who you're running from?"

"Yes. That was who I was running from when you picked me up."

"But that's not all, is it?" he asked.

"No. And I don't care how much you want to protect your aunt, I'm not willing to discuss anymore. Let's just say, my cousin destroyed my life in ways you could never imagine. And I'm in trouble for something I haven't done."

I lifted my head from my knees, not caring that he saw my tears.

"Now I would like you to leave this room. I pay for it and I have rights. If you can give me a couple of days, I'll find somewhere else to stay."

He nodded his head and stood. In silence and without glancing at me, he left the room. I curled on my side and cried myself to sleep.

The following morning, I showered and dressed, then snuck out of the house before anyone was up. I grabbed a newspaper and found a small coffee shop at the other end of the town. I sat at a table in the corner and scanned through the ads, hoping I'd find a room for rent. I also looked for another job. It wasn't that I would leave the diner, but I needed to work more hours just for another couple of weeks if I could manage to stick around that long. I wanted enough for airfare. Where to? I had no idea, but hitchhiking out of town wasn't going to get me far enough away. I'd never purchased an airline ticket before; I guessed it couldn't be that hard. I had no idea where the nearest airport was, but again, it shouldn't be difficult to find that out. Perhaps the librarian could help me with that.

I left the coffee shop and headed to the library. Unfortunately, the librarian I had met before wasn't around, a young guy stood behind the counter.

"I know this might be a strange question, but where is the nearest airport?" I asked.

He gave me a strange look, as if I'd asked him the most outrageous question. "International?" he asked.

"No, I don't think so."

"You don't think so?"

"I just want to fly to a different state," I tried not to get exasperated.

"Then I guess you'd want Tulsa."

"How far from here is Tulsa?"

He shrugged his shoulders before returning his gaze back to a pile of books on the counter. I wasn't sure I was going to get any useful information from him so decided to find a map. It was a library; they must have maps, mustn't they?

I scanned the shelves, and eventually found what I was looking for. I found the town and tracked across the page until I located their airport. On paper it didn't look that far, but in reality, I guessed it was way more miles that I'd be able to manage without planning. Maybe there was a bus service that I could take.

I hadn't noticed any public transport, in fact, there wasn't even a train station locally. I'd have to head back to my old home for that, something I wasn't prepared to do. I closed the map and replaced it on the shelf. If Beau wanted me gone, then he'd have to help.

It was with a shadow of sadness that I completed my shift. I knew Rose thought something was wrong, I saw her glance at me on more than one occasion. I did everything I was asked to do, with a smile to each customer, but I guessed that smile didn't quite meet my eyes. I didn't get the afternoon shift as Kacy had returned, and since it had been a quiet lunchtime, my tips jar was fairly low.

"Are you okay? You look a little distracted today?" Rose asked, as she handed me my wage envelope.

"A little tired, that's all. I didn't sleep well last night."

"You look like you've lost a little weight as well. Are you eating regularly?"

"Of course. Honestly, I'm fine." I gave her the smile she needed to stop her questioning.

I didn't head back to the house after my shift. Instead, I found a small park and I sat on a bench. It wasn't the weather for sitting out for hours, but I had no desire to sit in the bedroom knowing I wasn't welcome. I'd caused an argument between Beau and Cecelia and that troubled me. I just sat and watched moms and children play on the swings and slides. I watched dog walkers, some reluctantly, parading their pooches around. A couple walked past holding hands and laughing. It wasn't a cold day but I shivered and slipped my hands up the arms of my sweater. When my ass was numb from sitting for so long, I took a slow walk around the town. I discovered some back streets and a courtyard with a small fountain. I sat on the edge and dangled my fingers through the cold water. It did nothing to warm me up, but there was something comforting about the sound of rippling water. Maybe, when I figured out how I was going to leave, it would be to somewhere on the coast. I'd never been to the sea. The closest I'd gotten to open water was a dip in the murky, rat piss-infested lake back home.

I was growing bored, and tired. Tired through lack of sleep and tired of not knowing what was around the corner. There had been no fresh news about Philip, and I guessed the silence from Damien was because he, hopefully, was still helping the police with their investigation. I prayed for the day he would be officially arrested, maybe then I would contact the police and claim ownership of the shoe. I would lie, of course. I didn't want to tarnish Philip's name, and I certainly didn't want to be named as a trailer trash prostitute who had shared his bed.

———

The small convenience store was about to close when I barreled through the door.

"I'm sorry, I just need a couple of things," I said. The storekeeper smiled and let me in.

"You're working at the diner, aren't you?" she asked. I nodded as I grabbed a pre-made sandwich, a couple of bags of chips, and a bar of chocolate.

I fished out some money and paid for my dinner, trying not to make any further eye contact. "Thank you, and I'm sorry for keeping you open," I said, and then left.

She followed me to the door and I heard bolts being slid across as she prepared to lock up. I snacked on the chocolate on the walk back to the house. For the first time, I actually sighed as I walked the path to the sun deck and the front door. It was always unlocked and I hesitantly pushed it open. I could hear Cecelia humming to herself in the kitchen, and not wanting to appear rude, I called out to her. She asked me to join her for a cup of tea.

I left my dinner on the first stair with my sneakers and walked into the kitchen. I was thankful that Beau wasn't home.

"Sit, I don't feel like I've seen you for days. Tea?" Cecelia asked.

"That would be lovely, I'm all 'coffeed' out today," I said with a laugh.

"You've been working hard, and you look a little tired," she said, mirroring Rose's comments from earlier in the day.

"I had a restless night, nothing more."

"Is the bed uncomfortable, I can give you another room. One with a larger bed, perhaps?"

"Oh, no. The room is perfect, thank you. I just had a few things on my mind, that's all. I'm sure I'll sleep like the dead tonight."

Rose placed a cup, her pot, and the jug of milk on the table before sitting herself.

"So tell me about your day?" she asked as she poured.

"The diner was a little quieter than usual, but I took a walk around town. I found a nice park to sit, and a courtyard with a fountain. I thought I'd do a little exploring today," I said, forcing a smile.

"That sounds good. Beau lives near that fountain, in one of the townhouses."

He didn't spend every night at Cecelia's but it hadn't occurred to me that he lived elsewhere either.

"Oh, I thought he lived here," I said.

"No, although he stays over often. He really should sell that house after…"

She didn't finish her sentence and I didn't press. It wasn't my business to know why he should sell his house. We sipped our tea in silence for a little while.

"Charlotte, if there's anything you want to tell me, you can. I know you haven't known me for long but…" She left her sentence hanging.

I sighed and took another sip of the tea. "Cecelia, I don't want to involve you in whatever problems I have. I appreciate your offer of help, I really do. But it's my mess to get out of."

"You're so young, I just want you to know that you have support."

I wished I could open up; I wished I could tell Cecelia everything that had happened, but I believed her first response would be for me to go to the police. It would have been the right thing to do, but I had the added anxiety of Damien. I'd lied more in the past week than I thought I had my whole life. Lying wasn't something that came naturally to me and if I went to the police, I'd have to tell them everything. If Damien wasn't arrested for being my pimp, let alone murdering, if he had, Philip…Well, I didn't want to think how my life would turn out. It was better that I just ran.

"My *problem*, Cecelia, is complicated. It's best I don't involve

64

anyone."

I wondered whether Beau had relayed our conversation from the previous evening. Maybe he'd even told her that he was the one to pick me up from the roadside and bring me into town.

She nodded her head and I thought the furrowed brow might be worry. I was damned if I did, and even more damned if I didn't tell. I doubted for one minute Cecelia, Rose, Beau even, had any idea of the enormity of my *problem*.

————

It was the following evening that part of my *problem* caught up with me.

After a double shift at the diner, Kacy was sick again, I refused Kieran's offer to accompany me home. It wasn't a long walk, and I'd been doing it day after day to be able to find my way back blindfolded. I was distracted, looking at my sneaker lace that had come undone and debating whether I ought to tie it before I tripped over, when a pair of headlights momentarily blinded me.

A car engine rattled, it didn't purr or roar, it rattled, as if in desperate need of repair. The car jolted forward, cutting across the road toward me. At first I was frozen to the spot, my body way behind my brain in reaction time. Over the engine noise, I heard a man call out.

"Harlot, is that you?"

There was only one person who called me that. I spun on my heels and ran in the opposite direction. It wasn't a conscious decision not to alert Damien to where I was staying, just pure instinct in wanting to get away. I darted down the first side street I came to, ran across the road, and then down an alley not wide enough for the car. I dodged dumpsters, and a cat that screeched in fear of my manic presence. I didn't look behind me, not once. I kept on running, zigzagging my way down side streets, doubling back up others. Eventually, I found myself in the courtyard with the fountain, and nowhere obvious to hide. I crouched to one side of it, not sure if Damien was following me on foot or in the car, or from which direction he'd arrive. I took some deep breaths to quell my racing heart and feed my screaming, oxygen-starved muscles.

Other than my gasps for air, it was quiet. I strained to hear even the softest footsteps, not that I thought Damien capable of creeping quietly. I heard nothing but the scream I let out when a hand grabbed my shoulder. I leapt to my feet without looking who owned the hand. I tugged my shoulder from its grasp, clawing at the skin with my nails.

"What the fuck...?" I heard. It hadn't immediately registered that it wasn't Damien's voice.

I wrenched myself away and stumbled to my knees. I crawled to a nearby wall and used it to support myself. My legs had turned to mush. My vision was blurred with unshed tears when Beau stepped in front of me.

"What the fuck are you doing here?" he asked.

I swiped my arm across my eyes. At first I couldn't answer, my breaths were too ragged to form words.

"I...Was..."

"Breathe, Charlotte. Slow down, take some deep breaths," he said. I wasn't dumb enough to think there was any sympathy in his words. He probably didn't want to deal with me passing out.

Before I could, car headlights swept across the courtyard. I grabbed Beau, turned us so my back was to the wall, and pulled him to me. We had the shadow of the wall to conceal us. If Damien had seen us, I hoped he would have thought it was just a couple making out. I held onto the front of Beau's jacket, keeping my head low and turned away from the source of the headlights.

"One last time, Charlotte, what the fuck are you doing here?" Beau asked, his voice laced with anger.

"Please, just...please," I mumbled against his chest. Whether I'd tapped into what small amount of empathy Beau had, I wasn't sure, but I felt his body relax just a little.

We stayed that way for a minute or two. Until I was sure the vehicle had moved away for good. I let go of Beau's jacket and he took a step back.

"Trouble caught up with you, huh?"

All I could do was nod my head. "I'll pack my things and leave tonight," I said.

"And go where? How?"

"There must be a bus stop somewhere. I'll get the first one that comes along."

I made to step around him, but he blocked my way.

"You're not going back to the house, whoever that was might be waiting out there. I will not allow you to take your trouble back to Cecelia's."

"I need my things," I said, protesting.

He grabbed my arm and roughly pulled me along the sidewalk. We stopped outside one of the townhouses, and before we climbed the three stone steps to the front door, Beau scanned the courtyard. Satisfied, he led me into his house.

He let go of my arm and walked down the narrow hallway. To one side was a staircase, and the other held two doors. He paused at one, and then beckoned to me. I followed him into a kitchen. I stood with my arms wrapped around myself, not because I was cold, but to stop my body from shaking. Beau shrugged out of his jacket, placing it on the back of a high chair that stood beside a countertop. He rounded the counter and opened a cupboard door. I watched as he retrieved two mugs and poured coffee. He didn't ask me how I took it but slid a cup of black coffee toward me.

"Drink," he said.

I reached out and picked up the cup, thankful it wasn't full. My hand shook as I held it to my lips. It was hot, bitter, rocket fuel strength, but I welcomed it. Beau gave me a couple of minutes before pointing to one of the chairs.

"Sit down," he said, without any nicety.

I did as I was told. He leaned against the counter and stared hard at me.

"This will be the last time I ask you this, Charlotte. What the fuck are you doing here?"

"Hiding."

"Why?"

I blinked back tears, not wanting Beau to see how upset I was. I placed my cup on the counter, wincing at the rattle as the ceramic hit the marble.

"I don't..."

"If you're about to say you don't want to tell me, then I'll kick you out right now, and you can take your chances against whoever you're running from. You were terrified out there. Why?"

Beau held himself rigid, his arms were crossed over his chest, his face was hard but, and whether it was just wishful thinking on my part, it seemed that worry lines appeared on his forehead.

I felt myself slump; I reached out and grabbed the countertop to stop myself from toppling off the chair. As hard as I tried, I couldn't stop the sob leaving my mouth. That sob was followed by another, and for the first time since my grandmother had died, I cried hard.

I held my face in my hands, not caring about the tears that seeped through my fingers and dripped to the counter. Beau didn't say a word, he just stood where he was and let me cry myself out. When my sobbing had stopped, I felt something soft against the back of my hand. I parted my fingers to see a tissue being held out for me. I took it and wiped my eyes, my nose, and my cheeks.

I didn't look at him, I couldn't. At first, when I opened my mouth, the words wouldn't come but slowly, and quietly, I began to speak.

"My mother abandoned me, I know nothing about her. My grandmother wouldn't speak of her; I don't even know what she looks like. But that was okay, I was brought up well, until my grandmother died." I stopped to take in a deep breath, knowing Beau already knew this about me.

"A cousin I'd never met was appointed my guardian, all he wanted was to get the house my grandmother had left me. He drinks, takes drugs, he..." The words dried up.

"He what, Charlotte?" Beau asked, that time there was gentleness to his voice.

"He gave me to his friends. They raped me, beat me. I don't know how, but he lost the house, I imagine he owed money, but I was kicked out."

"Back up a minute. He *gave* you to his friends?"

I kept my gaze focused on the cup. "He forced me to have sex with his friends, and he took money from them for that." Only then did I look up at him and I wished I hadn't.

Beau's face clearly displayed the disgust he felt. I wasn't sure if that disgust was directed at Damien or me.

"He made me prostitute myself, for years. He wouldn't let me go to school, he isolated me from anyone, other than his friends."

"Where did you live?"

"Back in Whiteling, in a trailer on a park full of the dregs. So now you know, that is who I'm running from."

"But that's not the whole story is it?"

"No. But it's as much as I'm willing to tell you right now, Beau. I can see the disgust on your face, I know you don't like me, and now I've given you enough to hate me. Like I said, I'll leave as soon as I can get my things. Those clothes, that quilt my grandmother made me, are all I own."

My voice was hoarse, my throat sore from the crying, and my eyes were half-closed. I wanted to laugh; I'd always been an ugly crier.

I slid the chair back and stood. "Thank you for the coffee. I'll make sure he's gone before I go to Cecelia's. If he hasn't, I promise you, I won't go there."

"Where will you go, Charlotte?"

I shrugged my shoulders, that was something I'd decide at the time. He sighed before pushing himself upright.

"You'll stay here. That way I know you're both safe."

"I can't stay here, Cecelia is expecting me."

"I'll call her. No arguing. There is a spare bedroom this way."

He walked to the door and turned to look over his shoulder to make sure I was following, I guessed.

His house was on three levels. He led me up the stairs to the second level and along a small corridor. He opened a door and then stood to one side.

"The bathroom is along the hall. I'll be downstairs."

"Is there a bedroom downstairs?"

"No, but I've slept on the couch more nights than I've slept anywhere else."

"I'm putting you out," I said.

"Yes. But it's better than knowing that prick can turn up at my aunt's house during the night."

It was yet another comment of his that stung. I wasn't at his house so he could protect me; I was there simply to keep his aunt safe. I nodded in reply and then walked into the room. He closed the door behind me.

The room was beautifully decorated and a complete contradiction to Beau. The walls were painted a soft lilac, a wooden bedstead stood proud against one wall with a cream and lace quilt, matching lilac pillows were placed artistically at the headboard. A solid wooden chest of drawers was against the opposite wall. Sat on top was a vanity mirror, a glass vase with flowers that, only by touch, I realized weren't real, and an empty picture frame. It seemed at odds with the room. I wondered if it had housed a photograph at one time and it had been removed.

I sat on the edge of the bed and kicked off my sneakers. I crept to the bedroom door, needing the bathroom. I guessed Beau to be in the room directly below, and I didn't want creaking floorboards to disturb him. The bathroom was decorated in a similar, feminine way to the bedroom. Perfectly folded, pristine white towels were placed on a rack. A shelf above the sink held hand moisturizer and sweet scented soap. I used the toilet, washed my hands and face, and scrubbed my wet finger over my teeth. I had no choice but to disrupt the perfectly folded towels and was at a loss as to what to do with it after. I hung it over the edge of the roll top bath. I looked longingly at the bath; I hadn't been able to soak in a tub for years.

I undressed, folded my clothes and placed them on a chair beside the window. The bed was deceptively comfortable. I'd imagined, when I'd sat initially on the edge, that the mattress would be firm, as unforgiving as the dark oak bedframe. As I sank down into lavender smelling pillows and pulled the duvet over me, I knew a woman had lived in this house.

Although I woke a couple of times during the night, it was probably one of the best night's sleep I'd had in ages. I'd kept the drapes open so as not to oversleep. Reluctantly, I climbed from the bed and smoothed out the pillows and quilt. I dressed, not wanting to overstep my welcome with a bath, and quietly walked down the stairs. The door to what I presumed was a living room was closed, as was the kitchen door. I reached for the front door latch, deciding to leave before Beau woke, to find it locked and no key visible.

"Shit," I whispered.

There was no furniture in the hallway, nothing that would allow a set of keys to be left on it. After standing for a minute or two, not knowing what to do, I headed to the kitchen. I gently pushed open the door to see Beau already sitting at the kitchen table; he had earbuds in and was scrolling through his iPhone, selecting music I guessed. He was dressed for a run.

"Hi," I said, tentatively.

"Did you sleep okay?"

"I did. It's a beautiful room."

He nodded. "I'll let you out," he said, and then rose from his chair.

Without another word, he walked me to the front door, pulled a key from a breast pocket and opened it. We both walked out in the morning sunshine.

"Erm, thank you. What did you tell Cecelia?" I asked.

I did not want her thinking I was staying at Beau's because we'd become friends, or worse.

"You stayed at mine."

"But why did I stay at yours?"

"She didn't ask, I didn't tell. I'm late for my run."

With that, he closed the front door and locked it, before leaving me standing there and jogging away.

"How can you be late for a run?" I said to myself, as he was out of earshot by then.

I started the walk back to Cecelia's. A thought occurred to me halfway. Beau had been insistent that I stay at his so as not to lure Damien to his aunt's house. Why would that be different during the day? What made Beau think Damien wasn't sitting around the corner waiting for me? It didn't add up, and I made a mental note to ask Beau when I saw him next.

Thankfully, Damien wasn't sitting around the corner and I made it back without incident. Cecelia was sitting in the kitchen when I arrived. I called out to her, telling her I was heading for a shower, and then I'd be back down. She told me she'd have a nice cup of tea ready and waiting for me.

I was showered, hair washed, and dressed in record time. I also packed my bag. I wanted to head to Ellie's store before showing up for work. I was fed up of being asked if I was tired, and more importantly, being sneered at by the local girls. I wanted to buy some makeup. Not that I'd worn much of it before, but I knew it would help to make me look a little older as well.

"Here, have some tea," Cecelia said. I took a seat at the table.

"I won't be coming back, but I want to thank you for letting me stay," I said.

"Why? Aren't you happy here?"

Before I could answer, Beau walked through the back door. He still wore his running clothes, sweat coated the front of his t-shirt, and his hair was standing on end as if he'd just run his hand through it.

"I am, but I need to find somewhere else." I didn't want to tell her about Damien for fear of worrying her.

"Beau, talk to her. She wants to leave."

"It's her choice, Cecelia," he said, not looking at me.

I reached over the table and took one of her hands in mine.

"I've loved being here, and I want to thank you for that. But it's time for me to find somewhere of my own."

Cecelia sighed. "There's the apartment over on St. James Street. It's not much but I'm sure we can work out a suitable rent."

"Cecelia..." Beau said.

"Beau, I want to know Charlotte is safe and if that can't be here, for whatever reason..." She stared hard at him when she spoke. "Then she can rent *my* apartment."

"I don't want to cause any more problems than I already have. I'll be fine, I'm sure I can find..."

"No, I'll hear no more of it. Charlotte, I know you're in trouble and I want to help you. If you really feel you have to leave, then the apartment will be perfect for you. I'd rather someone was living in it anyway. Beau will take you over there, and I'll pop on over once I've done my chores."

I had half an idea that she knew Beau was the one that had instigated my leaving, and that was probably the reason why she'd insisted he show me where the apartment was.

"I'm not sure I can afford an apartment," I said.

"Then maybe we can come to some kind of an arrangement. I'll think about it. At least, for the next few days, stay at the apartment, please?"

I was torn. I knew the reason I had to leave, and I agreed with Beau in wanting to protect Cecelia. But I had nowhere else to go, and not enough money to get there.

Cecelia stared at Beau long enough for him to sigh and then look at me. "Let's go," he said.

Cecelia glanced at me and gave a wink. I followed Beau to the front door where he collected a key from a box on the wall and I picked up my backpack.

He didn't speak as we walked a block to the apartment. I say walked, I jogged to keep up with him. The apartment was the top floor of a townhouse, similar to the ones in the courtyard. Beau opened the front door and took the stairs, two at a time. On the landing was another door. He opened that and stood to one side. I walked in first, he followed. Perhaps the ass had some manners after all.

"It's…"

"Not ideal but it's short term, right?" he replied.

I nodded. I was going to say, the apartment was the most amazing space I'd set foot in. It was mainly open plan, with a kitchen to one side and living space opposite. There were two doors and I headed to one. It was a large bedroom with an iron framed double bed, a dresser, and an ornately carved wooden wardrobe. I placed my backpack on the bed and looked through the other door. It was a small bathroom but perfect for my needs.

Beau stood in the middle of the room with a set of keys dangling from his fingers. I walked over and reached out to take them. Before I could, he snatched them away.

"Short term, Charlotte."

I didn't respond but grabbed the keys from his fist, making sure I dragged my nails along his skin, again.

Fuck you, prick, I thought.

I then walked to the front door and opened it, making sure Beau understood that I wanted him to leave. I was done with taking his shit. He paused as he passed me.

"I've been controlled and bullied by a man for a long time. Don't think for one minute you can replace him," I said, making sure to hold his gaze.

He opened his mouth to speak, and a flash of confusion crossed his face.

"Thank you for walking me over here, but I think I can cope from now on," I said. I shut the door after him with a satisfied grin on my face.

There were large sash windows on one wall and I walked over to open them. The apartment didn't have air conditioning, not that I was used to that or needed it at that time of the year. I much preferred to have a gentle breeze and fresh air. The sheer drapes started to ripple. I checked out the kitchen, opening cupboards to see what I needed to buy. I counted out my money, surprised that it was a little more than I'd originally thought. I could buy some basic dishes, cutlery, and stock up the food cupboard and fridge. The bed had linen but I only noticed one towel in the bathroom. I'd pop into the general store after my shift at the diner.

I decided to take a quick shower before heading out. I wasn't sure of the time and added a clock to my mental list of things to buy. Although the shower wasn't as powerful as the one at Cecelia's, it was enough to wash my hair. I noticed the color run from my hair and added more dye to that list. I scrubbed the towel over my head, wincing at the dye that stained it, before wrapping it around my body. As I left the bathroom I stopped in my tracks.

Sitting on the kitchen counter was a black object that wasn't there earlier. I walked over and picked up a cell phone. Beside it was a note.

Use this in emergencies. I've programmed my number and Cecelia's. Beau

He'd added a list of instructions on how to use the cell. Although I'd never owned one, I knew how to use them. I switched it on and scrolled through the contacts. There were the two he'd said. I was more pleased to have an object that told me the time, than allowed me to communicate with the ass. However, I was disturbed that he appeared to have a spare key. I took the cell into the bedroom with me and dressed.

Before I left the apartment, I divided up my money into four separate piles and found four hiding places for each one.

"Good morning," Rose called out as I entered the diner. "You're early."

"I wondered if I could have a word," I said.

She motioned to a booth and then grabbed two cups of coffee. "What's wrong?" she asked.

"Nothing's wrong. I've moved into Cecelia's apartment, so I wondered if there was the chance of extra, permanent shifts? I know

I've not been here long, but I could do with earning a little extra. If not, do you know if I can pick up work elsewhere, obviously outside my hours here?"

"Mmm, well, Kacy is a little hit and miss right now. I'd hate to let her go, though; she's a single mom and needs the money. But, let me have a think, I'm sure we can sort something out."

"You are the champion of the needy," I said, with a laugh.

"I'll let you into a secret, I was where you are right now, once." She took a sip of her coffee.

"I kind of want to say, 'I'm glad,' but I know that's not the right phrase. But, I'm grateful to you," I said.

She chuckled. "So, you know you're an hour early?"

"I didn't. I don't have a watch, but Beau left me a cell so I'll know the time from now on. I have a little shopping to do, for the apartment, so I'll head over to the store and then be back, if that's okay?"

"Of course it is. Maybe you can pick up a couple of items for me?"

I nodded. She pulled her pad from her apron pocket and wrote a list, then fished in her jean pocket for some money.

"That should cover it."

I folded the bills in the note and stuffed it into my pocket, drained my coffee, and then told Rose I'd see her soon.

I grabbed a cart and wandered up the aisles of the general store. I had to go with the cheapest items I could find, but they would do. I wasn't planning on staying around and I certainly did not want to have to take it all with me. I grabbed a newspaper, hoping for more news on Philip. I paid for Rose's bucket and cleaner separately, then bagged up my own. I struggled back to the diner with four bags, two of which were heavy and clanking when dishes and cutlery rolled against each other. I handed Rose her bag, the receipt and her change, then left my purchases under the counter.

"Eat first, I want you to try this," Kieran said, as I entered the kitchen.

I looked at the pasta dish he'd placed in front of me. One advantage of being chief food tester, as Kieran had dubbed me, was I didn't have to purchase too much food for the apartment.

"What is it?"

"If I tell you that, I'll have to…"

I laughed, cutting off his standard response. Whatever it was, it was delicious and I devoured the whole plateful. There was no doubt that would fill my stomach for many hours to come.

"Loved it, is it going on the menu?"

"Maybe, now, get your backside out there, lunch rush is starting."

He cranked up his music and wiggled his backside as he flipped burgers.

My shift flew by, my tips jar overflowed. With my daily wages, I pocketed nearly fifty dollars that day. It was the best day for tips I'd ever had. If I could have more days like that, I'd be happy.

"Charlotte, tomorrow, if you're happy for a few extra hours, get here about eight?" Kieran shouted, as I was about to leave. I nodded enthusiastically, and again, wondered what his input in the diner was.

Despite it being the middle of the afternoon, I checked before I left the diner for anything unusual, or a beat up car. I looked over my shoulder many times on the journey back to the apartment, especially when the hairs on my neck stood on end at one point. I gave myself a mental kick up the ass and put that down to paranoia.

I looked at people passing by, wanting to see if they even so much as glanced at me. I began to doubt what I'd heard, had that been Damien? Had he called out my name? I knew one thing, though. I couldn't relax until he was charged with Philip's murder and I was in the clear.

"Charlotte," I heard, as I rounded the corner toward the house.

I looked up the street to see Cecelia walking toward me. She carried a couple of bags.

"I wanted to wait until you'd finished work. I have some things for you."

I raised my bags and laughed. "I have *things,* too," I said.

We walked up the stairs and into the apartment together. It was the first time that I notice Cecelia struggle a little. She seemed more out of breath than I'd normally see and she winced once or twice.

"Are you okay?" I asked. She waved off my question as she placed her bags on the kitchen counter.

"Now, I have some meals for the freezer, you will eat them, won't you? I also have some spare plates, cups, and..."

She opened one bag and gave me the sneakiest peek of a coffee maker. I could have kissed her, instead I threw my arms around her neck and hugged her close.

"You didn't need to do that but I can't say I'm not happy," I said, unboxing the machine.

I showed her what I'd bought and together we filled the cupboards.

"Now, we need to talk about rent," I said, trying to swallow down the nerves at her answer.

"I've been thinking about that. I need some help at home, Charlotte, and I know this might not be what you wanted to do with your life, but I'm happy to let you stay here rent-free, in return for some help around the house. Beau is often away for long periods with his work, and the house is just too much for me to manage."

I hadn't thought about Beau having a job, and I wondered what he did that kept him away for periods of time.

"Cecelia, I'd help you regardless but I'm not comfortable with staying here free. Can we come to some arrangement?"

She pursed her lips. "I thought that would be your response. So, I'll pay you one hundred dollars a week for ten hours to help me clean the house, tend to the yard, and you'll pay me one hundred dollars a week for rent. Sound fair?"

I had no idea if she was overpaying me, undercharging me, but it all worked out to what she'd offered initially. I chuckled as I shook my head and then held out my hand to shake on the deal.

"Ten hours a week it is then. But, if you need me beyond that, you just ask and I do it for free. I get the feeling I've gotten the better end of the deal here," I said.

I'd make sure I worked more than ten hours a week. I doubted a cleaner could command ten dollars an hour normally. For that small moment I felt like a grown up, I felt like I could make this new life work.

CHAPTER 6

Another week passed without any news on Philip. That surprised me, considering how popular he'd been. The odd report that I had found simply stated that the police were unwilling to release any more information and were working on leads. Part of me was pleased, they were clearly not close to identifying the shoe, and part of me was in turmoil at not knowing what was going on.

I decided to visit the library again and see if I could find anything on his family. I'd seen a photograph of his son, daughter-in-law, and their children, and thanks to a previous report, I knew his name. I Googled him to find he was some big shot in a law firm. That didn't bode well. I couldn't find any information on the family feud, although I didn't really expect to. I did read up about Philip's wife. It seemed she had died of breast cancer and was what I imagined her to be, a typical mayor's wife. She supported many charities, was very well liked, judging by the comments from friends, and looked to be a friendly person. She reminded me a little of a slightly younger version of my grandmother.

When I'd done my research, I asked the librarian for registration documents. I wanted to see what was required with regard to ID. I didn't have my birth certificate, I'd never learned to drive, or owned a passport. Damien knew someone who could produce fake ID; I'd seen a stack of driver's licences with a rubber band around them in the trailer. Contacting him, obviously, wasn't an option.

I wanted to check out books to occupy my evenings instead of buying them. I could give an address, and I assumed I'd get some utility bills at some point. In fact, I made a mental note to talk to Cecelia about bills; she hadn't mentioned those. I folded the registration form and slipped it into my back pocket.

I hadn't seen anything of Beau and I'd been to Cecelia's a few times to help clean up the yard. I'd raked, weeded, and fixed the fence. I finished painting the sun deck railings, and was sitting in the kitchen with a cold soda, taking a break.

"I have some furniture to move in the den, if you can help me?" Cecelia said.

"Of course, how heavy is it? Do we need help?"

"I don't know, it's an old leather chair that belonged to my father, it's taking up way too much room in there. I thought I might put it outside and see if anyone wanted it. Seems a shame to throw it away."

"Let's have a look," I said.

Cecelia opened a door to a room I'd never visited. It was a little dark with the shutters closed, but once I opened them, I gasped. I stood and slowly turned in the most gorgeous room I'd ever visited. The walls were wood paneled to halfway up, silk wallpaper, although old and faded, gave the room a luxurious look.

"Oh, wow, Cecelia."

"It was my father's office, and then my husband's for a little while. I don't like to sit in here, although I'm not entirely sure why. Anyway, it's this old chair."

She walked to a dark red leather armchair. Although the arms were worn, and the leather slightly cracked, it was a beautifully made chair.

"Oh, wow," I said, again. "I love it, why do you want to get rid of it?"

"I thought I might turn this room in something more useable for me, and this isn't comfortable."

I sat and felt so small as I sank into the leather seat. I curled my legs up under me.

"This would be a perfect reading chair."

"You can have it, if you want."

"Really?"

"I was hoping someone would take it, like I just said."

"I don't think I'll get it to the apartment on my own, maybe I'll ask Kieran."

"I'm sure Beau can organize it."

Maybe it was the look on my face that I'd tried hard to conceal, but Cecelia cocked her head to one side.

"You two don't get on, do you?"

"I don't think he likes me very much, but it's okay. I don't want you to worry about it."

"Do you know why? I might be wrong, but..." She strode to the other end of the room and selected a photograph from a shelf. She walked back and handed it to me.

I stared at Beau with his arm around a woman, they were laughing. What had my eyes wide was that woman could very well have been my sister. The resemblance was uncanny.

"You look like her. She destroyed him, so I don't think it's that he doesn't like you. I think he still hurts so deeply, and you remind him of her."

"What happened? No, sorry, don't answer that. It's not my business."

"It's not a secret. He works away a lot, he came home one day and she was gone. No note, nothing. He had no idea why she'd left, they were happy. He spent a long time trying to find her, mourning her, even. Since then, well, he's never been truly happy and that breaks my heart."

"I don't know what to say," I said. As much as I had every sympathy for him, it was hardly my fault I looked like her. Then I cringed, inwardly.

"Oh, God. I got cross with him and I asked him, something like, *What did she do to you?* Because I thought he was cranky over a woman."

"I guess he didn't answer you."

"No. Cecelia, I'm not sure he'd appreciate me knowing this. Why don't I ask Kieran to help with the chair and we won't mention this again."

She smiled at me before putting the photograph back. "In the meantime, why don't I give this room a clean?" I added.

"I guess it could do with a sweep through. You are an angel, Charlotte, thank you."

I set about to clean the layers of dust that had grown over the years the room had been unused. I squared up a pile of papers that dated back years on the desk but avoided the shelf of photographs. Many were of Beau, some of Cecelia with her husband, and there was one very old one that I assumed to be her parents.

When I was done, the sunlight that streamed through the window reflected off the polished wooden desk. The room look completely different once the shutters were open. I picked up my cleaning materials, aware that my t-shirt and hands were filthy, and found Cecelia in the kitchen. She was sitting at the table, holding her cup of tea but staring into space.

"I'm done in there. It looks lovely now, not that it didn't before," I added, quickly.

"I thought it might make a nice room to sit and read. Or a communal space for my guests, what do you think?"

"I think a communal space is a great idea."

"I have a couple of small sofas in one of the outbuildings, I'm pretty sure they're still in great condition. Once we get rid of the chair, and the desk, we'll bring those in and arrange them."

"Of course, I'll speak with Kieran tomorrow."

I left her in the kitchen and took a slow walk back to my apartment. It was a beautiful afternoon but my back and shoulders ached. I'd been working hard over the past few days, often falling straight into bed fully clothed, before dinner. I paused on the corner of the block and raised my face to the sun; I hoped the vitamin D might give me an energy boost. The sound of a car backfiring caused me to dart forward and slam my back against the wall. A rattling old engine slowly cruised past the turn I was hiding in. I kept my head pressed against the wall with my face looking in the opposite direction. However, when I saw the shadow of the car pass by on the opposite wall, I slowly turned to look. A beat up, light blue car with a broken tail light and no registration plate drove slowly down the road. Damien's car was beat up with a broken taillight but I struggled to remember if it was light blue or silver. I took off at a run and didn't stop until I reached the front door of the apartment building.

I stripped off my clothes and stood under the shower. My heart was racing and I took in some deep breaths to steady myself.

"Get a grip," I said to myself.

I had to find some strength. Unless he physically kidnapped me, there wasn't much else he could do to get me back to Whiteling. Was he capable of kidnapping me? Probably. But being able to and actually doing it were two different things. He scared me; he'd threatened me for many years. I had to keep in mind that, at the end of the day, he was a bully. He ruled with fear. He was certainly a fucking pervert and not right in the head, but in just the couple of weeks I'd been away, I was a changed person. He couldn't force me to do anything I didn't want to. I just needed to make sure I wasn't alone on the streets at night. I couldn't leave myself in a vulnerable position at any time, and maybe I should open up a little to those that seemed to care for me.

With a new resolve, I set about to change the furniture around and make it more a home for me. I didn't need a TV, but some shelves that could house a book collection would be nice, as would a lick of paint on the walls. I made a list of things that I would chat to Cecelia about.

I cooked a meal that evening, it was the first time I'd actually cooked in a long time. Most of what I'd eaten in the trailer had been something defrosted and microwaved or I'd snacked. I diced some chicken, vegetables, and added a tomato sauce to the stir-fry. I sat, curled up on the sofa and ate, enjoying the silence. Beside me, on a small coffee table sat the cell. I picked it up and scrolled through the two numbers listed. I wondered where Beau was, and what he did for a job. I imagined the house he owned hadn't been cheap and the truck he drove was new. What kind of a job had him jetting off to wherever at a moment's notice? I placed the phone back and shook my head. I didn't want to be interested in him. I wasn't attracted to him, but he did intrigue me, and that annoyed me a little. I thought back on what Cecelia had said. To come home and have his partner just disappear must have been hard. People didn't disappear for no reason, though.

————————

It was three days later that I saw Beau again. I'd covered Kacy's shift, and although Kieran had insisted on walking me home, I waved him off at the corner. I could see Beau further down the street, illuminated by a street lamp and about to turn the corner into the courtyard. At the same time a car pulled up beside him. I watched as his back stiffened and he slowly turned. He placed his hands on the roof and leaned down to talk to the passenger. Although I watched him, I continued to walk to my house. I saw him slam his fist on the roof and then I was stunned into paralysis. He reached behind him, to his waistband, and pulled out a gun. He leveled the gun at the passenger window but didn't fire. The car roared off, and I ducked down the pathway of the neighboring property, hoping their planting would conceal me.

I peered through the bush and watched as Beau looked up the street while replacing the gun in the waistband of his jeans. It seemed that he hadn't seen me, thankfully, he rounded the corner and was out of sight.

People carried guns, Damien often played around with one, I got that. But there was something in the way he pulled that gun from his jeans, the way he held it steady that had me thinking he was quite used to handling one. I stayed hidden in the bush, knowing that Beau had gone, but trying to understand what I'd just seen. I shivered, not sure if that was from the dip in temperature over the past couple of evenings, or fear.

I stood and cautiously stepped around the bush. Sure that the coast was completely clear, I headed up the steps to my building's front door. I passed the door to the downstairs apartment, it was empty according to Cecelia, and climbed the stairs to mine. For the first time, I felt a little uneasy being in the house on my own. I retreated down the stairs and double locked the front door.

I decided I'd get a safety chain, or some other form of security for my apartment front door. It wasn't seeing Beau with a gun that had prompted that decision, but the fact he could draw that gun in the street without, as it seemed to me, a care of being seen. Obviously, people of this town didn't look out for each other. For the second time, or the third, I'd lost count, I wondered who the fuck he was.

———————

I was woken by someone grabbing my arm and dragging me from my bed. I screamed out and tried to fight him off. I knew it was a 'him' by the strength of the grip on my bicep.

"Calm the fuck down," Beau said.

"Calm the fuck down? Let go of me, you fucking…"

He did, and I fell to the floor. I rubbed at my arm.

"What are you doing?" I shouted at him.

"Get dressed."

"No, what the fuck are you doing? And why are you in my house?"

"My aunt's…"

"I rent this, you have no right to just come in here, in the middle of the night and drag me from my bed. I should call the police." My voice rose further on every word.

He held out his cell to me. "Go on, call them. In the meantime, get dressed, I need you out of here."

"I'm not going anywhere." I shuffled until my back was against the bed and drew my knees to my chest.

I wanted to get up and turn the light on, my eyes hurt with the strain of seeing him in the darkened room.

"Charlotte, get up and get dressed, otherwise, I'll throw you over my shoulder and carry you out."

"I'll scream with every fucking step. Get. Out." I was glad I was the only tenant; my shouting would have had everyone up.

Beau walked toward the dresser and wrenched open a drawer so hard it fell to the floor. He grabbed a pair of jeans and a t-shirt. I rose, but not quickly enough, before he opened another drawer and pulled out a pair of panties. I grabbed at his wrist as he rifled in the drawer.

"What the fuck are you doing?" I said, through clenched teeth.

"Looking for a bra, obviously."

"There's nothing obvious about what you're doing."

We wrestled with a black bra until he let go and I stumbled backward. In any other circumstance, I would have laughed at the absurdity of it all.

Beau gathered up my clothes and in one swoop, he had his arm around my waist and before I could take in the breath I needed to scream, I was hanging over his shoulder. He kicked open my bedroom door, and then wrenched the front door. How he managed to keep hold of me as he walked down the stairs, I wasn't sure. I wriggled; I pummeled his back with my fists, and kicked my legs. I heard him wince at one point when my bare foot connected with some part of his body.

Once we left the building and I saw the reason for him wanting me to leave, I was subdued. He placed me, none too gently, on the ground. I was conscious of the fact I was in my panties and a tank, but it wasn't the cold that had me wrap my arms around myself. Scrawled in spray paint, I thought, across the front door was one word.

Harlot

I closed my eyes, holding in the sob.

"Tell me that has nothing to do with you," he said, thrusting my clothes at me.

I couldn't. Harlot was the nickname Damien had for me. Obviously, it wasn't a nickname of affection.

"Charlotte the harlot, he calls me," I whispered.

"Then he knows where you're living."

"I'll leave. I'll clean that up in the morning, and then I'll go."

I knew that I'd promised him I would leave before, but I thought I'd resolved it in my head. Damien couldn't hurt me. I hadn't anticipated the mental pain he was able to inflict. I felt defeated. Although it had been only a few weeks, I thought I stood a chance of freedom.

"Shit, shoes," he said.

I looked down at my bare feet. I didn't get the chance to respond before he picked me up again, gentler that time, and carried me down the steps. He set me on the hood of his truck while he opened the door. Before he could pick me up yet again, I slid off and climbed in the truck myself. I had no idea why he felt the need to carry me no more than the few steps I would have taken to reach his truck.

I watched him lock the front door before he walked around the truck and climbed in the driver's seat. I wasn't sure what to say to him. For a while, he sat looking stonily out the windshield. He sighed before starting the engine and we drove the short distance to his house.

I had started to shiver by the time we entered his home. I stood in the hallway and pulled on my jeans and the t-shirt. I wished I'd had the chance to grab the one sweatshirt, his sweatshirt, that I had. He didn't speak as he walked to the kitchen door and I waited to see if I was expected to follow. He looked over his shoulder before he entered the room. I took that as an invitation to join him.

"Beau, I..."

"I'll deal with the door tomorrow."

"Will you tell Cecelia?"

"No. I don't want her worried, she's not in the best of health."

He poured two cups of coffee and slid one over to me. I climbed on the same stool I'd sat on just a few days ago.

"How did you know?"

"I was driving home, I saw the door. I panicked a little, I guess."

If that was an apology for dragging me from my bed, I'd take it. I wasn't going to inflame the situation any further with a smart remark.

"Will you tell the police?" I asked.

"No. If I thought you'd actually corroborate the story then I would. What are they going to do anyway? Some fucking punk spray painted a door, doubt they'll put much effort into finding out who."

"Why did you panic?"

"The word, it's a bit obvious it was directed at you, Charlotte."

He hadn't actually answered my question. "You hurt my arm," I said quietly.

He slowly nodded, again, I guessed that was as much of an apology as I was going to get.

I sat up straight and took a deep breath in. "I'm going back," I said.

"What do you mean?"

"I'm going after him. I'm not living like this anymore. I don't want to keep running, I love it here. I want to be able to live my life without him, and the only way I can do is to show him I'm not scared of him anymore."

"Are you? Not scared of him anymore? Because from where I'm standing, you're terrified. I can smell the fear, Charlotte, so will he."

"He isn't that intelligent. Regardless of what you think you know about me, which is very little, I'm a fucking good actress, Beau. Believe me, that's one skill I mastered when I had to lay and pretend I was having a good time."

He screwed his eyes shut, again, in disgust.

"You can be as disgusted with me as you like, but I'm not a victim anymore. I didn't ask for, or deserve, anything I went through."

"I'm not disgusted with you. I..."

"You what? Feel sorry for me?" I laughed, bitterly.

"I feel sorry for you, why is that so wrong?"

He took me by surprise. "How old are you? And don't give me the crap you gave my aunt. That guy has fucked up your life so far, and I can tell you now, without even knowing him, you go back there, and you won't be leaving."

"What do you suggest then, huh?" I stood from the stool, annoyed at his lack of belief in me.

"You tell me the truth, and I'll help you."

I stared at him with a bunch of words on the tip of my tongue, none of which he'd want to hear.

"I don't know you."

"What has that got to do with anything?"

"I don't know you enough to trust you with why *I* need to deal with this. You've done nothing but be rude to me. You've openly displayed your distrust of me, yet you want me to tell you my secrets so you'll help?"

"You talk like the twenty-one-year-old you pretend to be, older in fact, but I know you're not that age."

"How old do you think I am?"

"It doesn't matter how old I think you are. If you want my help, I have to know everything."

"How can you help, Beau? I saw you earlier, is that the kind of help you think I need?"

It was his turn to be silent for a moment.

"You don't know what you saw."

"I saw you pull a gun on someone in a car. I'll tell you, after you've told me why."

He laughed. "You're feisty, I'll give you that." He leaned toward me, his face just a few inches from mine. "That was work."

"Work? What kind of work means you pull a gun on someone?"

"The kind of work you don't need to know about."

I stood, taking a step away from him. "Thank you for the coffee. Like I said, I'll clean the door in the morning and then I'll deal with my problem."

"Good luck, Charlotte."

I walked to the kitchen door and then realized, I had no way of getting back in the apartment. I turned and held out my hand.

"I'll need your key."

He raised his eyebrows, a smirk formed on his lips.

"Since you're the one that dragged me from my bed, didn't give me a chance to at least get dressed and gather my things, it's the least you can do."

"What if he's out there?"

"I'd rather take my chances with him than you. I know him; I know exactly what he'll do, if he's sober enough to do anything, of course. You're unpredictable. Your words and blatant dislike of me, hurt more than his punches."

He tossed his keys toward me. They landed short, I took a step forward and picked them up from the floor.

"You make me feel like he does, worthless," I said, quietly.

"I'm fucking nothing..."

I didn't hear the rest of his sentence. I left the house and started the walk back to the apartment.

"Charlotte, wait," I heard. I kept walking until Beau caught up with me.

"I'm sorry, okay? I'll walk you back."

I nodded but didn't reply. Beau made me feel like the piece of shit Damien always told me I was. By the time I was at the front door, I was struggling to hold back the tears. I reached out and gently touched the paint on the door. It was dry, for that I was thankful. At least it meant he had long gone, or so I hoped.

I had the door opened and was about to close it behind me when I heard Beau speak.

"I'm sorry, Charlotte. I..."

"I know. Thank you for your apology."

I locked the door and headed up to my apartment. It was only once I'd locked the apartment door and dragged a chair to wedge under the handle, that I allowed the tears to flow.

I didn't want to go back to bed, so I curled up on the sofa and wrapped myself in my grandmother's quilt. I sat and watched the sun rise, not knowing how long I'd been there. My neck ached, my knees had locked from being bent for so long. I stretched out and, trying not to hobble, made my way to the shower.

With a bucket of hot water and some detergent, I set about to scrub the front door. By the time I'd gotten most of the paint off, my hands were screaming with pain from gripping the sponge. I wiped the door to dry it and then realized I was going to have to get it repainted. Where I'd cleaned it, I'd taken a layer of the blue paint off as well.

"I'll sort that," I heard from behind. I sighed. I didn't need to deal with Beau on top of being tired and aching all over.

"If you can just tell me where to get the paint, I can do that after my shift at the diner."

"So, you're not going all renegade after your cousin today, then?" He chuckled as he spoke.

"No, not today, that would be way too obvious now, wouldn't it?"

"As well as your slushy romance, I suppose you read crime novels, too?"

"No, I don't in fact. I just have some common sense. Beau, I'm too tired for this today. Please, just leave me alone for a while."

"You're nineteen, Charlotte, and Johnson isn't your surname," he said.

I spun around. "How...?"

"Lucky guess, and now you've just confirmed it." He gave a half salute before walking away.

"Prick," I called out to his retreating back.

———

By the time I returned from my shift at the diner, had sat and eaten yet another mystery dish concocted by Kieran, the front door had been repainted. There was no evidence of any earlier graffiti, and for that, I was thankful.

I didn't know whether to laugh or cry when I walked into the apartment to see the dark red leather chair left haphazardly in the center of the room. Obviously, the keys I'd taken from Beau weren't the only set available. I didn't have the energy to rearrange the room, so I just sat and thought. I needed to show Damien that I wasn't scared, nor was I ever returning. Would that be enough, though? To say I wasn't scared to confront him would be a lie, but I didn't know of any other way.

I also had to think of a way to physically return. Whiteling was way too many miles for me to walk back, and as I'd discovered, there was no public transport. The slow realization that I'd have to take up Beau's offer of help, even if just for a ride, dawned and with it, another sigh. I scrubbed my hands over my face, scrunching my nose at the smell of bleach on my skin. I growled out an expletive with frustration.

"My name is Charlotte Kenny. I'm nineteen, however, it's my twentieth birthday in a few weeks' time, I think. I don't actually know my real date of birth; my grandmother decided the day I was left on her doorstep with a note, would be my birthday. It's very probable I'm already twenty. I don't know my mother, or my father. And I don't know why my grandmother had no relationship with her daughter. I do know she was very young when I was born," I said, when Beau answered the call.

"Well, Charlotte Kenny, probably twenty-years-old, does this mean you are looking for my help?"

"Don't be an ass. I need a ride, nothing more."

"You know I can't just drive you back to wherever you came from, sit around and wait for you to take on a dirt bag, then drive you back, don't you?"

"I don't want to involve you any more than necessary."

"That's very honorable of you, but not happening. Now, I'll be there in ten minutes and you can tell me the rest." He cut off the call. If I didn't need the cell to be able to know the time, I'd have thrown the fucking thing across the room.

I rose from the chair reluctantly, since it was the most comfortable thing I'd sat in, and filled the coffee machine with water. I scooped some ground coffee in and set it to brew. I wasn't going to tell Beau about Philip, I'd be out on my ass in an instant if he thought he, and his aunt, were about to be caught up in that level of trouble, but I had to come up with something. More lies started to form in my head.

"Can you please at least knock before you come in? I do have a formal arrangement with the owner of this property, someone that isn't you," I said, when Beau strolled into the apartment.

"Since I get left this, that *arrangement* is partly with me."

"Not so. And I mean it, knock next time."

He gave me just one nod of his head. I already had a cup of coffee but I waved my hand toward the machine, he could pour his own. I walked to the chair and sat.

"You like the chair? I remember my uncle sitting in that every day before he died."

"Where are your parents?" I asked, somewhat randomly.

"Dead, to me."

"Oh...I'm..."

"No need. Now, shall we get down to business?"

"What I've told you is true. However, on the night you picked me up, I was running…"

"Obviously."

"Obviously. I was running because Damien had wanted me to show his new *friend* a good time, at a cost, of course. I didn't want to, I didn't like the guy, he scared me, so I didn't show up. I knew Damien would be fucking furious and the mood he'd been in, I'd take a beating. I'd had enough, I packed my things, and I ran."

Beau stared at me, his brow furrowed and his head slightly cocked. A smirk played on his lips.

"Tell me about the *friend*?"

"I think he was a drug dealer, big time. I'd heard some awful things about him. He bought girls, some were never seen again. I didn't want to be one of those girls."

The only part that was a lie was me showing Cody Groves a good time. He existed, he was a drug dealer, and rumor had it, he abused then disposed of woman all the time.

"Do you know his name?"

"I don't, and I'm not sure why that's important."

"I guess it's not. So, that's why you ran?"

"Isn't that a good enough reason?"

"Of course, but why wait all this time?"

He stumped me then. I bit down on my lower lip, gently sucking it into my mouth; it was something I did when I was caught out, something my grandmother called my 'lie detector fail.'

"Honestly? I don't know. I was scared of him for such a long time. I was caught between staying and taking my chances with the drug dealer, or running and hoping not to get caught. I did the latter."

"And now you want to go back to show him what?"

"That he can't scare me anymore. That I'm not afraid."

"And when the big bad drug dealer knows you're back, bearing in mind he may have already paid for you, do you think just telling Damien you're a big girl now and have moved on, will be enough?"

I slumped down in the chair and let my head fall against the backrest.

"Then I guess I need a ride to the airport. I think I have enough money for a flight."

"Where to?"

"I don't know! For fuck's sake, Beau. I can't stay, I can't confront him, and I don't know what to do."

"Is Kenny your real name?"

"Yes," I replied.

"And Damien is his real name?"

I opened my mouth to speak, instead I let out a large sigh.

"If you don't believe me, just help me get to the airport. I'll figure it all out from there."

"Damien Kenny, from Whiteling, drug user, dealer perhaps, pimp and trafficker," he said, more to himself than me.

I had no idea what a trafficker was, but nodded anyway. Beau gulped down his hot coffee, placed his cup on the coffee table, and then stood.

"Okay, get some things, you're staying at mine. Although you did leave your panties and bra on the counter."

"I don't..."

"Get your things. I'm not asking, Charlotte."

"You know, you act like my fucking father."

"I'd be *thrilled* to have you as a daughter, although I'm not old enough, Miss 'I Think I'm Twenty Years Old.'"

It was clear that was sarcasm and I added that to the list of comments that stung.

"At this rate, I'll need an anti-histamine," I said. By the look on his face, he didn't get my meaning.

As I walked to the bedroom, I called over my shoulder, "How old are you?"

"Possibly eight years older than you."

"Twenty-eight. Sheesh, life has been hard on you, hasn't it? I'd have put you at way more than that. No wonder you're single, no woman would put up with your style of cheerfulness." Satisfied my parting shot had caused him to huff, I closed the bedroom door while I grabbed a few things.

In reality, I was surprised he was only twenty-eight. I thought he might have been early thirties. It was as I sat on the bed, I thought on my earlier comment. Cecelia had told me his girlfriend, had run out on him, causing him great pain.

"Shit," I said, quietly so he couldn't hear. I really needed to think before I spoke.

I packed a few clothes and then headed to the bathroom to gather some toiletries. I stood in the living room, waiting for Beau to lead the way. As he walked to the door, he snatched his set of keys from the counter. I waited until he was near the door before opening a kitchen cupboard and picking up one of my cash bundles.

"Not the best hiding place," he said.

"Best I've got. Shall we go?"

"Get the rest of your money, if your douche of a cousin breaks in here, you'll lose the lot."

"Turn around then."

"Really? Just get your fucking money, Charlotte."

I grabbed the other three piles and stuffed them in my backpack, cursing him under my breath as I did.

————————

Beau directed me to the bedroom I'd slept in before. I left the backpack on the bed and joined him in the kitchen. Sitting proud on the counter were my panties and bra. I stuffed them in my jean pockets as I sat on a stool.

"Now, plan of action. You stay here, you go to work, and act as normal as possible. But, you don't go out at night, you don't do the late shift, and you sure as fuck keep a look over your shoulder so you don't lead anyone back here, okay?"

"What if I need to go to the store?"

"Then I'll take you."

"What if you need to work, or whatever it is you do?"

"I work when I want to work."

"You have an answer for everything, don't you?"

"Yes. Any other questions?"

"Why are you such an ass to me?"

He fell silent; I raised one eyebrow waiting for his answer.

"Because I don't like you."

I blinked, not expecting that answer.

"Not for the reasons you think, though," he said, walking over to the coffee maker.

"It's not my fault that I look like her," I said, quietly.

I watched as he rested his hands on the counter and bowed his head. Slowly, he straightened his back and turned to me. His features were hard.

"Don't speak about her again," he said.

"I..."

By the look on his face, that line of conversation was over. I shut my mouth and slid from the stool.

"If you don't like me, for whatever reason it is, why are you helping me?"

"I told you, Cecelia isn't well. I don't want her caught up in all this."

"Is that all?"

He didn't answer.

"I guess we're all lying, Beau."

With that, I walked to the back door, opened it, and stepped out into his small courtyard. There was a small wooden table with two chairs around it. To one side was a row of ceramic pots filled with dead, sad looking plants. I crouched down and pulled out some weeds. Not that I knew about plants, but those looked a lost cause.

"Her name was Rachel, we'd been together a couple of years. And yes, you could be her sister, you look so alike. It throws me, brings back memories I'd rather not have. You cause me to lose focus, Charlotte, and I don't like losing focus."

I didn't answer, not sure what I could say to help. I was naïve, I wasn't as worldly as I should be, and as much as I used to be proud of my smart mouth and range of vocabulary, I knew I'd just say the wrong thing and inflame the situation.

I heard the scrape of a chair. "Your coffee is here," he said.

I stood and then sat in the chair opposite him. "Thank you, and I'm sorry to hear what happened. I don't suppose Cecelia should have told me anything, it's none of my business."

"It's not a secret, the whole fucking town knows. She just left one day and that was it."

I wanted to ask if he had any idea why, but I didn't. He'd crossed

103

his arms over his chest and looked away, effectively closing down any further conversation.

"I'll deal with Damien," he said.

"I don't want you to. I'll just leave, Beau."

"That won't stop him coming back here, like I said, Cecelia doesn't need to be caught up with this."

"Then let me speak to him. I'll tell him I'm going to the police if he harasses me."

"You should have gone to the police anyway."

"You think that small, hick town police force in Whiteling would believe me?" I laughed, Beau was as naïve as I was.

"He's a drug user, is he not?"

"Yes, so are most of the residents. I don't have a great reputation back there, Beau. People knew what I did, they didn't know I was forced to do it, though." I swallowed down the hurt at the thought of the ridicule I'd received.

I'd been called all sorts of names, from whore to slut, on a regular basis. I remembered a woman spitting at me once, when she'd caught her husband trying to pick me up. I wasn't interested in him; I wasn't interested in any of them. I was forced to do what I did because, for a long time, I just didn't see a way out.

"Do you know what it's like to be taunted every day of your adult life? To be called names, have people look at you with disgust? Do you know what it's like to be forced to do something that caused you to cry every single day? You can't ask me why I didn't run earlier any more than I've asked myself. I hate myself, Beau, because I'm weak, because I didn't do something about my situation earlier. I had no money, no clothes, no friends, I was totally isolated and reliant on him for a long time."

"What changed, Charlotte? Something did."

"I can't tell you that. If I did, you'd drag me from here in the blink of an eye. I'm scared to."

"So there is more?"

"Yes. And when I know how to deal with it, I will tell you."

"You don't know that whatever *this* is might help with getting Damien off your back. So, make your decision on whether you tell me sooner rather than later, Charlotte."

I sipped at my coffee and pondered on his words. I thought it had been Damien that had been helping the police with their investigation, maybe I was wrong. I was still convinced he'd been the one to kill him; I just needed a way to confirm that.

"I have to go," he said, looking at his watch.

"What do I do?"

"Read, watch the TV, whatever you normally do. Just stay inside."

"I can at least sit out here, can't I?" I looked around the courtyard with its high brick walls.

"Yes. And don't go snooping, most of the rooms are locked up."

He walked back into the kitchen, leaving me staring open-mouthed at him. He really didn't trust me at all. Yet more fucking tears pricked at my eyes. I wanted to hate Beau. For a little while, I'd thought he treated me the same way Damien did, but Beau was worse. He had no reason to trust me, I'd been around for less than a month, but his barbed comments hurt, and the lack of empathy he showed should have me telling him to go fuck himself. There was something about him, though. He was like an onion, he made my eyes water regularly, he was bitter and strong, but there were so many layers that I was sure, if I could peel some back, I'd see a sweeter side to him.

I laughed at the analogy, sure that he'd be mortified to be compared to something as basic as an onion.

I fixed myself a second coffee and tested the only other door on the ground floor. I would respect Beau's home, not that he did mine. I would never go snooping in anyone's house. The door opened to a small living room. A sofa was pushed against one wall and under the only window. It was a large brown leather one with cream scatter cushions. The opposite wall had me surprised. Row upon row of books was stacked neatly on wooden shelves. I walked over to look. The collection ranged from the slushy romance he'd mocked me for, to crimes and thrillers. There were biographies and travel books. Somehow, I doubted they belonged to Beau; he didn't seem the reading type. I selected a couple and settled on the sofa. I kicked off my sneakers and curled my feet underneath me. The sofa was comfortable and I snuggled into the corner. I looked around for somewhere to place my cup, not wanting to use the highly polished coffee table. I set it down on the wooden floor, hoping it wouldn't leave a mark.

I thumbed through the novel, loving that it had been read many times judging by the creases. It surprised me to see passages underlined in pencil. Obviously those words had meant something to the reader. I decided that I would read the book and flicked back to the beginning.

When my bladder had decided I'd had enough time reading, I put the book down and headed upstairs to the bathroom. Although I'd used it once before, I hadn't noticed the range of female products that were still lined up, in order of bottle size, on a shelf. While I washed my hands I studied them. They were product brands I'd never heard of but looked expensive. I picked up a hand cream and read the label before squirting a little into my palm.

I hadn't taken too much notice of my surroundings previously, but when I thought about the bedroom, it seemed to be that Rachel hadn't been removed from the house at all. I wondered if that meant Beau was hoping she might return. I didn't know how long she'd been gone, but from instinct, I didn't think her leaving was a recent thing. Was he still pining for her?

My stomach grumbled as I descended the stairs. Beau hadn't mentioned helping myself to food and bearing in mind how particular he was, I decided to text.

Is it okay for me to make myself something to eat? Or should I pop out?

Of course it is! Why couldn't you? he replied.

"Because you're an ass who doesn't actually want me here," I said to the cell.

Thank you, I typed, ignoring his question.

I opened his fridge and pulled out a loaf of bread, a carton of orange juice, and a plate of cooked chicken. It seemed that Beau ate very healthily. There was nothing processed or what I'd consider junk. I made myself a sandwich, washed up the utensils, and poured a glass of juice.

I sat at the kitchen counter and slowly ate my sandwich. I took in a slight layer of dust on the ridges of the cupboard doors, on some pots that hung from a rack above the stove. I guessed the kitchen wasn't a room Beau used that often, despite a full fridge.

When I'd eaten, I headed back to the living room and picked up the book. Despite it being the end of fall, the courtyard was a little suntrap. I pulled off my socks and rested my feet on the chair opposite as I settled at the garden table. I looked at a line of underlined text.

This is for you, not me, for you, please remember that.

It seemed an odd line to highlight. I continued to read. The story wasn't as captivating as other books I'd read. It was a pretty straightforward romance, one set in a small town, two high-school lovers that couldn't seem to get their act together. It was the to and fro in their young relationship that had me wanting to roll my eyes. I had a policy though, no matter how I had to work at reading, I would get to the end.

I'd gotten through another five or six pages before I saw another underlined passage.

I have to run.

The sentence was referring to the character needing to jog but it was only those four words underlined. It puzzled me to the point that I decided to forgo reading and flip through the next few pages to see if there were any more. The next one had my heart stop.

He will kill me.

These words weren't highlighted because the reader loved them, because they wanted to remember those particular parts of this mediocre book, I was absolutely sure of that. I wanted a piece of paper and a pen. I rushed to the living room and opened the top drawer of a sideboard. I didn't care whether Beau would be angry I'd disturbed his things, I rifled around. Not finding what I wanted, I went to the next drawer, and then the next.

I climbed the stairs two at a time and ran to the bedroom I was allocated. Each drawer in the cabinet was empty. There was another flight of stairs to a third floor and that time, I took them one at a time. I hesitated in front of the only door on that floor. I placed my hand on the doorknob and gently turned it. Beau had lied; the door creaked open.

That room was obviously the master bedroom. A huge bed with wooden bedposts and ornate finials dominated the room. The whitewashed wooden floor creaked as I walked across. At first I stood in the middle of the room. Floor to ceiling sheer drapes were artfully arranged over a large window. The pool of white material as each met the floor reminded me of a lake. Two large wooden wardrobes, similar to the one in my bedroom, stood against one wall. It only occurred to me then, they looked like something I'd see in a chateau or stately home. I remembered a magazine I'd scanned through, on homes across Europe. This room seemed to be modeled on one.

I backed out, not wanting to intrude any further. There was serenity about the room and I felt like I would tarnish that if I disturbed anything.

There had to be a piece of paper and a pen somewhere. I headed back to the kitchen and opened drawers. One contained some mail. I hesitated but decided I needed to write these lines down. I wasn't sure what was compelling me so much, but somewhere I just didn't accept this was underlining passages that were liked, more that they meant something.

A thought occurred to me. I ran back to the bathroom and opened a cupboard under the sink. I found what I was looking for; a makeup bag that contained an eyeliner pencil.

I sat at the kitchen table and started the book from the beginning. I flicked through each page, writing all the underlined text until I had a list. As it was, it didn't make sense but my blood ran cold. It was a message, I was sure of that. I sat and reread it many times. I debated whether to call him or not.

CHAPTER 7

Frustrated, I left a message on Beau's voicemail. I tried to keep my voice calm and simply told him that I found something in a book I thought he should take a look at. I paced, sat, pulled more books off the shelf, and flicked through many pages. I paced some more, constantly checking my cell to see if Beau had replied.

I could have called Cecelia but she wasn't aware I was at Beau's house, and I didn't want to alarm her, or give her any reason to think we'd struck up a friendship.

I picked up the envelope and turned it over. It was addressed to Rachel Summer, I guessed they weren't married after all.

I sat and watched the clock, getting more impatient by the minute. Darkness crept over the kitchen until, eventually, I turned on the lights. The more time that passed, the more I wondered if I was overreacting, if I'd come up with something so far wrong, Beau would laugh at me.

"No, it's a message," I said aloud.

"What is?"

I screeched. "Shit, Beau. Why the fuck are you creeping around? Did you get my message?"

"I'm not creeping, it's my house, I can walk around however I want, and yes. Which is why I'm here."

He walked toward the kitchen counter and picked up the envelope. "Where did you get this?" he asked, angrily.

"Turn it over. I'm sorry, I needed something to write on, I wasn't snooping."

He flipped the envelope over and read.

"What is this?"

"Look, I found those lines highlighted in a book." I picked up the book, he took it from me.

"That was Rachel's favorite, she read it over and over. So, I'll ask again, what is this?"

"In the book are lines of text that have been underlined. I didn't think anything of it at first, until I got to the third one. I wrote them all down. Why would someone underline that?"

"What is that?" he asked, pointing to something on the envelope.

"Let me show you."

I took the book and the envelope from him and turned to the first line that had been highlighted.

"*This is for you, not me, for you, please remember that.* It's been underlined in pencil, see?" I then listed the others.

I have to run.

He will kill me.

I want to keep you safe.

I hope you'll find / this / one day.

I love you, never forget that.

One day / I'll come / back.

"What are the slash marks for?"

I flicked through the book until I came to the right page.

111

"See here, someone underlined that little piece of text, skipped the next, underlined that bit, as if to make up a whole sentence."

Beau pulled out a stool and studied the envelope. "And you found this book where?"

"On a shelf in your living room. I just wanted something to read, I wasn't..."

He waved his hand cutting off my sentence.

"What the fuck?" he whispered, I guessed to himself.

"It's a message, isn't it?"

"I don't know."

He placed the book and envelope on the counter and the scrape as he pushed his stool back across the tiled floor set my teeth on edge. I followed him back to the living room and watched as he pulled book after book from the shelf. He flicked through each one, dropping them to the floor when he was done. The more he didn't find what he was looking for, whatever it was, the more aggressive he became. He started throwing the books around the room, eventually, when he'd run out of books, he kicked his way through the pile, scattering them around the room.

Without looking at me, he walked back to the kitchen. I jogged to keep up.

"Is it from Rachel?" I asked.

"How the fuck would I know?" he spat.

"It was her book..."

"I know! Just..." he shouted, and raised his hand to silence me. "I know, just let me think, please," he added, gentler.

I listened to him read aloud the words, slowly, as if digesting every syllable, every letter. I let him be and as quietly as possible, sat back down. It felt an eternity; eventually he looked up at me.

"It's a message, for sure."

"How long has she been gone?"

"She left a year ago, nearly to the day. Which is why, when I first saw you, it freaked me out a little."

"But you weren't freaked when you picked me up?"

"It was the only reason I stopped to pick you up. I saw you dart into the woods, the way your hair moved, your body. The way you closed your eyes, as if you couldn't see me, I couldn't see you. I thought it was her."

"What shall we do?"

"We?"

"Sorry, I mean, I'd like to help if I can."

He didn't answer but fished his phone from his jean pocket. He swiped his finger over the screen and dialed a number. He looked at me before he spoke, then picked up the envelope and left the kitchen. He obviously didn't want me to hear what he had to say. I waited until he returned. He moved around the kitchen like a man possessed. Opening drawers until he found a set of keys, undoing the buttons of his white shirt and shrugging it off his shoulders, he also kicked off his shoes. He grabbed a t-shirt from a pile off the counter. Despite the situation, I couldn't help but watch his stomach muscles tighten and ripple with the movement. I had to turn my head when he grabbed a pair of jeans from the laundry pile and started to undo his trousers.

"Boots," he mumbled to himself.

His tan work boots were by the back door, still muddy from when he'd worn them previously at Cecelia's, I imagined.

"Stay here, you hear me?" he said, finally acknowledging me.

"Beau, what can I do?"

"Nothing, just stay here. I don't need to be worrying about you on top of this."

Worry? I thought.

"Okay, I'll stay here."

He left, not before picking up the book as well. From the whirlwind that had just occurred, the calm that came with his absence unsettled me. At first I wasn't sure what to do. I looked at drawers left open, the pile of laundry in a mess, and decided to do the only thing I did well. I cleaned his house.

I refolded his clothes, occasionally getting a waft of a fresh smelling detergent; I wiped down the dusty cupboards and the pots hanging over the stove. Then I started in the living room. I replaced all the books back on the shelves, adjusting them in height order. I picked up my phone, surprised to see the time. It was getting close to eleven p.m. Maybe it was seeing the time, but I failed to stifle a yawn. My head had begun to pound, partly from hunger, mostly from tension. Stress headaches were something I'd suffered from since a young age.

After turning on a couple of side lamps, I sat on the sofa and picked up the TV remote control. I flicked through channels of crap until I found the local news. There had been no new reports about Philip's murder for over week. I didn't believe the community or the press had forgotten about him and wondered why no one was shouting for an update. Even his son had gone quiet. I turned it off and just sat in the dimly lit room.

————

I wasn't sure what it was that woke me, maybe a snuffle or a snore? I had fallen asleep on the sofa and now found myself covered with a quilt that hadn't been there before. The room was dark as I tried to stretch out my legs, I stilled when I hit something, or someone. I shuffled into a sitting position, and once my eyes had adjusted to the darkness, I saw Beau sleeping at the other end. He had his arms crossed over his chest, his head rested back. He looked very uncomfortable and I imagined he'd have a stiff neck in the morning.

I stared at him for a little while, noticing all the French features I'd not seen before. He had a straight, 'Romanish' nose and light olive-colored skin. Dark stubble framed his jaw. His bicep strained against the cuff of his t-shirt sleeve, and my thoughts were instantly taken back to his sculpted stomach. I shook my head gently to rid myself of any unwanted thoughts. Even if I weren't the person I was, if this was a different time and place, there would never be anything between us.

I rose, picking up the quilt with me; I wanted to place it over him. The room had chilled significantly, but I also didn't want to disturb him. I took the gamble. I pulled the coffee table slightly closer and raised his feet to rest on it. He groaned as I did, I thought that he'd mumbled a name but wasn't sure. He shifted down the sofa a little, and as he did, my eyes were drawn to a line of dark hair that ran from his navel to the top of his jeans. When I thought he was a little more comfortable, I draped the quilt over him and left the room.

The kitchen was colder than the living room and I shivered as I refilled the coffee maker. Its gurgle and hiss of steam as it percolated was a welcome disturbance to the silence. I wrapped my arms around myself and rubbed some warmth into them while I waited for the coffee to brew. On the kitchen counter were the book, the envelope, a set of keys, and a wallet. I picked up the envelope, and in the dim glow of an under-cupboard light, I read the list again.

This is for you, not me, for you. Please remember that. In my mind, that was Rachel telling him she had no choice but to leave, another line, further down seemed to confirm that. *I want to keep you safe.* From what, or whom? Was she in fear of her life, or his?

I stared at the last line the longest, *One day / I'll come / back.* That line brought me back to thinking that she'd been gone a year, and yet hadn't made it back, that wasn't good. The coffee maker beeped, letting me know it had finished, and I poured myself a cup. The light of the fridge as I opened the door caused me to squint against the brightness; I reached in and grabbed a carton of cream.

"I take mine black," I heard. Beau had startled me enough that the cream slopped from the container down my t-shirt.

"Shit," I said, placing it on the side and grabbing a cloth.

"What are you doing?" he asked.

"Chucking cream down myself," I replied, scrubbing at the stain.

He chuckled, and it was a pleasant sound, not one I heard that often from him. I poured the cream into my cup before pouring another coffee and handing it to him.

"I was reading the list again," I said, not that it wasn't obvious, I was still holding it.

He leaned on the counter and took it from my hand. He placed it at an angle so we could both read.

"This is for you..." he said, reading aloud. "What was for me?" I didn't think he was asking me the question.

"Was there anything that happened just before she'd left?"

He gently nodded his head. "She was pregnant, and I wasn't happy about it."

"Not happy?"

"I wasn't convinced the child was mine, I was always so careful.

We argued over it."

"Why would you think the child wasn't yours, mistakes happen?"

"Because all the while she was with me, she was also with someone else."

"Did you know?"

"Do I look like someone who would date a woman in a relationship?"

I could feel the hurt in his voice disguised as anger. I shook my head. Whatever Beau was, I believed him to be fiercely loyal, so, no, I didn't think he'd deliberately date someone who was an adulterer.

"When she left, did you search for her?" I thought either he or Cecelia had said he'd spent ages searching for her.

He didn't answer, but he did take a deep breath in and released it slowly.

"Of course I did. Not immediately, though. I think it was after a week when she hadn't returned for any of her things. That was odd, she didn't return for any clothes, toiletries, nothing."

I remembered the makeup bag and realized it was strange to have left home without it. Unless she was in a major rush, of course.

"Did you fight really bad? Scare her?"

He stared at me. "She fucked someone else, got pregnant, and I'm the bad guy? No. We argued, and I left for work. When I got home, she was gone, simple as that."

"You looked at her family, obviously, to find out if she'd gone home?"

He raised his eyebrows at me. "I've searched every single inch of her existence, trust me with that. Not just to find her, but to find out who the father was as well."

"Someone was after her, though. Maybe the father of the child? Perhaps she ran from him, too," I said, quietly.

"I need to sleep." He drained his cup and left it on the side.

I picked up the book and stared at the cover. *Why this book?* I thought. Beau had said it was Rachel's favorite and being a reader myself, that seemed strange. There were books on those shelves far superior to this one. I turned it over to read the back.

There was nothing remarkable about the story. A young couple fall in love. His father is the small town sheriff, and doesn't like her family. Like I said, nothing remarkable about it at all. I blinked a couple of times, wondering if the light was playing tricks on my eyes. I ran my finger over the words, feeling the slight indentation in the paper, which confirmed what I thought I was seeing.

"Beau," I said, sliding from the stool and rushing from the kitchen. We collided in the hallway.

"Look," I pointed to the word, 'sheriff'. "It's underlined."

"How can you see that?"

"Pencil doesn't show on gloss covers but you can just about see the indentation, feel it."

"Why would she underline sheriff?" he asked.

"Maybe that's who she's running from?"

"I doubt it, I know him well. In fact, we were all in high school together. They dated before we did."

"So?"

"Charlotte, I'm tired. I can't think about all this right now. She cheated, and then she left me."

He turned and walked back to the sofa. I watched as he lay down and dragged the quilt over him. He turned his back to me, I guessed as confirmation our conversation was over. I climbed the stairs to the first floor bedroom but was too fired up to sleep. I lay on top of the bed just thinking. The list had been a welcome distraction from my own troubles, but I knew I'd have to address those soon. I needed to let go of Rachel, she was Beau's problem, and concentrate on my own.

————

Beau was gone the following morning, I decided that I didn't want to stay cooped up in his house, so I packed up my things and walked back to my apartment. I had work to do, I had to be at Cecelia's that morning, and then I was on the late shift at the diner. I wasn't complaining. I was working to pay the rent on the apartment and my savings pot was growing nicely.

I showered and changed into what I'd kept aside as my working clothes, an older pair of jeans and a slightly washed out t-shirt.

"Good morning," Cecelia said, when I walked into her house. After everything that had happened I was wondering how to broach the subject of her locking her front door.

"Morning, where do you want me to start today?" I asked.

She handed me a cup of tea, one of the reasons I arrived ten minutes early, so as not to spend working time drinking tea.

"I need to strip down the beds in the guest rooms. I've got one guest arriving later. I haven't decided yet, but I might have a rest from taking in guests for a while."

"Okay, I'll get on that straight after this," I said, raising my cup.

Cecelia usually took in no more than three guests in three single bedrooms at a time. I supposed she did it more for the company than the money. I drained my cup and gathered up the cleaning materials before walking up the stairs. It often disgusted me the state some guests left their room. Cecelia was a lovely woman, way too trusting, and I sighed as I saw bed linen strewn across the floor, damp towels left on the bare mattress, and a dubious looking magazine poking out from under the pillow. I opened up a plastic trash bag and emptied the wastebasket. Using just my fingertips, I picked up the magazine and stared at the cover. Two naked women entwined stared back at me. I placed it in the trash bag.

I swept and washed the wooden floor, dusted down the furniture, and then made up the bed. I repeated the process with the other two rooms, thankful they weren't in as much of a mess. Next on the list was the bathroom. I was always very particular, making sure to bleach down all surfaces, aware of how many strangers shared the room. I loved the smell once I'd finished. It reminded me of the one time my grandmother had taken me to the local swimming pool. The chlorine smell, that I knew would hang to my hair and clothes for hours after cleaning, gave me a sense of better times.

Cecelia was in the front yard talking to a neighbor, I assumed, when I headed for the utility room. I set the bed linens on to wash and decided I'd make a start in the kitchen. It was the most used room in the house and always took the longest to clean. Cecelia would normally help, but I'd noticed over the past few days she'd seemed more out of breath, less active. Beau had said she wasn't well and I wondered what was wrong. I felt I had a good enough relationship with her to ask. I decided to make her a cup of tea, the first time I'd tackled tealeaves and a pot, but a break and a chat would be good.

I had the teapot on the table, the jug of milk, and her cup and saucer as she walked in.

"Tea?" I asked.

"Oh, that sounds like a lovely idea. The kitchen looks great, you should have waited, I would have helped."

"It's what I'm here for, Cecelia. Now sit, you don't look as well as normal."

She sat heavily, wincing as she did. "Cecelia, are you okay?"

"No, Charlotte. I'm not, really. Beau is in a panic about it all, but it's just my heart. It doesn't function as well as it should, I get breathless and lightheaded sometimes. Old age, Charlotte, don't get old!" she said with a laugh.

"I don't think I can stop that process, but I'll try."

She chuckled as she poured herself a cup of tea. I watched, waiting for the smile of approval I was hoping for. Once she'd poured her milk and had taken a sip, she closed her eyes and smiled.

"Perfect," she said. It seemed silly, but just to be able to make her a cup of tea, exactly how she liked it, made me feel great.

"You remind me of my grandmother," I said quietly.

"How?"

"She was kind, helped everyone anytime they needed her. I miss her."

"I'm sure you do, darling. I bet she's extremely proud of you, though."

It was a comment that should have had me smiling, instead it brought tears to my eyes. Not from nostalgia, but I suspected I'd be the biggest disappointment to my grandmother if she could see me now. I was lying to people that cared for me, I was trying to do anything necessary to save my own ass, and I was hoping that would be at the expense of Damien.

Cecelia reached over and placed her hand on mine. "You know, we all do things maybe we're not proud of, but it's called surviving, and for that...what is your grandmother's name?"

"Esther."

"For that, Esther would be proud. Don't believe otherwise."

Whether Cecelia had some physic ability or her and Beau had been chatting. I wasn't sure which; maybe paranoia was something I needed to add to my character that I should work on.

"What happens when you're tired of just surviving?" I said, not expecting an answer.

"You start living, Charlotte. You set your own rules, you have dreams and goals, and you reach for them. What you're doing right now is existing. There's a big difference."

I stared at her for a while. Like my grandmother, she was a wise woman. Existing is all I'd been doing for four years, ever since Damien had been appointed my guardian.

"Now, help me up, let's take a look at those sofas I want for the den."

I cleared the table and then held her elbow as she stood from the chair. We walked out the back door and to one of the outbuildings. Thankfully, it was a little more orderly and cleaner than the one we'd been in before. In the corner were the two small sofas covered in white sheets. I made a pathway large enough, I hoped, to be able to push, or drag, one closer to the entrance.

"Oh, it's on wheels," I said, as it slid that effortlessly across the floor, I fell flat on my face.

It was nice to hear Cecelia laugh. I climbed to my knees to see her lift the white sheet.

"Wow, Cecelia!" Underneath was a plush purple velvet sofa. The back was dotted with silver studs, which I was sure would polish up nicely.

I ran my hand over the material, loving the feel and the way the fibers moved to give a slightly lighter shade.

"These must be nearly a hundred years old. I remember them in my mother's *boudoir*, and I'm pretty sure she'd had them for years."

"It's in amazing condition."

"I had them in a spare bedroom for years, but they seemed too nice to leave for some of the houseguests I seem to get now," she laughed.

"I think they will look perfect in the den, and yes, it does seem a shame to waste them on guests," I laughed with her.

I pushed the sofa, running from front to back to guide it through the back door and across the kitchen. But then we were stuck. I needed to lift the sofa to angle it through the kitchen door and into the hall. I didn't want to climb over it, so ran around the side of the house and back in through the front door. With a little wiggling, huffing and puffing, and me telling Cecelia constantly to stop trying to help, I managed to get it in the den. We placed it under the large sash window and in the sunlight, the velvet looked even more opulent.

"I worry the sunlight might bleach out the color, Cecelia. Maybe we need to move this."

Although there were shutters on each window in the house, sheer drapes as well, the sunlight would be a killer to that material bearing its age.

"I guess I could put these in the living room, guests don't get to use that room. Then we can keep them just for us."

The living room had a three-piece sofa in a cream floral print. Although not to my taste, I thought it would be more practical for the den.

"I think we need help to move that sofa, although I could probably get the chairs out myself."

"Beau is away for work, maybe we could ask Rose?"

"How long does he stay away for?" I asked, curiosity getting the better of me.

"Sometimes just a day or so, sometimes it can be weeks. He works for the government, all secret I imagine. I never know where he is, he can't tell me."

I didn't respond but my mind was running overtime. *The government?*

"I'll ask Rose when I do my shift later, but in the meantime, I'm sure I can move these chairs, and although it's going to look odd, we'll get the purple one in."

It took another half-hour of scraped knuckles from handling furniture that only just made it through the doorway, and we had two floral chairs in one room, a purple sofa and a floral one in another.

"Phew!" I said, flopping down on the beautiful purple sofa. "I think we'll leave the other one in the outbuilding until we can move that one," I said, looking at where Cecelia had sat.

"These will look perfect in here," she said, looking around.

The walls were covered in cream wallpaper that felt silky to the touch. The dark wooden floor contrasted with the walls, making the room feel so much bigger. A large, ornately framed mirror hung from above the fireplace. I stood to look at it. Its bevelled glass was golden with age.

"That was my mother's as well. She came from a very wealthy family, they had a home in Paris, as well as a winery in Bordeaux. The best French red wines come from Bordeaux, one from my family's vineyard."

"Do you still have family there?"

"Of course. My brother and his family run the estate now. I've traveled to France many times, not so much in the last couple of years, sadly."

"You're brother, as in Beau's father?"

"Yes. Although he refuses to have any contact," she sighed when she spoke.

"I didn't realize Beau wasn't born here."

"No, he was born in Paris, his parents sent him here to live with me when he was very young. Unfortunately, that is the cause of the rift. I tried for years to have them reconcile, but the more I argued with him, the further he dug his heels in."

"Is he an American citizen now?" I thought on his *work* for the government.

"Now he is, of course. Anyway, how about I make us some lunch?"

"Sounds good," I replied.

Cecelia was a master at the art of making soup. Each day I was there, I'd be presented with a large bowl of various flavors. That day, it was squash with chunks of bread torn off a loaf that had recently come out of the oven.

"I'll get fat at this rate," I said, spooning soup into my mouth.

"You could do with a little weight on."

"I've always been skinny, I guess I'm one of the *fortunate* ones who can eat anything and not put on weight. It was awful when I was young and in school. I was called all sorts of names, accused of having an eating disorder at one point."

"You have a high metabolism, I assume," she said.

I shrugged my shoulders. There had been a time I'd looked awful, not that I thought myself beautiful anyway. My hip bones had jutted out, ribs could be counted, and my collarbones made me look like I was starving myself.

"I can never find clothes that fit well, hence the jeans and t-shirts," I said with a laugh.

"Every woman should have a wardrobe of pretty dresses, handbags, and shoes."

"I don't own any of those." I raised my leg to show off a battered sneaker.

I finished off my lunch and with a kiss to both cheeks, as was Cecelia's custom, I left to prepare for my late shift. I needed to shower off the cleaning chemicals and dust before I started at the diner.

―――――――

"Afternoon," I called out when I pushed through the diner door. A couple of customers greeted me in return.

I grabbed my apron and poked my head over the counter into the kitchen.

"Kieran, I'm here."

"Girl, am I glad to see you. Rose is unwell, you're on your own, do you think you'll cope?"

Tuesday evenings were pretty quiet normally. "Of course I can. What specials do we have on?"

Once I'd written the specials on my pad, I checked on the few customers already seated and cleaned up used tables.

It was a quiet evening, which I was thankful for in one way, however it did mean tips were low. Once the last customer had left and I locked up, I helped Kieran clean down the kitchen. He'd bagged up some leftover meals for me to put in my freezer. I didn't remember the last time I'd had to do a food shop.

"What's wrong with Rose? I hope it's nothing too serious," I said.

"I don't know, to be honest. I can't tell you how many hours I've spent nagging the old woman to go see the doctor. She's had a terrible head for days."

"She never said, I could have covered more."

"She never tells anyone anything," he huffed as he spoke.

"You're very fond of her, aren't you?"

"Been best friends since we were toddlers. Shame we never managed to get it on," he laughed, and then coughed and patted his chest.

"You don't sound too good yourself."

He waved his arm, as if to dismiss my comment. "I'm old, that's all."

"You're as strong as an ox, you are."

He gave me a smile, flexed his biceps a little and puffed out his chest.

"Kieran, I need to get to Whiteling, it's about eighty miles or so from here. Do you know of a bus service that could take me?"

I knew I wasn't being honest; I was being a little manipulative. I already knew there was no bus service.

"I doubt there's any public transport going that way. I can always drive you, if you can wait a couple of days."

"I can't ask you to do that."

"You can, and I've offered."

"Who will cover here?" Kieran seemed to work seven days a week.

"Got a young guy called Jack coming in tomorrow, take the pressure off me a little. If it's okay with you, we'll go one afternoon."

"That would be amazing, thank you. I can pay for the gas."

"Get away with you, girl. Now, let's get out of here."

Kieran walked me to the corner of my block and stood and

watched until I'd unlocked the front door. I waved before closing and locking it. A bulb was out in the hallway and I climbed the narrow stairs in the dark. I made a mental note to fix it the following day.

After my third shower that day, I climbed into bed and picked up my book. It reminded me of the one left at Beau's. I think I'd probably only managed a couple of pages before I fell asleep.

The cell ringing woke me. For a moment I lay still, totally confused as to what the sound was and where it was coming from. No one had ever called me before. I threw back the bedcovers and ran to the living room. The cell was sitting on the kitchen counter. Just as my hand reached for it, it stopped ringing. I cursed but scrolled to contacts to see who had called me. It was an unknown number.

It had to be a mistake. Only Beau knew the number, I doubted Cecelia would have called me, and if she had, her name would have shown. I couldn't, not that I would have, call the number back as it was unlisted. Instead I left the cell on the counter and switched on the coffee maker. I decided that I might as well get up, despite it being an hour earlier than I normally would have.

It was as I walked back to the bedroom the cell rang again. That time I pressed answer in time.

"Hello?"

The sound was muffled although I could hear a voice.

"Hello? I can't hear you," I said.

"Charlotte?"

I could barely hear, let alone recognize the voice, and suspected that was to do with a poor reception.

"It's Charlotte, can you hear me okay?"

The call disconnected. I doubted it was Beau and that only left

Cecelia; maybe she had called from her landline. I ran to the bedroom and dragged on the previous days clothes. Grabbing my keys and the cell, I ran from the apartment and didn't stop running until I was at her front door. For the first time since I'd been in town, the door was locked. I bashed my fists against the wood, placed my ear to it to see if I could hear her. I called out her name, I didn't get any response. I ran around the side of the house and wrenched on the back door handle. It was also locked. At that point I knew something terrible had happened. I cupped my hands around my face and peered through the glass. The kitchen didn't look to be disturbed.

To the side of the back door was a plant pot. I picked it up, initially hoping I might see a spare key, there was nothing, but while it was in my hands I knew what I had to do. I threw it at the glass panel in the door. Although the glass shattered, it stayed in place. Using the heel of my hand, I bashed the glass over and over until it eventually gave in. I wiped my bloodied hand on the front of my t-shirt and then reached through to open the door from the inside.

"Cecelia," I called out.

I ran through the kitchen, and looked in the living room, it was a mess. Furniture had been upended. I checked the den to see the same before rushing up the stairs. I hesitated at Cecelia's bedroom; my hand shook as I reached out to turn the handle. I pulled the cell from my pocket ready to call Beau.

"Oh, God, what have you done?"

Cecelia was lying on her bed motionless, her face was pale, so very pale. Sitting on the edge with a shit-eating grin was Damien. He waved Cecelia's cell in the air. I guessed that was where he'd obtained my number.

"Hello, Harlot. Think I wouldn't find you?"

"What the fuck have you done to her?"

I rushed to the side of the bed at the same time as he stood. He grabbed me around my waist, but all I could see was Cecelia. I fought him hard, scraping at his skin on the back of his hands until he moved one enough for me to spin in his arms. I kicked out but I was too close. I clawed at his face, tried to punch him. He pushed me away and then punched me straight in the face. I could feel blood run from my nose. I flew at him.

Everything was a blur. I punched, kicked, bit, scratched; I even grabbed his balls at one point. He shouted, winced, slapped my face hard but I didn't care. I felt nothing but rage until he grabbed me by the throat. He walked me backward, tightening his grip with every step. I grabbed at his hands, trying to pull them away. I couldn't breathe, my lungs were screaming at me to gain a breath; my heart was racing so hard it hurt. Small black dots floated in my vision until there was nothing to see.

––––––––––

I could hear voices but they sounded so far away. I tried to open my eyes but they felt stuck together. I ached, all over. It felt like every bone in my body was protesting at being beaten. I was also cold and not sure why. It took me a moment, and a feel of my hand to realize I had no jeans on, no panties. Although I was numb, I cried knowing exactly what had happened to me.

I pried one eyelid open, it was dark where I was, but I could see slivers of light. It stunk of piss and shit, to the point that I started to gag. My throat was raw and the bile that rose aggravated that soreness. I heaved, as I did I placed my hand down on something wet, squishy, and foul smelling. I knew then where I was. On the trailer park was a communal, outdoor bathroom. Not that I ever used it, as it was never cleaned. I crawled toward the slivers of light. The bathroom was wooden, the daylight filtered in through the gaps between the crudely nailed together panels. Damien was outside with another man.

"She isn't worth that much, fuckwit," the other man said. "I already tried her out." He looked familiar, and it was only when Damien moved an inch and I could see his face that my stomach knotted.

Damien was talking to his drug dealer, the one who, rumor had it, bought and sold the girls that disappeared. I knew then, I was in way more trouble than just dealing with Damien.

"She's got experience, Cody. You fucked her while she was out cold!"

"She's got a cunt the size of a tunnel." He laughed and then spat on the floor. I watched as he lit what looked like a joint.

"A hundred then, she's worth that. Fucks like a rabbit, always had good reports back. Bareback, anal, she'll do whatever you make her."

"I'll come by later. I got shit to do right now. Make sure she's fucking clean, I don't want no crap in my car."

I wasn't entirely sure, but I thought I could see just a small section of a vehicle, a blue vehicle with some form of writing. I needed to find a way out. I scuttled to the back of the small room, trying hard not to breathe too deeply. I tried just breathing in and out through my mouth but my throat was too sore. I had to use my nose, and with that came the stench. I tried hard not to cry and not to think of Cecelia until I could safely get away. I didn't have time to break down. I prayed that someone had found her and that she was okay.

"Charlotte the harlot," I heard in a singsong voice. Damien was coming for me.

I did the only thing I could think of, I rolled around in the shit and piss, coating myself in it. No matter how much of a pig he was, he wouldn't want to get too close. Light flooded the room, and I screwed my eyes shut against the sting as it hit my bruised eyes.

"Jesus Christ, you fucking whore," he said. "Get the fuck out here."

I crawled toward the door, deliberately. "Get up," he said, taking a step back as he spoke.

I reached out as if needing him to steady myself. "Don't fucking touch me," he said, covering his mouth with his hand.

"I can't get up," I said. My voice was hoarse.

He reached down and grabbed the hair on the top of my head, then pulled me to my feet, wrenching out a handful of hair at the same time. I reached up, as I did, he kicked me in the stomach causing me to double over.

"Don't fucking touch me, I said, didn't I? Jesus, you stink."

He dragged me to the rear of the trailer I'd run from, letting go of my hair and kicking at the back of my legs until I fell to the ground. I was still reeling from the kick to the stomach; I could feel hot piss run down my thigh as my bladder gave way.

I screeched when a blast of ice cold water hit me. He'd turned on the hose and was spraying me with water. I covered my face with my hands; the water was like a thousand tiny pins pricking my skin at the same time. When he thought I was clean, he threw the hose down.

"Get inside and get properly cleaned up, you've got a job to do."

I didn't move, but was then dragged through the door of the trailer. Dripping wet, I was marched to the one bedroom. I sat on the very edge of the unmade and stinking bed. I guessed he'd moved back in when I'd left. Cigarette ash, joints, needles, and drug paraphernalia littered the floor. They were accompanied by empty and half-filled bottles of liquor.

The bedroom door opened, and Damien threw in the black, fake leather mini-skirt and Gypsy top that he thought made me look more desirable. He tore my t-shirt from my body when I hadn't moved quickly enough. I needed clothes, I had no choice but to put on what he'd offered. He stood and watched. All the while, my mind was whirling. I was never going to be handed over to his friend and a plan had started to form in my mind.

"Can I get a drink of water?" I asked, "My throat hurts."

"Should have opened your mouth when I washed you," he replied. "I like your hair, makes you look older. Put some makeup on."

Damien handed me a small cosmetics bag, I had no idea who it belonged to, and I doubted very much he'd gone to the trouble to purchase those items for me. I used a small compact to apply eyeliner, mascara, and dabbed my lips with a balm, forgoing the bright red lipstick that had clearly been used.

"What time is your friend coming back?" I asked.

"Later."

Damien lay on the bed, his hand reached for a bottle of liquor beside the bed. I watched as he unscrewed the cap and took a gulp. He wiped the back of his hand over his mouth before offering me the bottle. I shook my head. Despite being desperate for a drink, I wouldn't put my mouth around anything he had.

"You know the police thought I killed Philip?"

"Did you?"

Damien laughed. "No, course not. I went there to give him a

stern talking to, remind him he'd been fucking something that belonged to me and was a minor. Someone got there first."

"I wasn't a minor." I ignored the *belonged to me* comment.

"Yeah, whatever. You've been fucking him for a year, that makes you a minor when you started."

I didn't bother to correct him. Numbers or local law wasn't his strong point.

"Anyways, I didn't tell them about you, I saved your ass, Harlot. So, now you owe me."

"You should have," I said, hoping to show I wasn't scared.

"You was always the dumb one, didn't get any further than one town over." He laughed before taking another large gulp from the bottle.

Damien was a seasoned drinker; he wouldn't pass out with just the half bottle he held in his hand. I hoped his friend took his time and Damien might move on to something stronger.

"What did you do to Cecelia?"

"Ah, she was a sweet old woman, wasn't she? I booked a room with her. See, I've been watching you and it wasn't that hard to follow you about."

He made no mention of Beau, so I wasn't so sure he had been following me that frequently. At the thought of Beau and Cecelia my eyes filled with tears. He was going to be so devastated.

"Aw, why you crying? She remind you of Esther?"

"Yes, she was kind to me."

"You ain't got a need for kind." Although not drunk, his words had become slightly slurred.

I shuffled, it was to shift from sitting on a bruise. I guessed Damien thought differently. He sprung from the bed and grabbed my arm.

"I'm trying to get comfortable, that's all," I said, trying to slow my racing heart.

All I wanted to do was to curl up and cry, for Cecelia, for Beau, for myself. But I knew, to survive this ordeal, I had to pretend I didn't care. I had to act no matter how hard that was.

I sighed. "I'm bored," I said.

"Too bad."

Damien placed the half-drunk bottle to my side. He pulled a pack of cigarettes from his pocket and a lighter from the other. He lit his cigarette and laid the pack and the lighter on the bed.

"Can I?" I said, pointing to the bottle.

He shrugged, it wasn't a yes or no but I picked it up anyway. He watched me, bemused I thought, as I placed the neck of the bottle to my mouth. I took the largest mouthful of the fiery liquid I could, without choking. At the same time, I picked up the lighter.

What I did next would haunt me. I spat the liquor into his face and at the same time, I flicked the bezel and set him on fire. I threw more of the liquor at him and ran from the bedroom. The screams pierced straight through me. I covered my ears as a flaming body stumbled after me, catching everything close by on fire. Synthetic curtains went up with a whoosh. The smell was the thing that would stay with me. Burning, melting flesh, smelled like a hog on a spit.

I fell out the trailer door; he fell behind me. I screamed, he hissed and his skin popped and voice gurgled until he fell flat on the ground. I knew I should have moved, ran, but I was paralyzed as I watched the trailer go up in a ball of flames.

Tears rolled down my cheeks, not for him, though. I guessed it was shock.

CHAPTER 8

I wasn't aware of time. I had no idea if it was day or night, how long I'd been sitting on a cot in a windowless cell.

The police had been called, which I remembered finding very strange. No one called the police on that trailer park. I was pulled away from the smoldering body that had been Damien. I couldn't speak. I was spoken to, asked questions, but I'd open my mouth and no words would form. They knew my name, I guessed whoever had called the police had told them that part. They didn't know that it was Damien charcoaled outside the trailer.

I was made to stand and hold out a board, I didn't know what the board said. I continued to cry as they took my photograph, but I didn't understand why they needed to do that. I would look at the policeman, I would see his mouth moving, but I couldn't hear his words. The only sound in my head were my own screams. The only image in my line of sight, no matter where I looked, was Damien's melting face and his bulging eyes.

I knew I was in a police station and I knew I was in trouble. I deserved it, I guessed. I'd caused so much trouble. Other than that, I was at a complete loss as to what I should do. I just needed a little time to clear the noise from my head, to get my thoughts straight, and erase the image imprinted behind my eyelids.

I tried my hardest not to sleep, even holding my eyelids, unsuccessfully, open one time. No matter how hard I tried, I failed. The noise that was contained during the day, spilled out of my mouth that night. So much so, that finally a doctor was called.

It surprised me to learn I'd only been arrested the day before. It felt like I had been sitting in that cell for days. The doctor told the police officer standing beside him I was fine. I was fit for questioning. Maybe I was, except I couldn't remember much other than the last few moments. I knew Damien had hurt Cecelia but then it all became a blur, a mesh of images that I wasn't sure were real, or when they had occurred. The confusion frightened me.

They asked me the same question over and over, *Did you kill Damien Kenny?* Sometimes they didn't ask outright, they worded it so many different ways. They sympathized with me; one policewoman actually said she'd have done the same had she been in my situation.

I'd asked how Cecelia was; they would look blankly at me, not answering. No one seemed to know who, or how, she was. I was shuffled from cell to interview room more times that I could remember. Sometimes they were friendly, sometimes not. They got frustrated and shouted, slammed palms on desks, and sometimes their voices were so smooth, low, and singsong, I'd want to fall asleep.

Another day passed, or at least I thought it had. There were no windows in the cell, I lost track of time, but I had slept so assumed, when I was given something unidentifiable to eat, it was breakfast time. It was that day that clarity started to form. The fog that had misted up my mind cleared, and the screaming in my head settled down to just a whimper.

It was day three that things changed. I was sitting in my cell, disgusted at the smell that emanated from my sweaty body and the room itself when the door opened. A policeman stood and beckoned me to follow.

"Your lawyer's finally here," he said.

"My...?"

I hadn't been given an opportunity to contact a lawyer, not that I would know who to call anyway. It also dawned on me that, from the little TV I had watched, I should have been allocated one from the very beginning. I racked my brain to see what I'd said in those many interviews.

I followed him to a room. A gentleman in a dark gray suit stood. He smiled as I entered, walked forward and reached out with his hand. At first I just stared, not to be rude, but conscious of how grubby mine were.

I opened my mouth to speak but he hushed me, staring harshly at the policeman who was hovering around the door. When we were finally alone, he pulled out a chair for me.

"Charlotte, my name is Paul. I want you to tell me how you ended up in Whiteling, okay?"

I nodded. I started at the beginning, telling him about my grandmother, Damien's abuse, losing the house and running from Whiteling. I omitted a lot of information that might have been useful, but I didn't care to share absolutely everything with a man I had only just met. I then told him of the phone call I'd received and what I'd discovered when I'd got to Cecelia's.

"Please, tell me. Is she okay?"

He sighed, "No, unfortunately she passed away, Charlotte."

"No. Oh, God, please tell me that's wrong."

"She was very sick, her heart gave out."

"Her...? So, Damien didn't kill her?"

"No, not according to the initial coroner's report, anyway. Whether the fright of finding him in her bedroom can be attributed to that, I'll have a damn good go at. Has a doctor seen you?"

I dreaded to think what I looked like. "Sort of. I can't remember much."

"Good, let's leave it that way. Now, we're going into the interview room, and I don't want you to speak unless I give you the nod. If I don't give you the nod, no matter what they say, you don't answer."

Somehow, and perhaps it was because my mind was a little clearer, the prospect of sitting through another interview terrified me. However, I nodded my head.

Paul stood and rapped his knuckles on the door. It was immediately opened and two police officers walked in. I recognized one.

"First, my client had been denied immediate representation; second, she should have been given access to proper medical attention. Both of those will be officially recorded," he said, before anyone had settled in their chairs.

"Noted," the officer I didn't recognize said.

"Charlotte, can we start again? Tell us what happened?"

I looked at Paul; he shook his head. "My client was kidnapped and brought to Whiteling, somewhere she'd left some weeks ago. She has suffered immense trauma, physical injuries that should have been tended to. She is willing to give a statement, but right now her needs are to be met. I'm requesting she's taken to hospital for a check up."

"Did the doctor check you over?" I was asked. Again, I looked at Paul and he nodded.

"A doctor sat on the edge of the bed, he didn't physically examine me. I don't actually remember anything he said, other than I was fine."

The officer sighed and then switched off the recording machine. He asked his colleague to fetch some coffee.

"Paul, I know Damien Kenny. I know he is capable of causing your client terrible trauma. All I need to know is what happened. Off the record for now. You know me, you can trust me."

Paul looked at me, I wasn't sure what I was expected to say.

"He has physically and mentally abused Charlotte. The police in Aylesham have him on CCTV at an address where the owner, Cecelia Mercier was found dead. He kidnapped Charlotte from that address. He raped her, beat her, locked her in a shed, and was then to *sell* her to a friend for prostitution."

Just hearing it spoken out loud had tears coursing down my cheeks.

"And the friend is?" the policeman asked, and both looked at me.

"I don't know him, I just overheard a conversation."

"Charlotte, what happened in that trailer?" the police officer asked.

At first, I struggled to speak. "He drank from a bottle, some homemade stuff, he called it the original moonshine, I think. He made me take a sip but I don't like it. I don't know exactly what happened. One minute he was sitting there, drinking, he lit his cigarette and then he was on fire. I panicked and I ran. He ran after me, as he did the flames...they caught things on fire."

I choked through the words, genuinely distressed, despite my statement not being strictly true.

"Can we get that on record?"

I looked at Paul. "Only if I have assurance she'll get medical treatment. Look at her, Frank. He beat the fucking shit out of her. You know she shouldn't be here."

More tears pricked at my eyes; there was so much compassion in his voice that I didn't think he was acting, or being all 'lawyery.'

"I think my colleagues were a little... You know what I mean. Charlotte, just repeat what you've told me, on record, then we can begin to sort this mess out."

I watched as the recorder was switched back on, I was asked the same question and I repeated my answer. Probably not word for word, but I didn't think it mattered. Once that was done, and some paperwork was signed. I was escorted from the station. The sunlight hurt my eyes that at first I wasn't aware of the figure leaning against the side of a car. Paul took my arm and I was helped down the steps. It was as I got close that I recognized Beau.

"I'm so sorry," I said, trying hard not to break down.

He didn't reply, just nodded, but he did open the car door and placed his hand on my lower back as he helped me in. I was grateful there wasn't a hospital in Whiteling, Paul had instructed Beau to take me back to Aylesham. I watched Paul walk back into the station.

"I don't know what to say," I said, quietly.

"Say nothing, Charlotte. Let's just get you to the hospital."

"I don't have insurance."

"Don't worry about that now."

Sadness etched his face and when he looked at me, I knew he blamed me for Cecelia. I wanted to reach out to him, beg his forgiveness if necessary. I wanted to tell him everything but whatever friendship we had started to develop was gone.

It appeared I was expected at the hospital, I was met at reception and led away to a small room. I was introduced to a rape counselor and I wanted to laugh. I'd needed one of those four years ago, not then. I declined the *chat*. I was asked to remove my clothes, which were bagged up, and I was given a robe to put on. Paul must have called ahead, or perhaps the police. I guess they wanted evidence of what I'd said.

Swabs were taken, X-rays and blood tests performed. Eventually, I was told I had two broken ribs, was bruised internally and externally. I was given some pills to ease the pain.

"Charlotte, we need to have a conversation." I looked up from the hospital bed and saw the counselor in the doorway.

I nodded. Nicola took the seat beside the bed. "I know you've said you don't wish to talk about what happened to you, but we do need to consider whether you could have gotten pregnant. It's not too late for medication, but I want to talk you through your options, if you don't want to take it."

"I don't know if he actually raped me, I just don't remember. I know my clothes were missing."

"Someone did, honey. There's evidence," she said, gently.

"What evidence?"

"Slight damage and some bleeding. Although there is no evidence he ejaculated, it's best to be over careful."

I shook my head. I just didn't understand. I'd woken naked from the waist down and that had to mean someone raped me while I was unconscious. Then I remembered the words I'd heard spoken between Damien and Cody. I held out my hand for the medication.

"At the moment, we have to assume it was Damien. We will be able to confirm with DNA testing," she added.

I knew it wasn't Damien, and did it really matter who it was? I rested my head back and closed my eyes. I wondered if Nicola thought I ought to be sobbing, reacting in a manner I expect she was used to seeing, but in my mind, every second of sex I'd had in my short life was like being raped. Whether I walked into a bedroom or was dragged, it made no difference; I had done what I had without consent. I was immune to any feelings I was expected to display.

I closed my eyes, effectively ending our conversation. I wasn't ready to divulge my life to a stranger, especially since I had no idea if I was still under arrest or not.

An hour, or maybe two, passed before I saw movement at the glass window in the hospital room door. Paul looked through and I straightened myself up in the bed. He walked in followed by Frank, the police officer.

"Charlotte, Frank needs to ask a couple of questions. Obviously, I'm here if you need to speak to me privately about any concerns you have. Are you up to talking?"

I nodded, not sure what I was going to be faced with.

"Charlotte, did you know Philip Stanton?"

I was thankful that I was in the process of wincing through movement, otherwise I wasn't sure I'd be able to keep a neutral look on my face.

"Not personally, I saw a report on the TV. You don't think Damien was involved in that, do you?"

"Why would you think Damien would be involved?"

"I just assumed that's why you're asking me. I mean, I'd never met Mr. Stanton but wasn't he a governor or something?"

143

"He was the ex-mayor. No, we don't think Damien was involved. A woman's shoe was found in Mr. Stanton's bedroom." He stared at me but had the grace to look a little uncomfortable.

"Ah, I see. So, because I was about to be forced into prostitution, you think I had to be fucking the ex-mayor!" I raised my voice in mock indignation. Inside my heart beat a rapid pace and my stomach curled in on itself.

"No, but..."

I looked at Paul. "Am I actually under arrest for anything? I know they took my photograph but no one has explained anything to me."

Paul glanced at Frank with one eyebrow raised. Could that be another failing to add to the list?

"Not charged yet, Miss Kenny. At the end of the day, we can't ascertain exactly how Mr. Kenny died, other than it would have been horrifically." His frosty stare was met by mine. I guess he wasn't as supportive as I'd been led to believe.

"Then I think I need to go get my things from my apartment and make arrangements to find somewhere to live."

Frank left, Paul showed him to the door and then returned to sit in the chair.

"Charlotte, you can't leave yet, I'm afraid. I mean, you can leave the hospital when the doctor discharges you, but you need to stay local. I know whatever you did, it was because you had no choice. But let's not push our luck, okay? There is still the matter of Philip."

He stood and gave me a smile.

"How does this work, Paul? I mean, I have some money, but..."

"It's taken care of. Just get yourself well, Charlotte. I'll see you in a couple of days."

He turned toward the door. "Oh, you have visitors outside."

Not that I was disappointed to see Kieran and Rose, but I had hoped Beau might have been with them. I needed to talk to him, explain how sorry I was.

"Oh, sweetie, look at your face," Rose said, rushing to me.

Her kindness broke me. I reached out and she wrapped me in her arms. I sobbed, I guessed four years of absolute, utter desperateness poured from me. I even heard myself wail. She held me tight, rocked me, and whispered in my ear.

I felt completely spent when Rose gently lowered me back on the bed. She swept my tear sodden hair from my face. Kieran sat to one side, holding my hand and patting it.

"I'm so sorry," I said.

"You've got nothing to be sorry about," she said.

"Cecelia..."

"Cecelia had heart failure, Charlotte. Nothing you, or he, did, caused her death. It was only a matter of time. To be honest, she lived longer than she thought she was going to. She just didn't want anyone to know or fuss over her."

"Sweetheart, you don't have to tell us anything, okay? But we want you to know that we're here for you, when you're ready to talk," Kieran said.

———

Two days later, I discharged myself. I'd had a further meeting with Paul to learn that charges, not that I ever really understood what charges there might be, were not going to be brought. However, the police were still keen to talk to me should I remember anything further. I remembered it all, I just wasn't willing to put my life at risk by divulging any of it.

Rose drove me back to the apartment and it felt very odd to walk in, knowing it was probably now owned by Beau. I hadn't seen nor heard from him since he'd driven me to the hospital, and I guessed I didn't expect to.

I thought of him, and of the list I'd found. I thought of Philip and wondered why there was still a lack of news. I wondered what would happen to Damien's body and hoped I wouldn't be involved in any decision-making.

I didn't know what had happened to my cell. I guessed I'd dropped it when I fought Damien. Perhaps I'd ask Paul, he said he wanted to tie up any loose ends, when he visited later that day.

I emptied the fridge of stale food; cleaned until my hands were red raw and the apartment gave off that comforting swimming pool smell. I washed bed linens in the communal laundry room. While I piled the linens in the dryer, I wondered if Cecelia owned the whole house or just the one apartment. I wanted to know what was happening with her. I hoped I'd be allowed to attend her funeral and pay my respects. I was sure Rose would keep me informed.

Paul arrived later that afternoon; he was dressed casually in a button-down shirt and jeans. He placed a file on the counter and accepted the coffee I'd had ready.

"What happens now?" I asked.

"As far as Damien is concerned, you're in the clear. I have to say, I'm sure Frank thinks you might have been involved more than you've said, but proving that just isn't going to be possible. It's going to be classified as an accident. I know they are still keen to learn who the drug dealer friend is and, this is just my opinion, there is more of a reason for that than just wanting to know who your cousin was involved with. I'm going to dig a little there."

"I don't know if I thanked you. I really am grateful that you offered to help. But who is paying for this?"

"Beau is, Charlotte. Although I've offered my services at a reduced fee, we go back a long way."

"Oh, why?"

"That's something you'd have to ask him. I'm looking at the possibility of suing for wrongful arrest. There are certain procedures that also weren't followed."

I shook my head. "I just want to move on and get past this, Paul."

"That's another thing I have for you. Your grandmother's house is legally yours. At least let me get that back for you. Charlotte, I want to help. My daughter went missing a year ago, you've heard of her I understand, Rachel. You..."

Once I got over the shock, I cut his sentence off. "I remind you of her?"

He set his coffee cup down and sighed. "You do, but that's not the reason. I don't know what you know of my daughter. She was a good girl, a great person, until one day she wasn't, and I never knew why. I tried hard but you know, parents and kids..." Obviously he didn't finish his sentence because I didn't know.

"Anyway, she changed when she met Beau and the old Rachel returned. And now she's gone and I'm back to where I was years ago. The not knowing why is the killer. But you found that list, the message, so I kind of feel I owe you for that sliver of relief at least."

"And helping me will do what?" I didn't want to sound ungrateful, but I couldn't afford to stay around, and I didn't want to take his help and then leave him like his daughter did.

"I don't know."

"I'm grateful for your help, Paul, I really am, but I can't stay here, and I'm worried that you'll think I've run out on you as well." I decided just to be honest.

"There's no reason you can't stay, but I understand that. For now, shall we at least get that house back?"

The thought of getting my grandmother's house back was tempting, but I'd never live in it again. "Okay, but then it has to be sold, immediately. I don't want to go back there, ever."

He smiled and opened his file.

"Tell me what you remember."

I went through the evening I was evicted, explaining that I thought it might have been either a drug deal gone wrong or a lost bet. Paul wrote as I spoke.

"I don't suppose you have any paperwork, your grandmother's will for example?"

"No, but from memory, it was a local solicitor that dealt with it all, and of course, the court was involved."

"Then I should be able to get all the info I need from there."

"Paul, anything I tell you is confidential isn't it? You can't repeat to anyone what I say, can you?"

"It is, and no. Unless I think you're about to commit a crime, then the law gets a little gray."

I fell silent for a moment, deliberating.

"The police asked me about Philip Stanton, do you know why?"

"Only that a shoe was found and I guess they made a judgement about you based on where you lived and...." He shrugged apologetically. "They're assuming he had company and it might have been *paid for* company." He looked a little uncomfortable when he spoke.

"He did have company, but it wasn't *paid for* company. I was there."

He sat bolt upright. "Okay, don't tell me anything more just yet. Let me think."

He flicked through the pages in his file until he came to a piece of lined paper with scrawl. He read through and I was amazed he could decipher his own writing.

"What happened, Charlotte?"

"He was a friend, I mean, he was looking to pick up a woman but just to talk. He was lonely. We met up a few times and all we did was sit and talk."

"Did he give you anything, even as a gift?"

"Yes, he gave me one hundred dollars, but that was one of the last times we met, I think. He wanted me to buy some nice clothes. Not for him, for me."

"Did you have sex with him?"

"Once, the last time we met, and it was a mistake. He didn't force himself on me, I thought I was doing the right thing, for him."

It sounded so lame, even to my own ears.

"We didn't have an arrangement, or a relationship, other than friends, I thought."

"Tell me what happened that night."

"I went into the shower, he had a bathroom off his bedroom. I swear, Paul, I didn't hear a thing. I came out of the bedroom and..."

"And?"

"And he was sitting up in the bed, there was so much blood, up the wall behind him. He'd...He'd been shot." I tapped my forehead, not wanting to speak the words.

"You didn't hear or see anything?"

"No, and that's why I didn't go to the police. How could I have not heard? They would never have believed me. I panicked. I ran back to the trailer and Damien showed up some time later. He said, something like, *I know where you've been, you won't go back there, will you?"*

"What was your impression of what he said?"

"That he killed him. I thought he was the man helping the police with their investigation but I'm not sure now. Honestly, I don't know what happened. He was sleeping when I went into the shower and then he was dead. I didn't hear anything." I really wanted to reiterate that point.

"How could I have not heard?" I said, quieter.

"Why didn't you tell Frank when he asked you about Philip?"

"Because he wouldn't believe me." I could feel anxiety washing over me; I wasn't convinced that Paul believed me, either.

"How can I convince you I'm telling the truth?" I asked.

"Are you, one-hundred-percent, telling me the truth?"

"Yes. I've told a lot of lies I won't deny that. I told Cecelia my name was Johnson, because I was scared. I was terrified that Damien would come after me; I was frightened that I'd get arrested for Philip. I did call the police, I told them a man had been murdered and gave his address. I wouldn't have done that if I was guilty, would I?"

"I don't think Damien killed Philip."

"Why?"

"Because whoever did, was a professional. You were in the shower, they would have known that. A professional is paid to do one hit, unless you'd witnessed that, you weren't a target. Do you think Damien would have walked in, while you were in the shower, shot Philip and then left? Or would he have made you watch, or whatever?"

I hadn't thought along those lines at all.

"Why would someone kill Philip, though?"

"That's what the police are trying to figure out. It's all gone quiet, even his son has stopped his press activity and he's a lawyer. Something has been found, some background maybe, and it's being hushed up now."

"What do I do?"

"Nothing. You say nothing at all, other than to me. I need to do a little research."

I nodded gently, grateful for his help and guidance.

"What about the list, Paul?" I asked, referring to the message in the book.

"Well, we don't know exactly what she was trying to tell us, but to me, it was clear she felt the need to hide. Why? That's what I need to know."

He'd said *we* but then *me*. Did that mean it was both Beau and Paul and did the 'me' mean only Paul thought the same as I did; Rachel had no choice but to run?

"How do you find out more?"

"I thought I knew my daughter, her mother died and I brought her up, but maybe I didn't. Perhaps there were so many secrets and I want to seriously dissect her life. Especially the time she went off the rails before she hooked up with Beau."

"They were high school sweethearts, weren't they?"

"Sort of. They got together, then split, got back together, the usual teenage relationship, I guess."

That wasn't how Beau explained it. Or maybe he did, I couldn't recall what he'd actually said, if he'd said anything at all.

"I need to get going. I have to tell you, it might be that at some point we have to tell the police what happened…" He held up his hand to silence the protest that was about to leave my lips. "I can cover that, Charlotte. Leaving the scene of a crime is about the only thing you've done wrong, but we have good reason to suggest why."

"I don't know about this. I need to think."

"You think, let me get on with a few things. The house is our priority, then we'll deal with Philip."

Paul closed his folder and I walked him to the apartment door. He paused in the hallway.

"Like I said, you've given me something to believe my daughter is alive. I don't know if you understand how great that is."

He left before I could answer. Was it great? She'd been gone a year, I could only pray that she still was.

CHAPTER 9

Although I hadn't been given any shifts, I took a walk to the diner. I didn't expect to work, in fact, with the bruising to my face, it was an effort to be out in public. I was a 'stranger' in town, and that alone seemed to cause curiosity without drawing attention to myself by looking like I'd been ten rounds with a boxer. However, I needed to earn money. I wanted to put my life back on track as quickly as possible.

"Sweetie, what are you doing here? You should be resting," Rose said.

I would have loved nothing more than to tell her the truth. I'd been subjected to far worse in the past. The only things causing me problems were the broken ribs.

"I need to eat, and I want to get out of the apartment," I said, sliding cautiously into a booth.

"Then let me take care of you," she said, with a smile.

"No takers for Kieran's *experiment* today?" I said, wincing as I spoke.

Rose winked at me as she placed a cup on the table and poured a coffee. She slid into the seat opposite me.

"How are you, Rose?" I asked. She'd lost a good friend.

"I'm going to miss her. We've known each other many years. But, like I said, we knew this day was coming. I spoke to Beau last night to see what help he needed."

"How was he?"

"He's devastated, of course. He sounded a little lost, if I'm honest."

I wanted to reach out to him but wasn't sure of the reception I'd receive. While I pondered on what to do, Kieran's latest experiment was placed on the table. It looked like a chili, after one taste I found out it was heavy on the chili! I waved my arm and thankfully Rose understood. A large glass of ice water was placed in front of me.

"Good?" Kieran asked, taking the seat that Rose had vacated.

"Hot! But lovely."

"Maybe I'll go a little easier on the chili peppers for the next one. Anyway, how are you doing?"

"Okay. I met with Paul yesterday; we went through a few things. It was good to talk to him."

"Such a shame about his daughter," he said, shaking his head.

"I didn't realize he was Beau's...well, father-in-law, sort of, I guess."

"They don't really get on. I don't know what goes on with Beau sometimes, he tends to keep everyone at arm's reach."

"Oh, it was Beau who asked him to help me."

"Doesn't mean they have to like each other. I guess each blames the other for Rachel's disappearance."

Kieran was interrupted from any further conversation by Rose telling him she was getting backed up with orders.

"Soon as you're back won't be soon enough. The old bat is giving me a headache," he said, and then winked before leaving the booth.

For the second time I wondered what their relationship was.

"When can I come back to work?" I asked Rose as I stacked my dirty dishes and glass on the counter.

"Are you ready for that?"

"I need to get back to normal, as soon as possible if I can."

"Mmm, okay. Lunch tomorrow, it's not so busy midweek. I worry about you, Charlotte."

"I know you do, and thank you. Honestly, other than a little sore, I'm okay. I just really need to do this."

She gave me a hug, and I made a point not to cry out as she wrapped her arms around my poor ribs.

————

I'd gotten to the corner of my block before my feet took me in a different direction. It wasn't necessarily a conscious decision at first, not until I found myself outside Beau's house. His truck was nowhere to be seen, but I climbed the steps to the front door and knocked anyway. I waited, there was no response. Just as I turned to walk back down the steps I heard a bolt release. Beau opened the door looking disheveled.

"I'm sorry if I've disturbed you, I just wanted to check how you were," I said. "And to thank you."

He ran his hand through his messy brown hair, looked up and down the street before opening the door and stepping to one side. I took that as an invitation to enter. The house was dark and with a slight sour smell. The kind of smell I'd expect from a house that had been shut up for some time.

I followed him to the kitchen. Although the counter was clear, the sink was piled with dirty dishes. I stood and watched while he set the coffee maker on.

"How are you, Beau?"

"How do you think I am? She brought me up, she was more of a mother to me than my own."

"You're hurting, lost, maybe feel abandoned even though you know she'd never have left you if she didn't have to. You're probably angry, wanting something, someone to blame. That's how I think you are," I said, recalling every emotion I felt when my grandmother died.

He stared at me, realization dawning that I did know how it felt to lose the one person that was a mother.

"Do you want coffee?" he asked.

"Please. Can I wash those dishes for you?"

"Why would you want to? Don't you clean up enough after people?"

"I want to be helpful."

"Helpful would have been to have refused my offer of a lift that day."

My mouth hung open. I turned on my heels and walked away. Before I got to the door I felt a hand on my shoulder, I stopped walking.

That hand snaked around my chest and I stiffened at his touch. His chest closed in to my back, his other arm found it's way around my waist and eventually, his head rested on my shoulder. He didn't speak at all but by the movement of his body, he was crying. I gently turned and cradled him to me. He was an ass, rude, nasty even, but he was also hurting and as much as I wanted to, I couldn't walk away. I guessed that had always been my problem.

After a couple of minutes Beau pulled away. He looked

embarrassed and that hurt more than his snide comments.

"Shall I pour the coffee? Maybe I'll clean up the kitchen, you look like you haven't slept."

He just nodded. "Go sit in the living room, I'll bring the coffee in. Have you eaten?"

He shook his head before walking into the room next to us.

I washed the dishes and left them on the drainer. I wiped down the counters before I poured two mugs of coffee. The living room was still in darkness, despite it being midafternoon. The quilt was draped over the sofa, a pillow screwed up in one corner. There were dirty clothes and an empty bottle of something on the floor. I handed Beau his coffee and then pulled open the drapes. He shielded his eyes against the assault of light.

"I'll make you something to eat," I said, gathering up his dirty laundry as I spoke.

I wasn't sure what I was doing but I loaded his washing machine and hoped I'd selected the correct setting. I could imagine the fuss if his clothes were ruined. His fridge smelled a little like mine had when I'd gotten home from the hospital. Stale food was tossed and what was left was enough to make an omelet. I mentally made a list of foodstuff to buy before deciding that was probably overstepping the mark a little.

By the time I'd made the omelet and taken it through to him, he'd folded the duvet and straightened his clothes a little.

"Here, eat this. It's not much, I can pick up some groceries if you'd like me to."

"Thank you, this is fine."

I think that was about the first time he'd been pleasant in a long while. I stood, not sure what to do. Beau waved to the edge of the sofa. I perched on the edge and just stared at the bookshelf while he ate.

"The funeral is next Wednesday," he said.

"I'd like to attend, if you don't mind."

"That's why I've just told you the day," he said, not looking at me.

If it weren't such a sad time for him, I probably would have rolled my eyes, given a smart mouthed answer. Despite him being an ass, he had just lost a loved one, I reminded myself.

"You're too forgiving," he said, placing his plate on the floor.

I wasn't entirely sure if he was referring to how I didn't react to his rudeness or not.

"Maybe, but I'd rather be that way than fester in my bitterness."

"Do you think I'm bitter?" he said, turning toward me.

"I think you have issues..." His laughing, a harsh toned laugh, halted my sentence.

"Well, I just wanted to check on you. Perhaps I should go now. If you need anything, would you ask?"

Beau reached over to the coffee table. It was strewn with paperwork. He rifled around until he found what he was looking for.

"Here," he said, handing me the cell.

"I wondered whether the police had it," I said.

He didn't answer, so I stood. "Maybe I'll call you, see if you need any shopping done?"

"Sure."

There was no asking how I was, no mention of the bruising to my face, or the past week at all. I got to the living room door before I spoke again.

"Thank you, for Paul, he's going to deal with some things for me," I said.

His brow furrowed a little but I ignored him and carried on to the front door.

————————

Later that day I received a text message. I opened it and read.

If you could, I need some groceries. I have to go away for a couple of days but I'll drop a key through your door later, and some money. Beau

No thanks, or please, but at least it was semi-polite. I texted back.

Of course. If you want to make a list, otherwise I'll just get what I think you might enjoy. Charlotte

I wasn't sure why we felt the need to add our names; it was all so formal. I decided to make a list of things I needed to replace. I knew I was low on coffee and cream, my freezer meals from the diner and Cecelia had run out, so it was time for some real cooking. Halfway through chores, it occurred to me that I had nothing to wear for the funeral. Jeans and sneakers didn't seem appropriate. I added a dress and a pair of shoes to my list, not sure if I'd be able to find anything appropriate. If I got stuck, I could ask Rose for help, I guessed.

I felt in limbo. I assumed that once Beau took ownership of the apartment, as well as Cecelia's house, he'd probably sell them. He had no need for three properties, I imagined. That thought brought me to Paul, and I wondered if he'd found the documents he needed for me to reclaim my house. It had been over a year ago that I'd been thrown out. I wondered if it was even possible to reclaim the house. However, he was a lawyer, I'm sure he wouldn't have even suggested it had he not felt he could.

Maybe it was being in control of something I'd chosen to do, but I enjoyed cleaning the apartment. I'd enjoyed cleaning the house and the diner. I liked the smell of disinfectant, bleach, and polish. I liked the way the apartment looked when it was all tidy. I opened the windows, and although the sun was weak because of the time of year, it was nice to have the fresh air.

I walked back to the counter and added a coat to my list. I'd soon need one; Beau's sweatshirt was looking very worn. Winter in Whiteling had been late the previous year. It had stayed pretty mild right until December and then the snow came. It looked like that pattern was going to be repeated. I remembered having to traipse to the store in my sneakers with soaking and cold feet to buy boots.

I gathered the list and headed out. I decided to tackle the clothes list; Beau's shopping, and my food list would be done the following day.

Ellie smiled at me as I entered her store. Whether she remembered me from my previous visit, I wasn't sure, but in a town where everyone seemed to know everyone else, I thought her smile was genuine, not one saved for a stranger.

"Good afternoon. I wonder if you can help me?" I said.

I explained that I needed a dress and shoes for a funeral. Instantly she knew whose funeral.

"You know, I don't think Cecelia would like everyone in black. I have some pretty and classy dresses if you'd like to take a look."

She encouraged me to follow her to the back of the store. There was a rail of classic styled dresses and I was instantly drawn to a red one. I wasn't sure red would be appropriate for a funeral but I wanted to try it on anyway. I could probably afford to purchase a couple. I remembered Cecelia's words. She had told me that every woman needs a pretty dress and shoes.

The red dress had a square neck and three-quarter length sleeves. It hugged my waist, falling to just below my knees, and was the prettiest thing I'd ever worn. Ellie surprised me with a pair of red court shoes. Not too high that I was teetering, but high enough to give a nice definition to my calves. I hadn't looked at the price before telling her that I wanted them both. For the funeral, I picked out a navy blue dress with a rounded neck and long sleeves. It was fitted and fell to mid-calf. I panicked then.

"I think, as much as I love the red shoes, I should exchange them for a black pair."

Black would go with both dresses and I wasn't sure my finances should stretch to two pairs of shoes.

"Of course, how about a small clutch, in black? I've had this one lying around for a while, I can offer a discount on it."

I added the clutch to the pile, another packet of hair dye, and fished in my pocket for my money.

When I returned to the apartment I tried on the two dresses, one day I'd invest in some nice underwear but I didn't think Ellie's was the place for that. I hung the dresses in the closet and decided to give my hair a trim and redye it. Maybe I'd get a professional cut, but I liked the blunt messy style I had going on.

I curled into the leather chair and started a new book. Although only a few days since I'd left the hospital, a sense of well-being washed over me. I was finally free and that thought had only just dawned on me. I laid the book on my lap and just looked around the room. For the first time I'd fought back, and the only reason for that was Cecelia. In a strange way, she'd saved me. It felt cleansing to let the tears fall and know they were simply in grief for her loss. My life had been so complicated for so long, it was often that I had a multitude of reasons to cry.

Before the evening fell, I heard the rattle of the main front door. Knowing I was the only person in the building, panic bubbled inside me. I crept to the apartment's front door and placed my ear against it, listening. I couldn't hear anything. I wasn't stupid enough to want to investigate further, it would often make me cringe when I read a book where the victim left the safety of their apartment to investigate a noise, only to wind up dead in a dumpster. What I did was to pick up my cell as I ensured my apartment door was locked and bolted.

The cell vibrated in my hand.

I left a list and some money just inside the door. Beau

I breathed a sigh of relief. Why he couldn't just have brought it up to the apartment was beyond me. I unlocked the apartment door and, although cautiously, made my way downstairs. On the last, or first in Beau's case, step was an envelope. I took it back to the apartment, and even though I knew it was Beau rattling the main door, I still double locked and bolted mine.

The envelope contained two fifty-dollar bills and a list. His writing was a little hard to decipher so I picked up a pencil to rewrite it. I didn't want to be standing in a store trying to work out what he wanted. As suspected, the list contained mostly healthy food, some cleaning products, and toiletries.

———

I wasn't sure if I was imagining things but it seemed that as I walked around the store, I received glances and whispers behind cupped hands. Although there was still some bruising on my face, it wasn't so noticeable as to attract attention. I tried to ignore it as I pushed my cart and read from my list. I smiled at a young girl, whose smile faltered when her mother grabbed her wrist and pulled her close. Something felt very off.

I upped my pace, throwing the goods in the cart, wanting to get out as quickly as possible. I separated my goods from Beau's at the checkout, bagging and paying for his first so I could give him back the receipt. It was only when I left the store that I realized I'd never be able to carry the bags back on my own.

"Shit," I said, quietly to myself. I'd have to walk back with the cart and then return it.

As I walked, I was reminded of an old woman back home who strolled the streets all day with a shopping cart containing all her worldly goods. I'd often stop and hand her a few dollars. She always gave me a toothless smile but should anyone else get close, she'd scowl, shout obscenities, and rush away.

I unloaded the bags into Beau's hallway, leaving them there so I could return the cart. I rushed back to his house, not wanting to leave bags of shopping just inside his front door. The house was a little tidier than when I'd left just the previous day. I unpacked the shopping and wiped down the kitchen counters, not that they needed it.

I left the receipt and the change on the counter and resisted the temptation to give the house a good clean. I wasn't sure Beau would appreciate that. I locked up the house and carried the two bags of my own shopping back to the apartment. The plastic cut into my fingers, and my fingertips tingled when I placed them on the countertop. I shook my hands to get the circulation going. It was as I was putting some things away in a cupboard that I noticed it. A tin of coffee had been moved. It was only an inch or so to the right, but I'd placed that tin strategically because it shielded one of my money envelopes. Just as panic started to well because the envelope was not where I'd left it, I saw it tucked behind some mugs. I racked my brain trying to remember if I'd moved it, knowing that I hadn't but wanting some explanation as to why it had been moved. I counted out the money, it was all there, but I knew, not where I'd originaly left it. I opened the other cupboards; nothing had been disturbed.

I took a slow walk around the open plan area, studying every piece of furniture. My stare froze on a sideboard. There was a visible indentation in the carpet where it had stood, originally. It was a heavy unit and one I hadn't moved. However, I couldn't convince myself the indent hadn't always been there. I checked out the bedroom next. Maybe I was a little OCD, maybe it was because cleaning and being tidy was about all I had control over, but I knew someone had sat on the end of the bed. Each morning I'd make the bed to military standards. The quilt was slightly crumpled and whether it was to straighten it, or connect with my grandmother, I'd stroke the creases out of the quilt each morning.

The closet was the next thing I checked. Again, nothing looked to be disturbed but I wasn't sure I'd notice if it had. I walked to the bathroom and looked at the products on the shelf in the shower. A drip from the showerhead landed on my arm and I looked up at it. I hadn't taken a shower that morning, yet it was wet.

In the time I'd been out shopping, I became convinced someone had been in the apartment.

Cecelia and Beau were the only people, as far as I was aware, who had keys. Even if Beau put the property on the market, I couldn't image a real estate agent opening cupboards and moving tins. Although, I was sure he would have told me if someone had been to view or value the property.

I didn't sleep well that evening, it wasn't that I was scared of being in the apartment, but my mind was running on overtime. Whoever had 'visited' had gone out of their way to ensure I didn't know. What kept me awake was wondering what they were looking for. Whoever it was, wasn't looking for valuables, there had been no sign of a break-in, but I decided as soon as it was possible, I was having the locks changed.

CHAPTER 10

I found a card that Paul had left and called him.

"Hi, it's Charlotte. I think someone broke into my apartment yesterday. I'm having the locks changed but I thought you should know," I said, when he answered.

"Was anything taken, or disturbed?"

"No, but I just know someone has been in here. A couple of things have been moved."

"I think you should call the police," he said.

"No. I don't want to waste their time but I am changing the locks."

It wasn't that I didn't want to waste their time; I didn't trust the police or want to draw any more attention to myself than necessary. I still wondered why I had received strange looks at the store.

"Okay, but think on calling it in. At least it's on record if anything should happen again."

"I will. For now I just wanted you to know." In fact, I wasn't even sure why I wanted him to know.

"Have you told Beau?"

"No, he's away, I think. I won't worry him with this."

"Be careful around him, Charlotte. I'm sure you realize, he's a little unstable at the moment."

I assumed he was talking about Beau's grief but still found it a strange comment to make.

"I will, thank you," I said, not sure how to respond.

"I should have some information for you in a couple of days. Now I have your cell number, I'll call to arrange a meet up."

I thanked him again and said goodbye. I was due at the diner that day so decided to head in an hour earlier and ask Rose if she knew of someone to change the locks. I also wasn't sure on telling her someone broke in or that I'd lost my key. I didn't want to lie to her but she'd only worry about me.

I didn't get the chance to lie, or otherwise, to her. When I arrived at the diner, Kieran was running around in a panic, and Kacy was behind the counter.

"Hi, I'm Charlotte," I said, holding out my hand to her.

"Hey, I'm glad to meet you, finally. And am I glad you're here. Rose is off sick again and I really need to get going. I can come back later and help out, though. Just got to pick the kiddo up and drop him to my friend."

She seemed friendly enough. "You go, I'll start now," I said.

I wouldn't have said the diner was overly busy, but I didn't get a break to even pee for a couple of hours. Kacy came back and between us, we had it all covered. I enjoyed working with her and I could see why Rose liked her. She was a bundle of energy, singing away to whatever song she could hear on the radio. When the lunchtime rush had died down and we'd cleaned tables, she pulled off her apron.

"Maybe we could get together, grab a pizza or something, one day," she said.

"Yeah, I'd like that, thank you."

I hadn't had friends before, and although I was cautious, it was nice to even be invited to join her. I managed the afternoon shift and even offered to stay on.

"No, you've done enough. I'm just going to close up this evening," Kieran said.

"Okay, as long as you're sure." I helped power down the kitchen and prep for the following day.

"Do you know how I can get the locks changed at my apartment?" I asked him.

He looked at me with a cocked eyebrow. "I don't want to worry Rose, but I think someone broke in. Well, I say broke in, nothing was damaged, but someone was in the apartment."

"You sure it wasn't Beau?"

"He told me he was away, and it happened during the day while I was shopping. Nothing was taken, which is strange, but I know a couple of things were moved around."

"Charlotte, I don't like the sound of that."

"I told Paul. I just think if I get the locks changed for now, I'll be happy."

"Why did you tell Paul?" he asked.

"Because he's my lawyer, obviously."

"I thought he had just sorted out your...troubles. I didn't realize you were still using him."

"He's kind to me. He's hoping to get my grandmother's house back for me."

"Just be a little careful, Charlotte."

"Why?"

"Paul and Beau really do not get along, you don't want to get stuck between those two."

Beau and I don't get along, most of the time, but I didn't tell Kieran that. Beau was telling me to be careful around Paul, Kieran was telling me to be careful around Beau and Paul, Paul was telling me to be careful around Beau. Maybe I should just be careful of them all.

Kieran knew a guy who could change the locks and he decided to call him straight away. I guessed he was a little perturbed as to why I wasn't in the panic perhaps I should have been. I headed on home to wait for the locksmith.

"All done," the locksmith said. He handed me a couple of sets of keys. I guessed I would have to give one to Beau, as he technically owned the property.

"That's great. How much do I owe you?"

I wasn't sure if the seventy-five dollars was good value or not, but for peace of mind, it was a small price to pay. I would make a point to remember to bolt the main front door as well.

———

Paul had called and arranged a meeting. We decided on the diner as I could then start my shift straight after. I was seated in a booth and sipping on a Coke when he rushed in.

"I'm sorry I'm late, something came up," he said, sliding in opposite me and ordering a coffee from Rose, who seemed a little frosty with him.

"That's okay, I only just got here myself," I said.

"I found some documents that prove the house was left to you so the next step is to approach the court for an eviction order."

"Will they contest that?"

"Of course, but I guess they didn't know who owned the property initially and more foolish of them for not actually finding out. I also know there is a lot of utility debt, seems your *tenants* weren't paying the bills. Which poses a problem. The bills are in your name."

"So I'm responsible?"

"Technically, yes, I'm afraid. I'll work on that, though."

"How are the bills in my name? I was a minor when that house was left to me."

"I don't know, I guess Damien had them changed at some point. Forged your details, perhaps?"

"Then ask them to cut the utilities off." It seemed the most logical solution to me.

Paul nodded and wrote on his pad. I'd been out of the house for a year, I thought, so wondered how the hell the debt had been allowed to accumulate.

"Did you get the locks changed?" he asked.

"I did, yesterday. I got a couple of new sets of keys. I feel better about that, and I'm bolting the main front door as well. No one lives in the downstairs apartment so I don't have to worry about locking anyone out."

"That's good. Have you given Beau a set of keys?"

"Not yet, I haven't seen him."

"Might be best to hold on to both sets. You just can't be too sure."

"Do you know if anything more has happened with the list?" I asked, diverting him away from Beau, or so I thought.

Paul laid down his pen. Sadness crept over his face and he sighed. "I don't. Beau keeps everything too close to his chest. I just want to find my baby, Charlotte, but I'm not sure Beau is as keen."

"Why do you think that?"

"Oh, I don't know. I guess it's no secret that we aren't the best of friends since Rachel disappeared. Maybe he doesn't trust me, I mean, he doesn't actually trust anyone."

I knew that feeling. "Maybe I can find something out for you?"

"No, I don't want to involve you. Trust me, Beau can be an ass if he's cornered." He laughed at his statement.

"I want to help, though."

"Well, just keep your ears open, but don't probe him. I'm never sure if he's telling me the truth, he's so secretive."

"But she's your daughter."

He sighed again. "I know. Enough about me, let's get you sorted, shall we?" He gave me a broad smile and I reminded myself how lucky I was to have him on my side.

We chatted back and forth about the house and what I wanted for it. Paul told me he could arrange for the sale but I wasn't to get too excited. The eviction process could be lengthy. We talked about my job at the diner and the fact I was a little worried about how I was going to pay rent. I assumed Beau would want to charge me.

"Maybe I can help with that. I might know of a job vacancy, let me check it out."

"I don't want to leave the diner, though."

"This might be full-time, I don't know. Leave it with me," he said with a smile.

I hadn't considered leaving the diner at all, but if Beau was to charge rent, and I couldn't blame him if he did, I might need to find a full-time job.

Paul left and I started my shift.

"Good meeting?" Rose asked.

"Paul is trying to get my grandmother's house back for me. My cousin lost it in a bet, or something, but I'm the legal owner."

"That sounds good. Will you move back to it?"

"God, no. I'd want to sell it as quickly as possible, but it will certainly help me to have the money."

"What will you do?"

"I don't know. I mean, maybe I can buy a little house here, or at least rent somewhere."

"Won't you stay in the apartment?"

"I don't know what Beau would want to do with it."

"I'm sure he won't throw you out," she said with a smile. I wasn't so sure about that.

———————

Over the next few days I spoke with Paul frequently. I started to feel sorry for him, he just wanted to know what had happened to his daughter, and Beau didn't seem to be letting him in.

I decided to see if I could reconnect with Beau. Maybe I could help both of them.

I know it's the funeral tomorrow and wondered if there was anything you'd like me to help with, I texted.

All under control. Rose told me you're going with them. Beau.

It still baffled me as to why he needed to sign off with his name.

I am, is that okay?

Why wouldn't it be? Beau

You don't need to sign off with your name every time; you're the only contact in my cell.

I didn't receive a reply and wondered if that 'reconnecting' might be a little harder than I'd expected. Before I could consider what else to do, Paul called.

"Hi, Charlotte, I wondered if you had a minute to meet up?"

"I can meet before my shift, if that suits you?"

"That would be great. In an hour?"

"Okay, I'll see you there."

I didn't think it was a conscious decision but I'd rather meet outside the apartment. There had been no more strange happenings, though, and I had begun to doubt myself.

The meeting with Paul wasn't quite as I imagined.

"There have been some developments with the Philip Stanton case. My source tells me some new evidence has been discovered, in the bathroom. It could be a hair, I don't know yet."

I felt my heart start to race. "What does that mean?"

"Your details are on record, they could connect that to you. But I don't want you to worry right now. We can always explain it away."

"But you can't lie to them, can you?"

"Listen, right now I want to help you. Just leave it to me, okay?"

"I don't understand. They only just found it?"

"I'm not sure. They only just told me."

"But..."

"Charlotte, please. Maybe I shouldn't have told you. Leave it to me, it will all be okay, I promise."

I felt scolded for being worried, but grateful that he would take care of it.

"I can't go to prison," I said, quietly.

"You wouldn't, not for this. Like I told you, the police know Philip's murder was more than just a break-in gone wrong. I want you to be careful, though. You haven't given Beau any keys, have you? I'm wondering if I should have a set. If anything happened, I'd hate not to be able to get to you."

"Do you really think Beau broke into my house?"

"I don't know, sweetie, I just...you know. I just want to protect you."

We were back to his daughter and I guessed he had felt maybe he failed her so was being overprotective with me. I smiled at him.

"I haven't given anyone the keys. I'm actually wondering if I imagined the whole thing, to be honest. I could have moved those things while cleaning and just didn't realize."

"Well, think about giving someone you trust a set of keys."

Was he suggesting that I shouldn't trust Beau? He'd kept alluding to that fact and knowing how Beau was with me, I wondered if Paul had a point. But giving Paul a set of keys? That was something I needed to think about.

Paul left and I started my shift. I was concerned that Rose seemed overly tired of late. She'd had a couple of days off, which I believed was unusual for her. I tried to take the bulk of the work so she could just manage the counter and cash register. The hours flew by, I didn't take a break, and it wasn't until toward the end of my shift that my bladder reminded me I needed the restroom some time ago.

I was mopping down the floor when Beau surprised me by walking in. He didn't frequent the diner that often. He took a seat at the counter rather than sit in a booth.

"Hi, can I get you a coffee?" I asked.

"Yeah. Black would be good."

He looked tired, dark circles framed his eyes, and his hair stood on end as if he hadn't brushed it for days. I poured his coffee and slid a menu toward him. He glanced over it but didn't order immediately.

"I had to change the locks at the apartment," I said. Paul's words rang through my mind but ultimately Beau owned it.

"Okay, why?"

"I thought someone had come in, I'm doubting myself now. But

I guess I panicked a little and changed the lock. I wanted to ask your permission but you were away."

"What made you think someone had come in?"

"A couple of things were moved, a tin in one of the cupboards. It doesn't sound like much, and like I said, maybe I overreacted."

"Was there anything taken?" he seemed to have perked up, as if he was genuinely concerned.

"No, that's the strange thing. There was no break-in, so I didn't bother to call the police."

"You should have. You should at least have called me."

"I didn't want to bother you."

He shook his head, his earlier concern gone and replaced with exasperation.

"You'll need to make sure I have a set of keys," he said.

"Of course, I can get them to you tomorrow."

"In future, Charlotte, if anything happens, you call me."

He turned his attention to the menu and selected a burger and fries. I wrote up his order and passed it back to Kieran. While I waited for his food, I continued to mop the floor.

Rose served Beau his meal and I watched him eat. He ate fast, as if food was just a perfunctory act and he gained no enjoyment from it. I wondered if he even tasted the food, it was chewed and swallowed so fast. When I'd finished cleaning, I pulled off my apron and stored it under the counter. Rose handed me my earnings and I said goodbye before heading for the door.

"Wait up, I'll walk with you," I heard Beau call out as I opened the door.

Although his truck was parked outside the diner, he started to walk alongside me.

"Did you manage to talk to Paul about that message?" I asked.

"Why would I?"

"She was his daughter."

"He told you that?"

"Yes. I think he's a little concerned that you're not sharing information with him."

Beau laughed, although I didn't think it was in humor.

"Don't believe everything he tells you."

"If you don't like him, why did you ask him to help me?" I know I'd asked that question before, but I wanted to see if he gave me a different answer.

"Because he knows those fuckers in Whiteling. I might not like him, but that doesn't mean he wasn't the best man to help you."

"Do you *know* those fuckers in Whiteling?" I'd never asked Beau why he was on that road that evening.

He didn't answer, just looked at me. "I know one or two people, it is the next town over, Charlotte."

Yet again, his tone of voice and choice of words made me feel as if I'd just asked the dumbest question. He was quite belittling and I wondered if he realized that. There were times when I thought he had no idea how rude he came across, and other times when I felt he knew exactly what he was doing.

"Don't get too close to Paul," he said.

"He says the same thing about you," I whispered.

Beau stopped walking abruptly; he grabbed my arm so I stumbled as I turned to face him.

"He said what?"

"Nothing. What the fuck is wrong with you?"

"How many times have you met up with him? He was supposed

to get you out of the police station, nothing more."

"Jesus, Beau. The man is helping me, and right now I need a little help."

"Charlotte, I mean it, stay away from him."

Why? I thought. I didn't think there was a point in asking him aloud. I wasn't sure I'd get an answer.

"Can you let go of my arm?"

His hand dropped from my upper arm and although he hadn't hurt me, I rubbed at it.

"Oh, and a thank you for doing your shopping might have been nice."

He stared at me, as if he wasn't quite sure how to respond.

"Watch my lips...Thank...You," I said, exaggerating the words.

His lips twitched. "Go on, smile, or say the words," I added.

He rolled his eyes. "Thank. You."

I gave him a fake smile and turned on my heel. I heard his footsteps as he followed me.

The more I thought about what Paul said, what Beau said, the more confused I became. I felt as if I was caught in the middle of something that I had no knowledge of, yet I wasn't entitled to that knowledge because I didn't know either of them. I had a few *supporters* in town, but did I really? As I got to my main front door, I stopped and turned to face him. I guessed he wasn't expecting that when we collided. I pushed him back.

"You know what? I'm grateful to you, to Cecelia, and Rose, and everyone wanting to help but I don't know why. I don't know why you and Paul tell me the same thing because there's obviously bad blood between you, yet you both want to help me. I feel like I'm caught in the middle, and I'm not sure that I like it. That makes me feel guilty now, as if I'm being ungrateful."

"Let me just get tomorrow out of the way. There are things between Paul and me, things I can't tell you, but give me a break here. I've just lost my aunt; I was fucked up enough before that. I have a lot on at the moment without..."

"If you are about to say, 'without worrying about me,' don't. I haven't asked you to do that. I'm just trying to fit in here."

I didn't want to snap at him, and I was mindful that he had just lost his aunt, but he infuriated me sometimes.

"Fine. I won't. Just one thing, stay away from Paul, please?"

I nodded, although I knew that I wouldn't. I mean, how could I? He was still sorting out my house and there was the matter of Philip.

I left Beau on the doorstep and walked up to my apartment. I was more confused than ever. Maybe I'd pull back a little from Paul, I didn't expect to see or hear from him for a few days anyway.

———————

Rose and Kieran called for me on the morning of the funeral. I felt a little uncomfortable in my dress and shoes and held on to the hem as I climbed into the back of their car. Although we chatted, the closer we got to Cecelia's house, the quieter we became. I hadn't realized how nervous I'd be, how much my hands would shake as we exited the car and walked toward the house. Mourners were gathering in the backyard, returning there after the service. Beau, or someone, had erected a large tent and I, along with many I imagined, was grateful for that. The wind blowing off the farmland was chilly and gray clouds were rolling in.

The yard was filled with people of all ages, however I was drawn to an older man accompanied by a woman, who continually looked over to Beau. He didn't acknowledge them at all and it didn't take a genius to realize they were his parents. The similarity was remarkable. I also understood why he'd been so on edge. Not only had he lost his aunt, the woman who brought him up, he was in the same environment as parents he'd fallen out with.

"They haven't spoken in over fifteen years," I heard. Turning, I came face-to-face with Paul.

"Oh, I don't really know anything about that," I lied.

I was surprised he was there, if he'd fallen out with Beau, what had his relationship been with Cecelia?

"Did you come with Rose?"

"I did, she's just getting us a drink, and Kieran is chatting to someone."

"I think we're moving off soon. I saw the cars arrive just now. Do you want to ride with me?"

"Ah, there you are. We're ready to go," Kieran said, approaching me.

I turned to Paul. "Thank you, but I have a ride."

Paul nodded at Kieran, but I noticed that Kieran kept his face neutral. He didn't smile at all. Kieran took my arm, like the gentleman that he was, and led me from the house. Outside a black limousine stood beside another. I swallowed down the lump that had jumped to my throat at the sight of a light wooden coffin. A single array of white lilies lay on the top. Black suited men stood with hands clasped in front of them and heads bowed as we filed past. Beau stood at the second car, dressed in a black suit, a white shirt, and black tie. He glanced over to me and gave a ghost of a smile. He nodded to Kieran but was then distracted. His parents joined him, without speaking he opened the rear door and they all climbed in.

We followed the procession to the cemetery. We made our way

into a room and slid across a wooden bench toward the back. I sat with my head bowed throughout the service. Kieran handed me a small booklet and I flicked through. It contained an order of service, a couple of hymns, and a photograph of Cecelia on the back. That photograph brought tears to my eyes again. I thought fondly of her, her belief and trust in me, and her kindness.

I hadn't heard a word being said until a familiar low tone hit my ears. I looked up to see Beau standing at the lectern. He thanked everyone for being there and celebrating Cecelia's life. He spoke of his childhood with her, her family back in France, her parents, even. He talked about how gracious and kind she had been. While he spoke he scanned the room, coming to rest on me.

"Cecelia's purpose in life was to help others, something instilled in her from childhood and living in France through the war. She offered her house as a place of refuge for those in need but had decided to cut back on that when she fell ill. However, Charlotte Kenny arrived and breathed some life back, not only into the house, but to my aunt as well. For a little while, for the last few weeks of her life, Cecelia had someone to care for. She'd been given that last opportunity to live the role she believed she was destined for. So I thank Charlotte for that."

I let a tear roll down my cheek. No one turned to look at me; I doubted anyone other than Paul knew who Charlotte Kenny was. I dared not look at Rose and Kieran. I wasn't sure whether to curse or thank Beau for revealing my real name. I sat rigid and held my breath until I felt a gentle squeeze on my hand, and I looked down to see a hand wrinkled with age and hard work. I raised my head and saw Rose smile at me. She had unshed tears pooling in her eyes.

"We know," she whispered. I closed my eyes and sighed.

"I'm sorry, I'll explain."

"No need."

I turned back to watch Beau lay a single white rose on the coffin before taking his seat again. A hymn was sung before the mourners started to file past the coffin, and the service was over. Cecelia was to be cremated, and according to Rose, a private scattering of ashes was to be arranged in a few weeks' time.

We stood outside while people paid their respects to Beau and his parents. He stood slightly apart and held himself rigid. He looked uneasy, uncomfortable, desperate to wrench that tie from his neck and leave. I watched him fiddle with the knot, loosen it slightly. Although he wore a suit well, it didn't seem it was his natural attire. I walked over to him.

"Thank you, for your kind words," I said.

"I meant what I said. I hadn't seen her so *alive* for a long time. Although she hadn't known you long, she loved you."

"Oh, I'm not sure..."

"She told me that you reminded her of herself at the same age. She saw something in you, something good, and she didn't care that you were in trouble. She gave me hell for *forcing* you to move into the apartment," he chuckled a little.

"Well, you sort of did," I said, with a smile.

He gently shrugged his shoulders. "I don't get much right, Charlotte, but where you're concerned..."

He didn't finish his sentence before he was interrupted. He scowled at his mother, who had asked for his attention, cutting him off mid-sentence and completely ignoring me. She had harsh features, cold blue eyes, and a wrinkled mouth that seemed to be in a permanent scowl.

"I was talking," he said, grabbing my arm as I was about to walk away.

She answered him in French to which he replied. I hadn't heard French spoken before so had no idea if the language was animated or they were arguing. Regardless, I placed my hand on Beau's and gently released it from my arm.

"I'll speak to you later," I said, talking over his mother.

His mother reached out to touch his arm, maybe to guide him away from me. He pulled it back, trying hard not to make a scene. I decided it was best to walk away in case my presence aggravated the situation.

I joined Rose and Kieran at the car and we headed back to Cecelia's.

"Do you mind if I go home? I have a headache coming and I'm not great in social situations," I said.

"Do you need me to walk with you?" Kieran asked.

"No, please, I'm okay. I just find these kinds of things a little unsettling."

In truth, I was anxious not to cause trouble, I didn't want to be in the middle of Paul and Beau, and the whole day just brought back memories of my grandmother. I wanted to get out of the dress, throw on a sloppy t-shirt and jeans, and curl up in my chair.

Before Kieran could insist on walking me home, I gave him a kiss to the cheek, hugged Rose, and left.

———

I had been home for a few hours when I heard a knock on the apartment door. At first I froze and listened.

"Charlotte?" Beau called out.

I breathed a sigh of relief and rose to open the door. He stood there, swaying slightly from foot to foot and holding a half drunk bottle of liquor in his hand. His hair was disheveled, his tie missing, and the top two buttons on his shirt undone. He raised the bottle high.

"Have a drink with me?" Although he wasn't slurring, his accent was heavier.

"Have you maybe had enough already?" I asked, opening the door wide.

"Nope," Beau said, as he sat on the sofa.

I put the coffee maker on, just in case, and watched him unscrew the cap and sip from the bottle. Inside my stomach roiled, it was a sight I'd seen many times, and it didn't conjure up great memories.

"Tough day, huh?" I said.

"Yep. Made worse by the presence of my parents."

"I saw, I'm sorry for you."

"Don't be. I don't do sorry, or pity, or any of that fucking shit." He took another, longer swig.

I poured two coffees and placed one beside him on the coffee table.

"Just in case you fancy something different," I said, as I curled into the chair.

He let his head rest against the back of the sofa, and his eyes closed. The bottle of liquor dangled from one hand, and I hoped he wasn't about to pass out and drop it everywhere.

"They hate everything about me," he said, quietly.

"Are you sure about that?"

"Oh, yes. She tells me enough times." Without opening his eyes, he took a long drink and I began to worry he'd end up with alcohol poisoning.

"Why don't you have some coffee and tell me about it?"

He laughed, just the once, and not in amusement. "You don't want to hear about that."

"I do, Beau." I wanted to add that it might give me some insight as to why he was often an ass, not that his parents not liking him was an excuse, though.

He fell silent for a little while, and I wondered if he had, indeed, passed out. I slipped forward in the chair, waiting to catch the bottle if he let go.

"I killed my brother," he whispered.

He didn't say anything else but I saw his body relax and his fingers lose their grip on the bottle. I reached forward and took the bottle from him. I waited for a moment, wanting to see if he'd miss the feel of the glass in his hand, but he didn't stir. I walked to the sink and poured the contents down the drain. I didn't want hard liquor in my home.

I watched him for a while, his jaw fell open, and his breathing deepened. I gently pulled off his shoes and placed a pillow under his feet, resting them on the coffee table. I could have slid his legs onto the sofa but I didn't want to wake him. I was an expert at maneuvering drunks, I'd done it enough with Damien and not disturbed him, but I thought Beau was more emotionally exhausted than drunk. To one side of him was my grandmother's quilt. I'd last used it to snuggle under and read. I draped it over him and headed to the bathroom.

After a quick splash of water to my face, I cleaned my teeth and headed to bed. Before I opened my bedroom door, I turned off the main light, leaving just a small sidelight on in case he woke. I didn't want him stumbling around in the dark if he was disorientated.

It must have been an hour or so later, I wasn't fully asleep but enough to be startled by a dip on the edge of the bed. I opened my eyes, allowing them to adjust to the lack of light.

"Are you okay?" I asked, hoping he had sobered up a little.

"I was a twin. I don't know the technical term but I took all the nutrients, all the goodness while in the womb. My brother died but my mother had to carry us both until it was safe for a C-section. She had one dead baby in her stomach, and one alive. I imagine that was brutal for her. But she hated me for it."

"It was hardly..."

"My fault? I know. Oh, don't think I'm affected by what happened before I was born. I don't harbor any guilt for that, I mean, for fuck's sake, I could hardly have controlled that, could I?" His voice rose slightly in anger and I wondered if he truly believed that.

"She hated me the minute I was born. I don't recall a time she ever hugged me. I had a nanny in France, and as soon as she could, she shipped me out here."

"What about your father?"

"Too fucking weak to stand up to her. Anyway, I just wanted you to know."

I wasn't sure why he wanted me to know, but I was grateful for that snippet of his life.

"And before you go thinking that's my excuse for being an ass, it isn't. I don't try to be, I guess I have plenty of other issues to make killing my brother pale into insignificance."

"Beau, it's been a long day for you. I imagine you're exhausted. Why don't you lay down?"

Without saying another word, he lay on his back at the edge of the bed. I shuffled to the other side and pulled back the duvet.

"Where are you going?" he asked.

"I'll take the sofa."

"Lay with me, Charlotte. I won't touch you, I just need some company tonight."

It wasn't that I didn't understand, but I was uncomfortable with Beau in my bed. I had to remind myself that he'd had a real shitty day, past year, even. I lay back down keeping a distance between us.

I listened to him breathe an even rhythm, deep breaths in with slow exhales. The sound was therapeutic; it was as if he'd learned a technique to calm himself. Beside him, my heart was racing, which confused me. I wasn't sexually attracted to Beau; in fact I doubted I'd ever be sexually attracted to anyone. But there was something that had me wanting to reach over, to just place my hand on his chest and feel his heart beating. Whether it was a connection that ran deeper than I understood, or desire to comfort him, I wasn't sure. He didn't deserve anything from me, yet something pulled me toward him.

He was gone the following morning and I was grateful for that. I didn't want the awkwardness of waking up beside him. I threw back the duvet and climbed from the bed. I took a shower, and with a towel wrapped around me, walked to the kitchen. I smiled when I saw the coffee maker already on and the black nectar waiting to be poured. I grabbed a cup and took it back to the bedroom with me.

I dressed in jeans and Beau's sweatshirt, pulled on my sneakers and decided on a walk. The apartment felt a little stuffy that morning. The chill in the air reminded me I needed some warmer clothes. But the briskness of my walk soon warmed me. I headed for the small park and sat on a bench for a little while. Listening to the screams of delight from children that played ball and ran around had me smiling.

"I miss those days," I heard. I startled before recognizing Paul's voice. "Sorry, I didn't mean to scare you, I was taking a walk," he added.

"That's okay, I was miles away."

"May I?" He indicated toward the bench. I could hardly say no.

Paul sat beside me. He wore jeans and a sweater with a leather jacket pulled tight around him. He crossed his sneaker-clad feet and stretched out his legs. Although he'd worn casual clothes when we met at the diner, he seemed a completely different person out of 'lawyer' mode.

"I come here sometimes to remind myself that I'm still a father."

"You must miss her terribly."

"I do. Every day I talk to her, as if she's still here. I mean, she's an adult but she'll always be my little girl. I just wish I could see her. Sometimes I think I catch a glimpse of her. A few days ago, there was a blonde woman across the park, I ran over calling out her name but it wasn't her."

My heart squeezed at the sadness in his voice.

"It must be so hard. I don't really know what to say."

He smiled at me. "There's nothing to say. I just have to keep hoping Beau will let me in, share whatever information he has. One day I'll find her, I know that."

"Do you know why she ran?" I couldn't recall a time where he'd mentioned she was pregnant.

"No, I think there were problems with her and Beau. She never told me, but I think she was scared of him."

"Oh, he said he came home from work one day and she was gone."

"Then that may confirm it, might it? I mean, if she wasn't scared of him, why wait until he wasn't around before she ran?"

It did make sense, but although Beau could be a dick, I wasn't sure there was anything to feel scared about.

"Did he share the message with you?"

"Snippets. I'd love to be able to see it all. There could be something I might be able to decipher."

"Maybe I can get a copy for you?"

He turned to me and tears pooled in his eyes. For some reason, and I wasn't sure why, to see a man emotional made me feel uncomfortable. I didn't know how to deal with that.

"That would be amazing, Charlotte. I would forever be grateful if you could."

He picked up one of my hands and held it between his two. "You don't know how wonderful you are, do you?"

"I..." I wasn't sure what to say.

"I'm sorry, that was so inappropriate of me. It's her birthday today, I'm overemotional," he said, letting go of my hand.

Maybe that was partly why Beau wanted to lose himself in a bottle of liquor the previous evening.

"How old would she be?"

"Twenty-seven. I remember the day she was born." He smiled at the memory. "I ought to go, leave you in peace. I'm having a chat with Frank, the detective at Whiteling, tomorrow. I think I have a way to get you off the hook where the DNA is concerned."

I didn't know I was 'on the hook.' Paul had told me evidence had been found in the shower but not what or that it was connected to me.

"I'm going to do everything in my power to have this all 'go away' for you, Charlotte, you know that, don't you?" he said.

"I do, and I'm thankful. I'm not sure how I can repay you, though."

"You are repaying me. Just being here, letting me ramble about Rachel is enough thanks."

He rose and with a last smile, left.

CHAPTER 11

A few days later I slipped on the red dress and black shoes and walked to Paul's office. I had an interview for the newly negotiated part-time office clerk. I was still to speak to Rose about my hours at the diner but thought I'd find out what the deal with Paul was first. I might not like the job; he might not think I was suitable.

I found his office easily enough and was greeted at reception by an older woman. She asked me to take a seat while she let Paul know I had arrived. I tried not to wipe my sweating palms down the front of my dress, or fidget in my seat.

Paul walked into reception and held out his hands to me, I was unsure what he wanted at first until he helped me stand from the seat.

"It's good to see you," he said.

I followed him through a set of doors to an office. Another gentleman had his back to me; he was standing and looking out the window.

"Let me introduce Charlotte," Paul said. The man turned.

He had a broad smile and took a few steps toward me. His gaze ran over me, goosebumps rose on my skin and I wasn't sure why.

"Perfect, Paul," he said. I frowned.

He stepped forward and reached out with one hand. I took it in mine, shivering slightly at the coldness of his touch. I found it hard to hold his stare; it was as if his bore straight through me. He was intense, for sure.

"It's a pleasure to meet you, Charlotte. I'm Richard."

"Thank you. I'm eager to know about the job on offer." I wanted to get his attention back to why I was there.

"Of course, I'll let Paul give you all the details. I have to run." He turned to Paul. "A very good choice, well done."

I wasn't sure of the point in meeting Richard. Not that I'd ever worked in an office before, but I didn't think his *appraisal* of me was part of the interview process.

"Take a seat," Paul said, indicating to one. Instead of taking the one behind his desk, he sat beside me.

"Can you let me know a little about the job?" I asked.

"We're looking for someone who can help around the office. I know this is probably not where you wanted to start, but we're behind on filing, typing up some letters when Rebecca is overworked. It's menial stuff but a start, don't you think?"

I didn't know who Rebecca was, and could only assume he was referring to the woman on reception.

"I'm not sure on the typing thing," I said. I could type, I had in school, but whether my speed was up to what they'd require, I wasn't sure.

He waved his hand as if dismissing my comment. "I can sort that." It seemed he could sort a lot of things.

"Wouldn't there be a conflict, bearing in mind you're looking after my case?"

"No, it's quite okay. Like I said, I'll have all that dealt with shortly. Now, why don't I show you around?"

Was that it? Interview over? I rose and followed Paul as he walked through the small office. Rebecca, if that was her name, was the only other person there. Paul had an office, there was a spare, a small kitchen, and restroom. Outside his office was an area with a desk and computer.

"This is where you'd sit," he said, pulling out the chair for me to try.

"Okay. What about hours, and salary?" I asked.

"We can come to a suitable arrangement on hours, say four each day? The salary isn't great to start with, minimum wage I'm afraid, but I can have Rebecca type up a contract and you can take that away to look through."

Having never applied for an office job before, I assumed what he was offering was the normal procedure.

"Can I take you to lunch, to celebrate?"

Celebrate? "I have to get to the diner shortly, but thank you. Maybe I can get those details from Rebecca and call you tomorrow?"

"Of course, I think you'll do wonders here, Charlotte. We can work on your case, and there's plenty of opportunity to progress to a full-time position and a greater salary."

"Is Richard one of your partners?"

"He owns the company, Charlotte. He's a very influential man, someone to have on your side, if you know what I mean." He winked at me, actually winked!

"Oh, okay." I had no idea what he meant, of course.

Paul walked me to the front door. "How about I bring that contract over later. You'll be at the diner I take it?"

"Erm, yes, okay. Although I haven't spoken to Rose just yet. I'll do that later."

"I'll be discrete, don't worry."

Paul opened the door. "I'm excited, Charlotte, to have you working with us."

I wasn't, yet. "Thank you, I'll have a think on what you've said."

For the whole time it took me to walk back to the apartment, I wondered what it was about Richard that had my skin raised. Maybe it was the way he looked me over, as if I was piece of meat. He reminded me a little of some of Damien's friends. I shuddered at that thought and decided I'd push him to the back of my mind for the moment. I needed another job to pay the rent I was expecting to receive details of, and it didn't look like he physically worked in the office.

————

"Do you think I can have a word?" I asked Rose when I walked into the diner.

She dried her hands on a towel and grabbed the coffee pot and two mugs. We settled into a spare booth.

"What do you want to talk about?" she asked as she poured me a coffee.

"I have to take on another job. I was cleaning for Cecelia in return for the apartment. I don't know what's going to happen with rent now. I expect to pay something but need to earn more money to cover it. I don't want to leave here, and I know you don't have any more shifts, but I wondered if I could change my hours a little?"

"Have you been offered anything?"

"Well, Paul needs a part-time office help, although I couldn't actually see how, to be honest. It doesn't look like he's that busy. He said I could work four hours a day, but he hadn't said exactly what those hours would be. I wondered if I could start a little earlier so I can get to him in the afternoon. I totally understand if that's not possible. I can see if I can find something else that fits around my shift here."

I really wanted her to understand that I wouldn't be leaving the diner, but I was in a dilemma. I was working the lunchtime, which didn't give me many hours either side to find another job.

"I'd hate to lose you, so whatever we have to do, we will," she said, smiling at me. "To be honest, I think Kacy is struggling to find childcare. Maybe I need to have a frank talk with her and see if we can work something out between us."

"I'll talk to Beau and see what he wants to do about rent first."

Rose told me about Kieran's latest culinary experiment, and we laughed when I discovered I was the only one willing to be his test subject.

"Can I ask, about you two?"

"Ah, now there's a complicated subject. We were sweethearts at one time, a long time ago. We both went our separate ways, Kieran into the army and me...well, I guess I never got over him." She leaned forward to whisper. "We're very good friends, that's all. He rents a room from me and bosses me around here as if he owns the goddamn place."

"Which, technically, I do," a male voice said. "You see, Charlotte, I own all the buildings on this side of the street. Miss Rose here, just rents this place from me."

We both laughed as Kieran slid into the booth beside Rose. "Taco?" he asked, placing a plate on the table.

"What's in it?" I asked, it didn't resemble any taco I'd ever seen.

He tapped the side of his nose as I tentatively took a bite. Whatever the secret ingredient, it was delicious.

"Mmm, that's good," I said, licking my fingers after devouring the whole plateful.

With my experimenting done, I got to work. It was a slow day out front so I spent some time in the kitchen, cleaning down units and restocking the fridge and cupboard.

"Hey, Charlotte," Kacy said when she arrived for her shift. She always had a smile on her face.

"Hi, I'm just finishing up, do you want a drink?"

Kacy grabbed her customary glass of Coke and I poured another coffee. It was one of the perks of the job, free drinks when we wanted them.

"So, how's the delicious Beau?" she asked with a laugh. It was the first time I'd heard her talk about him.

"Delicious?"

"Oh, come on. You don't think he's a nice piece of ass? He's gorgeous! So mean and moody, never know what he's thinking."

I laughed at her words. "Erm, no, I mean..." I felt my face flush and not because I was embarrassed. She elbowed me.

"Aw, you got the hots for him?"

"No, honestly, I don't. He's my landlord, just a friend, I guess." I was never sure what he was.

"Well, send him my way if you're not interested." She drank down her Coke and headed for the kitchen to prepare for her shift.

I waved goodbye and left to do some shopping. I chuckled as I walked. Sure Beau was a good-looking man, if you took the scowl off his face. Maybe if he dropped the abruptness, or...I checked myself. Kacy could have him if he was interested. Her comments dipped my mood though. There had been a time when I would have loved the *Pretty Woman* moment. I wanted to be swept off my feet by someone madly in love with me, someone who wanted to save me from my life. It didn't happen, of course. The thought of having sex with someone turned my stomach. I didn't think I could have an intimate relationship anymore, not after what I'd been through. If I couldn't offer that side of me, I doubted anyone would be interested in me just for company.

I walked around the store, placing the few items I needed in my basket. I wasn't paying attention to my surroundings, but something caught my eye outside the large glass window. Richard was standing with Paul. I couldn't hear what was being said, but judging by the hand motions and the look on Richard's face, it looked as if they were arguing. Paul had both hands raised in front of his chest, his palms facing Richard as if trying to calm him down, or defend himself. Richard turned and walked away, and Paul not only dropped his hands, but his head dipped as well. I saw his shoulders rise in an exaggerated sigh.

As he turned toward the window, I ducked around the corner of the aisle. He could be, potentially, my new boss. I was sure he wouldn't want me witnessing an argument he was having with *his* boss.

———

"Would you like a hand with those?" I heard.

I had left the store and was making my way home. I turned toward the voice.

"Oh, thank you, but I can manage," I said, raising the bags to show they weren't that heavy.

"A lady should never have to carry her own bags," Richard said, taking the bags from my hands.

I didn't want him to carry my bags, and like before, my skin prickled, more so when his hands ghosted over mine.

"Really, it's not problem, I can manage."

"Lead the way, Miss Kenny. Or should I get my car?"

I had no intention of getting into his car but had no choice than to walk home. Paul knew my address; I assumed that meant Richard might as well. I ditched the idea of walking up the path of a neighboring property.

"Paul is looking after you well, isn't he?" His voice was commanding, although not loud.

"He is, thank you," I said, guessing that, since he owned the company, I ought to thank him as well.

"I took a look over your file, I've made sure that Paul knows how to have all the charges against you dropped."

"I wasn't aware any more charges had been brought against me." I stood still and looked at him.

"Further potential charges, my mistake, Miss Kenny." He smiled, and if you added his cold blue eyes, he had a wolfish look about him. "He's done a lot of work for you, Miss Kenny."

"And I'm grateful for that."

"I'm sure he'll be pleased to have you working with him."

We came to a stop outside the apartments. I reached forward to take the bags from him.

"I haven't made a decision on that just yet. It depends on whether I can work the hours around my current job."

He sighed. "I'm sure he, we, will be very disappointed, especially since he's gone to so much trouble for you."

It took a moment for his comment to register. Was that

blackmail? A threat maybe?

"Maybe I should ask Paul not to work on my case until I've made my mind up."

"That might be a good idea. I'm sure he can work out his billing for the hours he's done so far."

There was no way I could afford to pay him until the house was sold, Paul knew that. I know he'd said Beau had arranged for him to help me, but I expected that was just getting me out of the police station.

"I'll contact Paul today. Thank you for carrying my bags but it was completely unnecessary."

I left him standing on the sidewalk. I didn't need to look to know he was staring after me. My hands shook as I inserted the key and I couldn't get through the door quick enough. When it had shut, I slumped against it.

I placed my shopping on the counter and picked up the cell. I sent a text message to Beau.

When you have a minute, I need to talk to you about rent. I know it's still so soon, and I hope that you're coping okay.

I cursed myself after I'd pressed send. I should have asked after him first. My message seemed a little insensitive.

If I could find out what rent Beau wanted, I could make the decision on whether I actually needed another job. Maybe I would ask in some of the local shops, instead of considering Paul's offer, not that I'd officially seen it.

I walked to the window and peered out. Richard was still outside but he had a cell to his ear. I wondered why he hadn't moved on immediately. I ducked out of view as I saw him turn his head to look up at the front of the house, as if he had sensed me watching him.

It was an hour later that I heard a knock on the apartment door. I called out, asking who was there.

"Beau, open the door, Charlotte," came the reply.

I pulled the door open, just a little, and peered through the gap. Beau looked a little better than he had the previous time I'd seen him. I pulled the door wide and he walked in.

"You're a little jumpy still?" he said.

"Cautious, nothing more. Do you mind if I get a chain for that door?"

"If you want, not that a chain would stop someone kicking it in, if they wanted to."

"Well, that made me feel a whole lot better. Coffee?"

While I waited for the coffee maker to percolate, I leaned against the counter.

"How are you, Beau?" I asked.

He shrugged his shoulders a little. "Coping," he said. "You said you wanted to talk to me."

"We need to discuss rent. I have to find a second job so, I know you might not want to talk about this right now, I just want you to think about what you're going to charge me so I know where to start."

"There is no rent to pay. Not yet, anyway."

"What do you mean?"

"Cecelia has left provisions for you."

"Oh, I didn't know that," I said.

"Neither did I until yesterday. I had a call from her lawyer. There are one or two things to go through before I can see her will and know exactly what it is."

"Was that Paul?"

"Paul? No. She had the sense to use someone who actually knew what they were doing."

"Yet, you asked him to help me." I think I might have stated that once before.

"Only because he knows the police in Whiteling. But you're keeping away from him, aren't you?"

"Well..."

"Charlotte, I told you to stay away from him. You cannot trust him, at all."

"He offered me a job and I think I'm stuck."

"What do you mean?"

"His boss, Richard, said..."

"Wait. Richard was here?"

"Not in here, but he was at Paul's office and then I bumped into him outside the store. He carried my bags home for me. I didn't ask him to, I didn't seem to have much choice."

Beau seemed to have expanded in size. His chest bulged, and a vein pulsed on the side of his neck. His jaw worked side to side as if he was grinding his teeth.

"Exactly what did he say to you?"

"It was odd, to be honest. Paul has done some work to get my grandmother's house back, he also offered me a job. I think, if I don't take that job, I'm about to get a huge bill for all that Paul has done so far. And..."

"And, what?"

"There was another thing Paul was going to deal with for me, I don't know what's going to happen now."

"The real trouble?"

"Yes, the real trouble."

"And Richard knows about this real trouble?"

"I don't know, I guess so. He said he'd read through my file. He creeps me out, for sure."

"He's a dangerous man. Fuck!"

Beau pushed himself from the counter and started pacing. "Pack all your belongings, Charlotte."

"Why?"

"Because you can't stay here. Now, do as I say. You won't tell me your trouble, so don't ask me about this, not yet. Just, for once, trust me."

"You're scaring me, Beau."

"It isn't me you should be scared of."

I stared at him. Did I trust him? It surprised me to note that I did. I walked to the bedroom and pulled the backpack from the bottom of the closet. I filled it with my belongings and then headed to the kitchen and emptied the cupboards of food and my money envelopes.

"Am I coming back?" I asked.

"Let's just get you away for now."

"What about my job?"

"Charlotte, we can have a conversation about this later. If Richard is showing an interest in you, you need to be away from here."

"He said something, in Paul's office...something like, 'a good choice, well done.' I didn't know what he meant."

Beau grabbed the backpack and the two shopping bags from me in one hand. He pulled open the apartment door and then fished out his cell from his pocket. I followed him from the apartment as we walked down the stairs, and he raised the cell to his ear.

"They've started already. Charlotte this time."

He didn't say anymore, just switched off the phone and replaced it in his pocket.

"Who was that?" I asked.

"No one. Get in the truck," he said, opening the passenger door. He placed the bags in the truck by my feet, looked around before helping me in. He slammed the door behind me.

CHAPTER 12

Beau didn't speak as we drove through town. He continued on the road toward Whiteling and my stomach tightened as we passed the turn off. The sky had darkened a little and it looked like a storm was rolling in. We continued for another hour before he finally glanced over to me.

"Where are we going, Beau?"

"A little place I have that not many people know about. You'll be safe there."

"And isolated."

"Do you trust me? I know Paul would have told you not to, and I will tell you who that fucking piece of shit is when I know I've got you away."

"I don't understand what's happening."

"He's grooming you, Charlotte."

I had no idea what he meant. "*You* were the one to introduce him to me!"

"There was a reason for that. Now, hold on."

He turned off the road and drove through the trees. There wasn't a vehicle track but he weaved his way between them, clearly knowing the route he needed to take. He didn't even turn on the truck's headlights.

I stared out of the side window, and in the dim light, I thought I saw someone dart between the trees. Branches were swaying in the wind and I questioned whether it really was someone, or just the shadows.

We bumped over the uneven ground and I held on to the door handle. I closed my eyes at one point when we drove a little too close to a large tree. Eventually, we came to a halt in front of a wooden cabin. It was so isolated, I didn't think anyone would ever find it.

"Where are we?" I asked.

"My home."

"I thought the townhouse was your home."

"It is, so is this."

I waited until Beau left the truck and opened my door for me. I grabbed the backpack and he picked up the two bags. He fished around in his pocket for his keys, just as the rain started to come down. In the distance I heard a rumble of thunder.

The cabin was chilly inside and after I'd left my backpack in the hall I followed Beau through the open plan space to the kitchen.

"This is amazing," I said.

The downstairs was open plan with a staircase to one side. Wooden beams crossed the ceiling, down the walls, and I noticed some had intricate carvings on them. I walked over to a beam and ran my hand over the wood.

"The guy that built this for me is Native American, I guess those are symbolic to him. I really should have asked what they meant," he said, as he unpacked the shopping bags.

"This would be my ideal home. I don't know how you can bear

to leave here for the townhouse."

"It wasn't Rachel's ideal, unfortunately."

I walked to a window and although the sun had set, I could make out the woodland surrounding the cabin. The moon cast a glow over the trees, causing ominous shadows that would have children scared. In fact, they had me shivering as well.

"I'll get the fire going," Beau said.

I'd wrapped my arms around myself to keep in the warmth as he stacked the fireplace with logs, and lit the rolled up paper he used as kindling.

"If that storm hits us, it might knock out the power. I have a generator in the shed, though," he added.

I noticed half burned down candles on the mantel above the fire, on a sideboard, and the small table that sat between two sofas. I guessed the power going out was a regular thing. When the fire was roaring, I stood in front of it.

"Do you spend much time here?" I asked.

"Yes, I work from here."

I slowly turned in a circle. There wasn't a desk, or a workspace, that was obvious and I wanted to ask him exactly what work he did. I remembered Cecelia saying something about his work.

"What do you do?" I asked, chancing that he would actually tell me.

"I work for the government," he told me, with a slight smirk.

"That could be anything from a clerk in the town hall to a spy," I said.

"Somewhere towards the top of that scale." He left me staring at him as he walked back to the kitchen area to make coffee.

I sat on one of the sofas and waited for him. The cabin was

warming up nicely, and I could feel a flush of heat on my cheeks. Beau came back with two mugs of coffee, he handed me one and then sat opposite.

"You need to tell me what's going on, Beau," I said.

"Richard is someone I have to keep you away from."

"Why? You never actually answer my questions."

He sighed and rested back in his sofa. "Because I believe he's after you."

"*After me*? For fuck's sake, Beau, just tell me what's going on."

"You remember what you heard when your cousin was talking to his friend?"

"Stop talking around the question and answer it. What has my cousin, his friend, got to do with Richard?"

"Richard has his *associates* find women who look a certain way, Charlotte. He then provides fucking crooks, pedophiles, whoever, with those girls."

"I don't know what you mean, *look a certain way?*"

"Blonde, blue-eyed."

"I don't have blue eyes." Mine were a dark brown.

"Which is why I thought you were safe with Paul."

"What has Paul got to do with…?" Paul worked for Richard. "No, I don't believe it."

"It's true. We've been keeping a close watch over you; we thought you would be okay, especially when you cut your hair off. But then Paul seemed to show an interest beyond what I expected and…"

"We? Who, Beau?" I was starting to get agitated.

"Kieran, Cecelia, Rose."

"So, you're telling me that Richard, and Paul, and maybe my cousin and his friends, take girls and do what with them?" I knew the answer, I'd heard the rumors about Cody, but I wanted him to spell it out for me.

"Force them into prostitution, sell them to rich old men like Philip Stanton. That's what they did with Rachel's sister years ago."

I heard the click of my jaw as it fell open.

"What do you know about Philip Stanton? And what do you mean, Rachel's sister?" I asked.

"I know that you reacted badly when you saw the report of his death. Tell me what happened, Charlotte." His voice had softened a little, not answering my second question.

At that moment, I guessed there was absolutely no point in keeping Philip a secret anymore. Kieran had obviously told Beau.

"He was my friend. I met him at a bar; he just wanted company, Beau. I used to visit him at his home and we'd chat, nothing more, for a while, anyway. One night he was exceptionally upset, I assumed it was grief over his wife, so I took it a step further. We had sex, after I took a shower and when I came out of the bathroom…"

His eyes were wide, his eyebrows raised and his jaw worked side to side. I guessed I was about to get a snide comment about sleeping with a much older man. I squared my shoulders, waiting for his verbal attack.

"*You* were in the shower?"

"I just said that. Someone shot him in the head. I panicked and I ran. I think Damien killed him."

"Damien didn't kill Philip Stanton," he said.

"How do you know that?"

"Because I did."

———

Beau had decided we needed a break from talking and we

needed to eat. I was glad, what he'd said had my head in a spin. He had killed Philip but he hadn't said why. I curled my legs under me, not for comfort but I guessed it was instinct to make myself as small as possible. I'd done that every time I felt threatened. I wanted to scream at Beau, I'd gone through hell the past few months and poor Philip had been murdered. I blinked a few times, gasped as my breath caught in my chest. I slowly uncurled. I was in the same house as a murderer. I quietly stood, wondering what the fuck I was going to do. I needed to get out, but the rain lashing against the windows created a drum so loud on the roof that we'd had to raise our voices when we spoke. It was dark, it was stormy, and I had no fucking idea where I was.

Despite the fire that warmed the cabin, I felt chilled deep inside. I was beyond shedding tears but fear crept over me. Kieran, Rose, Beau, Paul, they'd all lied to me. They'd all known I was in danger, and yet they'd acted as normal as possible around me. Or had they? Small details began to filter in my mind. Kieran insisting on walking me home: Rose not being overly pleased to see Paul in her diner, in fact I lost count of the amount of times she'd been back and forth with that coffee pot as if to interrupt us: The strange looks in the store that day.

"There's nowhere you can run to from here, Charlotte. Whether you believe a word I've told you, you are safe here," Beau said. He placed a small plate with a chicken sandwich and another mug of coffee on the small table.

I started to shake my head. "You all lied to me," I said.

"No, we just never told you the truth. You're the only one who lied, Charlotte."

"Didn't tell me the truth? Tell me the difference! You put me in danger, why?" My voice had started to rise.

"Sit back down. Paul is friends with Frank, the detective in Whiteling. Frank works for me."

"That means fuck all to me. Explain."

"Frank is part of a team to dissolve, arrest, whatever, a ring of traffickers and pedophiles. Your cousin was under investigation, long before you stumbled into the middle of all this...."

"*Long before I stumbled into the middle of this*! Beau, I've been in the middle of this since I was fourteen-years-old." I broke then.

"You all knew about my cousin yet no one saved me. No one intervened. I was a fucking child; I was raped more times than I can remember. I was ridiculed, kicked, punched, spat at. I was a slave to those people in that trailer park and you all knew." I had started my sentence screaming at him, I ended it whispering.

I didn't care about the tears that rolled down my cheeks, I didn't care about the snot that dripped from my nose, or the fact my ugly crying would probably embarrass him. I just cared that someone knew what my cousin was doing and no one came to help me.

Beau rose from his sofa, he took the few steps needed to round the coffee table, and he knelt at my feet. He took my hands in his and it was the first display of comfort I'd ever received from him. I snatched them away; it was way too late.

"We didn't know about you, Charlotte. I swear, we didn't."

"Bullshit! If Frank, whatever his name is, knew my cousin, knew the ring of..." I couldn't bring myself to say the words. "Then he knew about me. I wasn't a secret, I wasn't kept hidden away. I walked the streets, I had to shop, I visited bars as a minor and got kicked out, regularly. Don't you dare tell me he didn't know."

"I said, we, as in me, Kieran and Rose. Cecelia didn't know about you and she knew about everything."

"I can't process this. I don't know what's going on. Frank works for you, yet you didn't know about me. I bet me turning up in your life was a fucker, wasn't it?" I laughed bitterly.

"No. It was hard, like I said before. But we did not think you were at any risk at all."

"Well, you all got that so fucking wrong, didn't you?"

I stood abruptly, causing him to fall back on his ass. I stepped around him and paced.

"Why did you kill Philip?"

"I can't tell you that."

"You can, and you will. You walked into that man's house, that kind, old gentleman, and you shot him in cold blood. Why?"

"Because I was ordered to. That *kind, old gentleman* used to buy young girls, girls about six-years-old normally. He fucked them, any which way he wanted. He kept them locked up in his house. I bet there was one there all the time you sat on his sofa, having a cozy chat. The grief you say he felt? Guilt, Charlotte. And not guilt because what he did was fucking repulsive, but guilt because he'd been caught. Except the government, for whom I have no respect, didn't want him to face trial. I don't know why. I get an order, I do a job, and then I get paid. I don't ask questions."

I spun to face him. "You murder someone and you don't even care to know what they did to deserve that?" I saw the spittle leave my mouth as the bitterness spewed from me.

"It's a job. It's not my place to question why. At the end of the day, that man ruined girls. Do you think he deserved to live?"

His comment stunned me. Not that I was a law-abiding citizen, not that I also had any respect for a government that had badly let me down, but I could never murder... I slumped on the sofa. Perhaps Beau and I weren't so different. I'd killed Damien. I didn't think, at the time, I'd intended to murder him. But when I saw his whole body on fire, I did nothing to help him because I knew he'd never leave me alone, he'd never go to prison, and he didn't deserve to live.

I covered my face with my hands and I sobbed. My stomach roiled at the thought there might have been a child in that house at the same time as I was sitting there chatting to, consoling, Philip. I then realised just how easy it was to be kept under the radar. Maybe Frank didn't know what was happening to me. I imagined they would be so focused on girls who were way younger than I was; I just slipped through the net. I wasn't the typical age for the victims they were concentrating on. I didn't have the right look for Damien to hand me over to Richard. I was just a teenage prostitute, like hundreds of others all over the county.

"When I was in the store the other day, people acted strange, people that I didn't know. Why?"

"I can't answer that. All I can say is that, one, you resemble Rachel even with your brown hair. Two, you're a stranger in a town that has one of the largest and most dangerous cults on its doorstep. Maybe they hadn't seen you around before and you spooked them."

"What?"

"Richard is the elder of a cult, housed in a compound outside of Ayelsham. They are some serious people that the FBI have tried to shut down for years, and failed."

"Pedophile, trafficking, a cult! Are you sure you haven't got stuck in a fucking crime novel? These things don't happen in real life...do they?"

"Yes, they do, and it happens right here, in Whiteling and in

Ayelsham."

"Why me, Beau?"

"The cult, years ago, believed in divine children, kids of angels or some shit like that. Richard now believes in drugs, guns, and catering to high-ranking officials and their sexual appetite for children. I guess that pays more than praying to God ever did. However, he has been able to convince the more gullible there are still divine children. So, he finds a blonde, blue-eyed girl, drugs them, and sells them. He holds all the power. Why do you think he has never been brought to justice? It isn't just ex-mayors he has the capability to blackmail."

"And you're job is to wipe those high-ranking officials out instead of bringing them to justice?"

He didn't answer; he didn't need to. "Be very embarrassing for the *government* if it all got out, I suppose," I added, sarcastically. "And I reiterate, I'm not blue-eyed."

"Then Richard had a different role for you. But believe me, he *did* have a role for you."

"I need to sleep. I cannot comprehend what you've told me. I don't want to believe any of it, but I do, and that makes me question everything. It hurts, Beau, so much it's physical. I could have been saved, maybe there was a child in that house with Philip, and I should have saved her. Maybe I..."

"Charlotte, if there was, there would have been nothing you could have done. I can't tell you how many people have lost their lives because they tried to take a stand against Richard, Paul, and Philip. As for you being saved? I'm sorry. I'm so sorry that you had to live that life. If you were younger, maybe you would have been on our radar. We fucked up; we missed you. You say you were visible, but not visible enough for us to see what was happening back then."

"When I was arrested, Frank knew I was Damien's cousin, didn't he? Couldn't he have connected the dots?"

"Frank wasn't involved, initially, when you got arrested, but as soon as I found your phone on the bedroom floor, I knew something had happened. I called Frank; he took over the case. I also called Paul, and I'll tell you why. Frank is undercover, Charlotte. He's not in as deep as I need him to be, but he's acting the rogue cop. It's the only way we can find out who is involved, where they are, what they're doing."

"So, you used me and my situation to help your cause?"

He sighed. "Yes. Yes I did, Charlotte, knowing the benefit of that would be your release. The Whiteling police force were all for charging you with murder. There wasn't one person, me included, who believed Damien happened to set himself on fire by accident. There was also the matter of silencing you. If they discredited you enough, I mean, you *were* a prostitute from childhood who murdered her pimp, no one would have believed anything else you ever said. Especially when it comes to Philip."

His words were harsh but honest.

"I killed Damien. I took a mouthful of his liquor, spat it over his face and then set fire to him. I splashed his one-hundred-proof shit all over him until the flames spread. I didn't think about what I did, I didn't even think I was killing him. It was…"

"Self-defence, Charlotte. Years of pent up abuse being released on the perpetrator. It was a justifiable murder. They happen, more regularly than you imagine."

He'd made his point and I slowly nodded. "Get some sleep, Charlotte. There are two bedrooms upstairs, take which one you want."

    I rose from the sofa, wearily grabbed my backpack, and climbed the stairs to a galleried landing. I could see Beau sitting on the sofa, and I watched him pull out a phone different to the one I normally saw him use. He glanced up before he dialed. I didn't care to listen to his conversation; I was exhausted, both emotionally and physically. I picked the first door I came to, and then realized I was in the bathroom. I took the next one and opened it into a large bedroom. I kicked off my sneakers, pulled back a comforter and climbed, fully dressed, under the cover. I closed my eyes, begging sleep to take me quickly.

CHAPTER 13

I woke with a start, and it took me a moment to get my bearings and for the previous evening's conversation to filter through my mind. I sighed and closed my eyes, disappointed it hadn't all been a dream.

I hadn't taken too much notice of the room the night before. I admired the woodwork, noticing the same intricate carvings on the rich oak beams that crossed the ceiling. The walls were painted a warm cream and the drapes matched the deep purple quilt I was laying under. Two small light oak cabinets stood on either side of the wrought iron bed, and the two wall lights above the headboard were still lit. A chest of drawers sat against the wall opposite the bed. I climbed from the bed, picking up my backpack and placed it on top of the sideboard. I needed to shower and rifled around inside for my toiletries and some clean clothes.

Snippets of the conversation from the previous night floated around my mind. It was just too much to take in and get a real understanding of what I'd landed myself in. I felt dirty; like all those times I'd been fucked against my will. I had an overwhelming desire to scrub my body with bleach to rid myself of the tarnished skin. The compulsion to wash was so great that I didn't even wait for the shower to warm. I stepped under the cold jets, welcoming the pain and then the warmth when it came. I scrubbed myself raw.

———

Beau was sitting at the kitchen table with a laptop in front of him. He looked up, alerted by my steps on the wooden stairs I imagined.

"Did you sleep?" he asked.

"I did, God knows how, though."

I passed him and poured myself a coffee. I didn't think to offer to refresh his cup. I sat at the table and silently sipped from my mug.

"How long will this storm be?" I asked, doubting it was a question he could answer.

He shrugged his shoulders. "Should ease up in a day or so, according to the forecast."

The sky was dark, the sun not having the strength to break through the thick rain clouds.

"So, you follow the weather?"

"It affects my job. Good weather isn't so great for surveillance or..."

"Murdering people. Yes, I guess a nice sunny day can put a stop to that."

"What was the sun doing when you *murdered* Damien? The only difference between what you did and what I did is, I earned a shitton of money," he said, staring me down.

I lowered my head and sipped on my coffee. He went back to his laptop.

———

I sat on a sofa, sipping on my second cup of coffee and ignoring my grumbling stomach. As hungry as I was, I wasn't sure I could eat and keep it down. The caffeine was flooding my body, but the lack of food was making me feel jittery. Although Beau had made me a sandwich the previous evening, I hadn't taken a bite from it.

"She's okay, she's processing at the moment," I heard. I looked over to see Beau hold a cell to his ear. He wasn't looking at me but his laptop. I hadn't heard his cell ring.

"I will, but I'm not sure she wants to at the moment. I'll let you know when she's ready. Yes…Yes! I know what I'm doing." Beau seemed to get agitated with whoever was on the end of the call. He sighed as he disconnected and laid it on the table.

"Kieran," he said, without looking up.

I gave him the finger, wondering if, since I hadn't asked who was calling and because Beau hadn't looked over to me once, if he would see. He laughed, and finally he looked up and slowly turned his laptop around. Not that I could see clearly, but his screen was a grid of small squares, live camera images.

I looked around the room there were no obvious cameras anywhere.

I heard the scrape of a chair and Beau came into the living room. He sat on the same sofa as me.

"How are you doing?" he asked.

"Were you told to ask me that?"

"No. Kieran, me, I don't think we're particularly great at the emotional stuff. We're 'doers', practical, I guess we don't take feelings into account."

"You don't say!"

"What do you want to ask me, Charlotte? You must have a ton

of questions."

"What is Kieran to you?" It wasn't one of the million questions I had floating around but the first that came to my mouth.

"He was my commander, when I was in the regular army. Then he was my commander when I joined the *irregular* army. He retired, and I took his role. He still thinks he can boss me around, though."

"Isn't he too old to be in the *irregular* army, and what is that, anyway?"

"That's why it's an *irregular* army. Most of the guys are ex-soldiers. He wasn't front line, but he had certain skills that the regular, or *irregular,* army didn't want to lose."

I noticed that he'd dodged my question. That was okay, because it was one I'd be sure to ask as many times as it took to get the answer.

"Let me get this all straight. Richard is a member of a cult. He employs Paul, Damien, and other crooks to deal his drugs, find him girls, and whatnot. I killed Damian, in *self-defence*; you used that opportunity to connect Paul and Frank because Frank is working undercover, just not undercover enough. It was a bonus that Paul is a lawyer and knows the police in Whiteling. Oh, oh, so that's why Frank said that Paul *knew* him, he could *trust* him. I suspect that was code of some kind because they didn't look like they knew each other when they first met.

"Anyway, you, Rose, Cecelia, and Kieran, and whoever the fuck else, all knew that Paul and Richard were the baddies. You bumped off Philip because he was a baddie, and then I came along after being overlooked for four years. You all thought I was great until Richard put in an appearance, which was pretty obvious, considering he was Paul's boss and I was thinking about working for Paul. But it wasn't real, was it? I was being groomed for a life as a prostitute for Richard, and I was about to be blackmailed. So, in you come, all knight on a white charger, and here we are."

I finally took in a long, deep breath.

Beau raised his eyebrows, cocked his head slightly, and nodded. There was a smirk to his lips as if he was impressed.

"That is about the best summing up I've heard."

"Oh, hold on, we haven't finished. I find a message, presumably from your ex-girlfriend, who also happens to be blonde with blue eyes, Paul's daughter, and missing. You haven't once mentioned that you think Paul might actually have something to do with his own daughter's disappearance, instead she ran because you said you weren't the father of her child, she was fucking another..." My sentence trailed off, my voice lowered to a whisper as realization dawned, and I saw the look of utter despair on his face.

"I'm so sorry, I didn't mean..."

Beau raised his hand to silence me. "Yes, she could have been sold by her own father, her sister most certainly was. Yes, her father, Richard even, could be the father of the child she was carrying, and she was too scared to tell me, so she left that message. She could be in the cult; she could have been in the basement at Philip's. She could have already been forced to sleep with other men. There are a thousand 'could haves' and I explored every one of them. I failed her, I wasn't about to fail you."

He rose and walked to the fire. "You know the old saying, Charlotte, keep your enemies close and all that. That is why I keep some form of a fake relationship with Paul. They don't know what I do; Rachel didn't know what I did for work. I believe she was scared of something, she ran not because of our argument but because she had no choice."

"What do we do now, Beau?" I asked.

"We eliminate the threat, once and for all."

"You can't take on Richard on your own, surely."

"I never said I'd take him on, not on my own."

Before I could ask him any more, we both heard a scrape on the deck outside the cabin. Although the rain still pummelled, the scrape was loud enough, it seemed to me to be the sound a piece of furniture would make if it were dragged. When we'd arrived, I hadn't noticed any furniture.

"Stay there," Beau said, and he reached behind him, under his white t-shirt and pulled out a revolver.

He quietly walked to the front wall, away from the window and placed his back between that and the front door.

"Keep your head down," he whispered. I curled on the sofa.

For a while there was silence, other the sound of my heart pumping blood at pace past my ears. Beau walked back to the sofa, he reached down, and grabbed my arm.

"Kitchen," he whispered.

I followed him. Just as he reached his laptop, to check the cameras I presumed, a small window in the back door shattered. I screamed as Beau pushed me to the floor. He raised his gun and fired back. His aim was off and his bullets hit the woodwork around the door. It was then that I noticed he was holding the gun in his left hand. The right side of his t-shirt, up by his shoulder, was red.

"Beau," I said.

"It's fine," he replied, but I heard the wince as he transferred the gun to his right hand and lowered to a crouch.

"Do you see that door under the stairs? We need to get there," he whispered.

I hadn't noticed the small door under the stairs, but getting there would mean exposing ourselves. "On my count, you run, okay?"

I nodded. Beau only got to number one before something was thrown through the window and smoke exploded into the room. It stung my eyes, causing them to immediately weep. I crawled toward the stairs, losing my bearings. I could hear Beau calling me, but in my panic I couldn't determine where he was.

I felt a hand grip my arm and I scrambled to my feet. I came face to face with a woman with long blonde hair and a plastic mask over her face. I was about to open my mouth and scream when she leveled a gun at my face.

The smoke began to clear and she whipped the mask off her face. She turned me to face away from her, and she placed the gun at my temple. It was then that I saw Beau. He stood with his gun pointing; we were at a standoff. Beau, without looking, keyed something into his phone and I prayed he was calling for help.

"Beau, I'm sorry but I have to do this," she said.

"You don't, Rachel, you know that. You're choosing to do this. Who is it? Richard?"

"It's me or her. I don't know what's so special about her but this is my task."

"I can help you, you know that. I could have helped you a year ago."

"How, Beau?"

"He works for the fucking government," I said, hoping to speed their conversation up a little. "He can help you. Think about your child, Rachel,"

The gun was pressed harder into my temple. "Keep your mouth shut," she said.

"What about your baby?" I said.

"I don't have a baby, not any more. We don't have a need for boys. Oh, Beau, he looked so much like you."

When she spoke to me, her voice was harsh, when she spoke to Beau it was soft and girlish. I laughed.

"She's talking bullshit, Beau," I said. I then winced as the pain escalated at my temple.

"I know she is, Charlotte. Rachel, if you shoot her you're not walking out of here alive, you know that. Let her go."

"She's just a piece of trash, why are you concerning yourself with her? This thing, and I do feel she is contaminating me by being so close, is just a fuck toy, nothing more. I mean, I visited the apartment, Beau, she has nothing."

I'd been called *trash* for years. I'd been a *fuck toy* as she called it, for years. And in that moment, I didn't care about a gun to my head. I stared at Beau and mouthed, *one, two, three*.

On three I elbowed her in the stomach, I slammed my head back into her face, I dropped to my knees at the same time as Beau sprang forward. It wasn't rehearsed but worked like a fucking dream. Before Rachel could figure out what was happening, Beau had her by her hair and forced to her knees.

"Now drop the fucking gun," he said.

I scrambled to the side, but not before she let off a shot at me. I heard it whizz past my head. I watched as Beau tilted her head to the side and shot her through the side of it. I opened my mouth to scream, but her blood and brain splattered over the front of my face. I was stunned into silence. A split second after, I heard another shot but I was paralyzed at the sight in front of me. Beau slowly folded to his knees. He let go of Rachel and she slumped to the floor just in front of me. A puddle of blood spread from below Beau's knees.

"The door," he said, it sounded as if he was forcing the words past a scream of pain.

I wasn't going without him. On all fours I crawled as fast as I could. I picked up the gun that he had let fall to the floor. I had held a gun once, though I'd never used one. Instinctively, I wrapped my finger around the trigger and faced it to the back door. I fired, surprised when the gun jolted in my hand knocking me back on my ass. I grabbed Beau by the arm.

"Please, I can't do this without you," I said.

"Go, now, for fuck's sake," he growled.

"Not without you."

I saw a shadow pass the window and fired again. I discovered that if I kept my finger on the trigger, loads of bullets were ejected. The problem with that was I was thrown all over the place. I felt Beau wrap his hand around my wrist. I dropped the gun and we crawled toward the stairs. A trail of blood followed us.

Beau reached up and opened the door to a dark room. "There are five steps, get down them," he said. I missed the first and fell down the rest.

I heard the clunk of bolts, metal against metal as a bar, it sounded as if, was slid closed.

"Find the light, Charlotte, it's on the left, a cord."

Since Beau couldn't see which way I was facing, I swung both arms until the fingers on my right hand brushed against something that moved away. I grabbed it and pulled. An orange glow flooded the steel lined room. When I turned to look, he was slumped against a metal lined door.

"Beau..."

He raised his good arm. "Open that cabinet. The code is seven-one-eight-four."

On the opposite wall was a large metal cabinet with a keypad. I keyed in the code and heard it unlock. When I pulled the door open an array of firearms greeted me.

"On the left," he said, his voice sounded strained.

On the far left was what looked like a rifle. "The clip," I heard.

I didn't know exactly what a clip was, but I'd seen enough pictures to know there should have been something hanging from the bottom of the rifle, something that contained bullets. On a shelf above the rifle was a black metal object. I lifted it to show him, he nodded.

I ran back up the small flight of steps and laid the rifle on his lap. The blood from the wound to his shoulder had spread across his chest and running down to his stomach.

"Shit, Beau. You're really hurt."

"You don't say," he said, wincing again as he inserted the clip.

We fell silent when we heard a kicking to the door.

"Help me down," Beau said.

I grabbed his thigh to straighten his leg and my hand touched hot liquid. "Just help me down," he said.

I wasn't strong enough to lift him but managed to slide him to the top step. He bumped down the steps on his ass, biting on his lower lip. The kicking of the door intensified.

"Is there a way out?" I whispered. Beau didn't answer. The fact he'd positioned himself facing the door suggested there wasn't.

I looked around the room. There were no windows; we were obviously in some kind of a basement, although the room didn't span the width or depth of the house. On one side was a desk with a computer sitting on it. Beside it, another screen and some electrical equipment I couldn't identify.

"You dropped your cell," I said, quietly.

"That's okay, Kieran knows what to do."

"How quickly can he get here?"

"Quick."

I hoped so because there was a pool of blood extending from Beau's leg. I ran back to the metal cabinet and grabbed a large hunting knife and a revolver. I used the knife to cut the jean from Beau's thigh. There was a large hole where skin should be.

"Oh, God. Tell me what to do," I said.

The kicking had stopped, but I didn't think for one minute whoever was up there had left. The silence scared me more than the noise.

"Get my t-shirt off."

I cut a section and then tore the front of his t-shirt. Like his leg, a fleshy wound seeped blood.

"Is the blood running fast, Charlotte?" he asked. I shook my head. "Good. Use the t-shirt, tie it around my thigh, above the wound."

My hands shook, my fingers slipped on the sodden material, but I thought I tied a tight enough knot. It was hard to tell if the blood was still running or not, he was covered in it.

"Have they gone?" I asked as I slumped beside him.

"No." Beau's voice seemed distant. When I looked at him, he was deathly pale. The hand holding the rifle on his lap shook, his stomach quivered.

Before I could panic that he was dying, the smell of smoke filtered into the room. I made to stand; we needed to get out of the room.

"The minute you walk out there, you're dead," I heard Beau say.

"We're dead if we stay here."

He shook his head. A small amount of smoke swirled through the tiniest gap under the door. It wasn't enough to make me cough but I felt my throat constrict in panic. I sidled closer to Beau, not caring that I was sitting in his blood. I held the revolver in my shaking hands, raised at the door. I heard Beau chuckle.

"It's not loaded," he said, his voice even fainter than it was before.

I threw it to the floor and only then, when I thought there was nothing we could do but die in that *dungeon,* I started to cry. Beau wrapped his good arm around me, leaving the rifle on the floor.

A second later an explosion happened outside the door, it buckled but held, although the gap underneath was wider. Smoke poured into the room.

"We're going to die, aren't we?" I said. He didn't answer.

CHAPTER 14

The lights went out and we were plunged into darkness. Neither of us spoke, but I felt Beau's arm tighten slightly around me. We sat in silence with just the crackle of a burning house for company. The room heated up, and I could feel sweat roll down my temple, the air became dense, and it was difficult to breathe. I wasn't sure how much smoke was making its way into the room but knew with each breath I took in, my throat and lungs burned. The smell had become acrid. I didn't sob or cry out, initially, but I let the tears roll down my cheeks and silently prayed. I felt Beau's arm loosen until it fell from my shoulders. He slumped sideways, only then did I cry out loud. I curled into his side, wrapping my arms around him, spooning into his back and whispering to him.

"Don't leave me, Beau," I said, over and over. He never replied.

I closed my eyes, hoping death would find me soon and it would be painless. I tried hard not to recall the images of Damien and knew this was my punishment. I could only hope the smoke would overcome me first. I held on tightly to Beau, I didn't know if he was alive or not but hoped that he could feel me, that he knew he wasn't alone. I couldn't hear him breathing, I didn't feel his chest moving, and the blood seemed to have stopped flowing. I lost track of time and, eventually, I slipped into unconsciousness.

———————

I didn't know if I was dreaming, if I was dead or alive. I felt someone lift me but I couldn't open my eyes. I heard distant voices but could not work out what was being said. I thought I saw brightness behind my eyelids and a woman's voice. I wanted to call out to my grandmother, I was sure it was her. Something was placed over my face, the air that I breathed in, or thought I was breathing in, felt fresh and clean, cold and with a slight earthy taste. Then it was all gone again, the darkness consumed me. I welcomed it.

———————

"Charlotte, can you open your eyes for me?"

I'd heard voices earlier, or maybe it was a while ago. I didn't want to open my eyes. I wanted to sleep some more.

"Charlotte?"

Fingers pried at my eyelids, and I fought against them. I think I groaned, maybe I said a word. I felt something in my mouth, in my throat. I wanted to swallow and I couldn't, it was in the way. I raised my hand to pull whatever it was from my mouth.

"It's okay, don't panic now. We're going to take this out," I heard.

The obstruction in my throat was removed and it was replaced with soreness. Every breath I took scratched.

Beau. I wasn't sure if I spoke the word, or thought it. I missed him already.

"She's doing well."

Who was? Me? But I was dead, wasn't I? Sparks of light would dance just out of reach, voices would float around but they were nothing more than a hum in the background. There was a constant beep and it began to annoy me. I wanted silence, nothing but silence and stillness. I hurt; with every breath I took my chest ached. I wanted the breathing to stop.

For periods of time I'd get my wish, all was quiet and calmness would wash over me. Until one day.

"Charlotte, I really need you to open your eyes, sweetie." It was her voice again, my grandmother's.

It was a man's voice that finally broke through the fog in my mind. "Rose, you've been here all night. Let's get some rest," he said.

Rose? Rose!

I tried to move my head. I strained against the stickiness that held my eyelids closed until eventually a sliver of light, so bright it hurt, penetrated through the small gap.

"She waking, call the doctor," Rose said.

I followed the sound of her voice.

"Sweetie, don't try to move. We're calling the doctor."

I grunted out a sound, I didn't seem to be able to form words.

"Don't speak, your throat is so burned."

Fire. There had been a fire. Beau. Beau had been with me. Panic started to rise inside, and I felt my legs thrash against the bed I realized I was lying on.

"Doctor!" she called out.

"Hey, Charlotte, can you open your eyes for me?" Why did they ask that? I was trying, couldn't they see that?

I managed to get one eye open further than the other. Everything was a blur at first. Colors were bright, searing my eye. When I managed to open the other one, my vision became a little more focused. There was a person standing to one side of me. I turned away from him.

"Rose?" I croaked out her name.

"Don't talk, sweetie. I'm here. Oh, God, sweetie. I'm here, Kieran is, too." It seemed she found it hard to talk. Her voice broke on every word.

I felt her hand on mine. I also felt her tears as they dripped onto my skin. I think I cried then. My vision blurred further and liquid ran down my temples.

"Can you sip on this?" I heard. It was the man to my side. I felt something press against my lips and opened my mouth slightly. Something plastic and small was pushed in. I sucked, it hurt, but the cold water soothed the hurt away.

People came and went, one minute there was brightness beyond my eyelids, the next it was dark. I would hear voices, and then it was quiet, save for the continuous beeping. The times I did manage to open my eyes, my vision was still blurred. Someone had said, or maybe they'd told me directly, I didn't remember, that my eyes were irritated by smoke. My lungs and throat were damaged from smoke inhalation. It took a few days, however, for me to really understand and remember.

"Let's get you a little more comfortable, shall we?" a nurse said.

I knew I was in the hospital, obviously, I just wasn't sure how long I'd been there.

"Do you know how Beau is?" I croaked out.

"I don't, honey. I'm sure your friends will be here soon."

She fussed around, tucking in the sheet and raising the back of the bed a little. I could still smell the acrid smoke of a burning house with all its contents, and with every painful breath I took in, a moment of fear washed over me.

"There she is," I heard. Rose came through the door. "Oh, sweetie, it's good to see you fully awake."

"How's Beau?" I asked. She didn't answer but did glance to the door. "Let's talk about that later."

A sense of dread settled over me, it was weighted down with sadness. I closed my eyes, willing some tears for him and to lubricate my eyeballs.

"What's wrong with my eyes?"

"It was the heat, and the smoke. Kieran will be here shortly. Is there anything he can get for you?"

I shook my head, aware that she had diverted me. I felt so tired, it was an effort to breathe and I was grateful for the oxygen pipe sitting just under my nose. I reached for my cup of water and took a sip. Just the few words I'd spoken had hurt my throat.

"We nearly lost you," Rose whispered. It was the sadness, mixed with relief that finally caused those tears I'd longed for to fall.

She reached over to take one of my hands in hers.

"They tried to kill us," I said, still none the wiser on who *they* were.

"We know. There are people here to protect you, Charlotte. You're not in danger here, you're safe now."

I didn't think I'd ever be safe. No matter where I ended up, trouble always found me. It was a horrible feeling, knowing I'd always be looking over my shoulder.

Kieran came into the room, holding a bag aloft. "I got you some clothes, I don't know if anything will fit, but you might be more comfortable in them."

I guessed everything I owned would have perished in the fire. The thought that my grandmother's quilt was gone saddened me.

"Where is Beau?" I asked him. He pulled a seat up close to the bed.

"He's gone, Charlotte."

I stared at him. "Gone?"

"He survived. God, Kieran, you'll give the girl a heart attack. He had surgery, a blood transfusion, but then he discharged himself. We don't know where he is," Rose said.

"I don't understand."

"Neither do I. Although I think this man here knows more than he's letting on."

"He called you, didn't he?" I said. Kieran nodded.

"I heard you scream, I knew where you were and I got there as quickly as I could. The whole house was ablaze, Charlotte. I'm surprised you survived."

"You knew *exactly* where we were?"

He slowly nodded his head. I remembered Beau telling me that Kieran had been his commander, I think the word was. There was something in the way he looked at me, a pleading in his eyes to not push for information. His eyes flicked to Rose. It was a conversation for another day.

———

It was another two weeks before the hospital discharged me, and that was only after I'd insisted, told them I had no money to pay so they might as well let me out as soon as possible. Kieran collected me and took me back to their house. I'd never visited their house before and was surprised by the size. Like Cecelia's, it was Colonial style with a wraparound porch. He held my arm as we walked up the path and through the front door.

"Sweetie, it's so good to have you here. Now, I've set up a

bedroom for you and we've bought some more clothes." I'd traveled home in the pajamas Kieran had brought to the hospital.

"Charlotte, you're going to have to talk to the authorities at some point. We've kept them away for as long as we can."

"I can't." Panic rose at the thought of talking to the police.

"I'm talking about the FBI. There is a guy called Corey Lowe, who is going to come visit. I know him, he can be trusted. I wouldn't trust the local police, especially Cody to deal with this," Kieran said.

"Cody? Damien's friend was called Cody."

Kieran looked at me. "Do you know his surname?"

I told him and watched as he closed his eyes and sighed. Cody was obviously part of the ring they were watching. I realized then, the car I'd seen was a cop car.

"What do you know, Kieran, about me?" I asked. My voice had changed pitch. I was told it would return to normal in time, but it still sounded strange to my ears.

"Everything," he whispered, glancing at Rose, who was making coffee to make sure she was out of earshot.

"How long have you known *everything*?"

"That's a conversation for when we are alone, if that's okay with you?"

I nodded. I guessed he wanted to protect Rose from the gory details. "I'm really tired," I said.

"Let's get you to bed," Rose replied.

She led me up a winding staircase to a bedroom at the back of the house. There was a large sash window that overlooked the fields at the rear, and I wondered if that was part of Cecelia's land. The room was beautifully decorated in pastel, floral printed wallpaper and a matching quilt was draped over a large wooden bed.

Rose opened a wardrobe to show me an array of clothes hanging on a rail and folded items on shelves.

"I wasn't sure what you'd like. Ellie helped me pick out some items, Kacy wanted to help also, but I didn't think her taste was the same as yours. Everyone's been so worried about you. It's been a shock to the town, Charlotte."

"I need to pay you back but..." I didn't have a cent to my name.

"Listen," she said, as she sat on the edge of the bed. "It seems that Cecelia wanted to take care of you, she left you some money. Beau has given all the details to Kieran. But even if she hadn't, I wanted to do this. You're important to us, Charlotte."

"But you've only know me for such a short time," I said, sitting beside her.

"I've know you a lot longer than you think. Not *you*, but girls like you. In a day or so, when you're settled, I'll tell you about this town, and about some of its people."

I wondered exactly what the fuck I'd stumbled into when I was driven into this town.

"I think you've been bombarded with so much information, Charlotte. And I'm sorry that we didn't tell you enough to keep you safe, but Richard showing an interest in you surprised us all. We're not sure why just yet."

"But you knew what he was, and Paul, didn't you?" She was the last person I wanted to make feel bad, and a wave of guilt washed over me at the look of sadness on her face.

"It will all make sense when you understand where you are. Now, let's get you out of those pajamas and into a fresh pair."

Rose fussed; she opened the drawer of the unit and pulled out a matching top and bottoms. She helped me wiggled out of what I wore and tactfully averted her gaze at my nakedness.

"There's a bathroom next door, just for you. I've placed some toiletries and a gown in there for when you want to shower."

Despite being washed in the hospital, I could still smell smoke in my hair and on my skin. A long shower would be most welcomed. First, I needed to sleep. My head had started to pound. I had been told in the hospital I might suffer the odd headache for a while. I climbed under the quilt and sank into the mattress. The pillow was like placing my head on a cloud, it was that soft. I vaguely remember Rose picking up my dirty pajamas, maybe she spoke to me before she closed the door, but that was it.

When I woke, the sun was setting over the horizon, throwing red and orange hues over the rich brown turned earth. As a child I'd watch the sun set, right until that last minute when I believed it waved at me. Just as the sun dipped out of sight, and, obviously it was an illusion, I'd see tiny flame-like arms. I'd wave back, bidding the sun a good night.

I pushed back the quilt and swung my legs from the bed. I pulled open a drawer to the unit and found a pair of fluffy socks that I didn't recognize. Once I'd pulled them on, I ventured downstairs. Rose was sitting in her kitchen, reading a newspaper.

"Hey there, did you sleep well? You've been out for the count for hours."

"I did, I can't believe how comfortable that bed is."

"I got some new linen but I had that bed as a young girl. They don't make them like that anymore; everything is so disposable nowadays. Here, take a seat. Now, I bet Cecelia had you hooked on tea, so how about I make some?"

I wasn't sure I was hooked on it, but it did make a refreshing change from coffee. What with the sleep I'd had, still feeling tired, and the headache, I didn't want to add strong caffeine to my system as well.

"Tea would be lovely," I said.

"I've made some soup and bread for dinner, I didn't think you'd want anything too heavy, just yet. It will just be us for dinner, Kieran is away for a couple of days."

Her comment surprised me; I couldn't recall a time when he'd taken a day off at the diner.

"What about the diner?"

"Kacy is covering your shift right now. We decided to close in the evenings for a little while; we do that in the winter anyway. We don't get the customers on chilly nights to warrant staying open."

"Who's cooking?"

"Jack, he's a college kid looking for some extra income. He's been with us on and off for a couple of years, although not the past couple of months. He decided to do some traveling but now he's back, just in time for us, thankfully."

"I guess the patrons will be pleased not to have to endure Kieran's experiments," I said, trying not to laugh in case it hurt my throat.

Rose chuckled as she ladled some soup into a bowl. The smell of leek and potato made my mouth water. We sat side by side at her kitchen island and ate. I tore off a chunk of bread and dipped it in my soup.

"This is delicious," I said.

"Soup. Heals the soul, my mom used to say."

"Kieran said I had to speak to some guy from the FBI. Do I really have to?"

"I'm afraid so, but you don't need to be afraid about this guy. He comes with Kieran's seal of approval."

"I don't want to talk to the sheriff." I wasn't sure what Rose knew, so tried to approach the subject delicately.

"Sweetie, what happened to you is way above his rank anyway. And no, we wouldn't let you speak with him. Cody, Paul, and Richard are the people we watch, very closely."

"So you know about them?"

She laid down her spoon. "Remember when I said I've known you longer than you realize? Maybe it's time we had that chat."

She turned slightly in her chair.

"I was in a convent, Charlotte. Except this convent wasn't a conventional one, not that I was aware of that, of course. It was run by a Father Samuel, Richard's father. The purpose of this convent was to farm out children to families to use and abuse. Some of us managed to get out in later life, some didn't. Some are so indoctrinated there is no hope for them. And some were killed. Corey, the FBI guy? He's been on the trail of a cult for years. That convent, that Father, was the start of a religious cult. I'm talking many, many years ago now."

"When did you get out, and how?"

"Oh, I was early teens, I think. I was told I was an orphan, I'm not entirely sure that was true, when I entered the convent. I was there for a couple of years until I was placed with a family. Sister Anna was in charge of those placements. Except the families were all part of the cult. They did terrible things to children, Charlotte. Things I won't speak of right now, I don't think you're ready to hear it."

"I know, Beau told me a little."

"Beau," she sighed when she spoke his name. "Vigilante Beau.

237

He's a good person, Charlotte, and I'm pretty sure, although I don't ask, he and Kieran worked, maybe still work, together. Anyway, Father Samuel was murdered a little while ago. One of his sons committed suicide, leaving Richard, another of his sons, and he has many, in charge. Richard wasn't satisfied with just abusing young girls, and he'd long since let go of the Father's belief in divine children. He got involved in drugs, in trafficking young women, lies, fraud, blackmail, you name it, he's involved."

"Why is he still out on the streets then?" I knew Beau had explained but maybe Rose had a different version.

"Because he has a lot of influential people in his pocket. And no matter what the FBI does, they can never pin anything down on him. It wouldn't have been Richard that came to Beau's. He's never directly involved in anything. It's all circumstantial, as far as the courts are concerned."

"Beau said something about this divine child thing."

"Father Samuel found a woman, I don't know the full story. She was blonde, so light she was nearly white-haired and with startling blue eyes. To be honest, I imagine her to be albino to some degree. She had alabaster skin, she was angelic looking, Charlotte. He knew he was a sinner, he thought if she was his mate, if he was able to produce children from her, he could create a line of divine children. That would ensure his seat next to God. He was quite crazy."

"Did you meet him?"

"Many times. One stare from him, Charlotte, and any child would fall immediately into submission. He was evil, and that evilness rolled off him like a gas, contaminating everything and everyone around."

She was looking off into the distance, lost to her memory. I wasn't sure whether to interrupt to bring her back to the safe present or let her be.

"I was placed with a family, made to work the land, cook, clean. It was nothing more than modern day slavery, but with the added bonus of being regularly abused by the family or the elders of the cult. I wasn't classed as a divine child; I don't have that look. Those children were revered, as much as an abused child could be."

"Are there any left?"

"One. And we've been working hard at getting her out."

"What do you mean?"

"She's closely guarded, protected. Once she was permitted to leave their compound and that was under armed guard. Her beauty takes your breath away, Charlotte. For a long time I wished they were angelic, they were divine, but it's nothing more than faulty genetics and indoctrination. I caught a glimpse of her, they had moved her because they'd been tipped off the FBI were about to raid. When they did raid, they found that nothing goes on in that compound; they have several dotted around the county. There is one where they make the drugs, another where the *families* live, and a third where the elders live. I'm sure there are many more. They are able to pick up and move in an instant because they are so spread out."

My soup was getting cold, but I was intrigued with what Rose was telling me. As she spoke, I popped small pieces of bread in my mouth to quiet the grumble of hunger.

"Anyway, we know the elders, we know where the children are, and we work at getting them out."

"We?"

"There are five women, we were six until Cecelia passed, in this town. We either came from the cult or volunteered to help the cause.

Ellie is one; I'll introduce you to the others. Kacy was one of our girls, Charlotte. When we managed to get her away from her adoptive parents she was pregnant. She's never spoken of the father to her son, but we suspect it was her adoptive father."

"How many girls have you managed to help, and how, exactly, do you get them out?"

"Oh, hundreds. I don't think we've kept a tally. We've been doing this for many years. Nearly all the girls move across the country. We keep in touch with some. How do we get them out?" She sighed, but I noticed a glint of something naughty in her eyes. She seemed to come alive.

"We have insiders, we spend time reeducating the child and then we snatch them."

"You snatch...?"

"They're not going to hand them over, Charlotte. We can only do this with a child who is willing; you understand that, don't you? We don't go around kidnapping kids who don't want to leave. And believe me, there are many that are either too scared, or too deep in the faith, to believe us when we tell them it's all wrong."

"What I don't get is how this can all happen. How can you live here with Paul, and Richard, and Cody on your doorstep and nothing happens to them, or you?"

"First, Richard, Paul, or Cody even, have no idea who we are. They know there is a group of people, who seem to disrupt their activities periodically but look at us. We're a group of old women, who would suspect us? And my time in that cult was years before Richard was born."

A group of old women; vigilante old women. Women whose knees creaked when they stood, who complained of arthritic bones, and still got blue rinse perms at the local hair salon.

"It's fucking genius," I said, finally letting out that laugh, not caring whether my throat was torn to shreds by it.

"It's worked for many years. And that's why we stay here, Charlotte, the cult is here."

"How did Beau become involved?"

"When he left the army he was a changed man, a damaged one. It took a long time for him to readjust. I don't know *exactly* what he does, I doubt it's legal, and I do know, despite his whispered conversation, Kieran is involved somehow, too. Did you know Kieran was his commanding officer? Beau couldn't cope when his best friend was killed. He was dishonorably discharged," she said with a laugh. "He took up with Rachel. Like his aunt, he has a good heart. He wants to *save* people, because somewhere deep inside him, he couldn't save his friend. I'll let Kieran tell you about that time, I only know snippets."

"Rachel told us it was her or me. I can only assume that meant Richard wanted one of us. But for what? Beau said they wouldn't pass me off as a divine child; I don't have blue eyes. Did they want me for their prostitution business?"

Rose nodded her head. "There are still the older generation who believe in their warped version of the faith. Richard tells them he'll give them a divine child, I think, but like I said, there is only one left and she belongs to him. Prostitution is a lucrative business for the cult, as are the drugs."

"I don't know if I can process all of this. I mean, this should be something I read in a crime novel, not something that goes on in real life."

"And where do you think those authors get their ideas from?

241

Mostly it's what happens in real life, sadly. Now, I think that's enough for tonight. You haven't eaten your soup."

"I've eaten a ton of bread, I could do with a rest though."

With what I'd learned from Beau, what I experienced at his house, and subsequently the information Rose had just given me, my brain was about to explode. I was still unsure on how Damien fit in, I guessed he had a hand in finding the girls, but why had he kept hold of me? Maybe he saw just how lucrative it was. Had I always been on the periphery of this cult? It certainly appeared that way. Maybe I was always destined to be dragged into it.

"What is her name? The divine child?"

"Allana. She'll be about twelve now, so time is running out to get to her before..."

"Can you get her out in time?"

"We're hoping so. Charlotte, my sister is still in the cult. She's older than me and she chooses to stay because she helps us."

"Richard must know who you are then?"

"No. We were separated as children, as I said, long before he was born."

There was so much to process, so much more to learn, I was sure. All I did know was, when I was able, I was going to help this group of vigilante old women, and I was going to redye my hair.

I pushed my chair back and stood. "You need a name, like a gang name or something," I said, shaking my head at the thought.

"We are the thorns in their side, for sure. Maybe it should be something to do with roses, since I started the *gang*."

I gave her a hug, placed my bowl in the sink, and turned the faucet on. "Leave that, it will all go in the washer," Rose said.

I smiled and left her in the kitchen. My legs felt heavy; I was weary as I climbed the stairs to the bedroom. Although I'd already slept for most of the day, I couldn't wait to climb back into bed. I wanted sleep to calm down the overload of information in my brain.

CHAPTER 15

I woke late the following morning. I hadn't pulled the drapes and the winter sun, although low in the sky, brightened up the room. It picked out the small, pastel-colored birds that shimmered on the wallpaper. I ran my hand over one of the small birds. They looked like hummingbirds about to take a dip into the head of a flower. For that moment I forgot why I was there. It was the sound of Kieran calling out as he walked through the front door, I imagined, that brought me back to earth.

I gathered a pair of jeans and a sweatshirt, some underwear, replacing the bra in the drawer knowing it wouldn't fit, and headed to the bathroom. I stood in awe at the huge shower. The water that fell from the showerhead pricked my skin. It made me feel alive. My skin pinked with the heat and the steam cleaned my sooty pores. I scrubbed my skin, shaved my legs, and washed my hair. When I emerged, I felt human again. I felt like the old Charlotte, prior to Damien. I had a determination that I hadn't felt for years. For the first time in a while, I didn't feel beaten down.

I stared at myself in the mirror as I rubbed the towel over my head. Did I have the courage and determination to help Rose? To be one of the *gang*? The woman staring back believed I did.

"Good morning. It is morning still, isn't it?" I said as I walked into the kitchen.

"Well, look at you, girl," Kieran said as he stood. He wrapped his large arms around my shoulders, engulfing me.

"Let her down," Rose said, slapping his arm.

I sat at the table as a cup of coffee was placed in front of me. Kieran held in his hand a large brown envelope. He fiddled with it, looking at me periodically and smiling.

"What do you have there?" I asked.

"Something that will set you up for life."

I cocked my head with interest. "Stop teasing her, Kieran," Rose scolded.

He placed the envelope on the table and slid it across to me. I ran a finger under the flap and shook out a bundle of official looking papers. I wasn't sure what I was reading.

"I don't understand..." It was titled 'Last Will & Testament of Cecelia Mercier'.

Kieran leaned forward and flicked a couple of pages over. He placed his finger on one section.

To the wonderful Charlotte Kenny, I leave my house for her to do as she wishes. The house comes with twenty-two acres of land. There is a codicil that gives the tenants of that land lifetime tenancy, all rents to be paid to Charlotte Kenny. In addition, I leave five hundred thousand dollars...

I couldn't read on. "This has to be a mistake, doesn't it?"

"No. Beau didn't want the house, he and Cecelia chatted about it and she wanted you to have it. They both wanted you to have a permanent base, should you want to stick around, of course. I know that Cecelia would equally be happy for you to sell it."

Prior to the previous evening conversation with Rose, I'd have disputed Cecelia wanting me to have the house. However, with the knowledge I'd gained, although still very surprised, I was overjoyed.

"Of course I want to stay, I'm joining the gang," I said, throwing myself at Kieran and then Rose.

I looked back at the document. I could forget about my grandmother's house. It was run down when I'd lived in it, and I had no desire to ever step foot back in Whiteling unless I was on a *mission*.

"We have a lot of work to do with you before you can join the *gang*," Kieran said.

"Like what?"

"All in good time. Right now, eat," Rose said, placing bacon and waffles on the table.

We chatted about the house; I brought up the subject of security. I knew I was still at risk but I was eager to live in my own place. Kieran would sort out what I needed. He also informed me that Corey Lowe, the FBI guy would be arriving at lunchtime. I trusted Kieran to steer me in the right direction, and when we'd finished eating, he informed Rose that he was taking me out on to the back porch to debrief me. She handed him a tray with a pot of coffee and some cups. She also wrapped a blanket around my shoulders before we headed out.

There were a couple of wicker sofas on the porch, I settled in one and Kieran, the other. He dragged a small table between us and poured the coffee.

"Corey Lowe has been chasing the cult for years. He's the FBI's top man in their cult section."

"They have a cult section?"

"Sure, although that's not its official name, of course. Since Waco, the FBI has very different techniques on how to deal with cults. Corey heads all that up. He's going to ask you to tell him everything you know. Tell him everything. He knows about Cody's involvement."

"Why hasn't Cody been arrested?"

"Because they have to be able to prove a crime has been committed and so far, Cody, Paul, and Richard, have been very clever. Richard hangs people out to dry and somehow the shit never sticks on him."

"What went wrong, Kieran? With Rachel, I mean."

He slumped back in his chair. "We don't know. She was abused by her father, passed around, from what we were told. I'm beginning to wonder whether any of it was the truth, though. I don't doubt she was abused and that fucked her up, I imagine, but I'm not sure she was scared for her life, or that she needed to get away. I think she was very much part of the cult and one of her tasks was to find the girls. I mean, think about it. You'd trust her before a guy you'd never met."

Kieran had a valid point.

"Where did I fit into this?"

"By accident, I believe. Your cousin, Damien, was on the outside but he bought drugs from Richard. Not directly, of course. Richard wouldn't lower himself to deal with someone like Damien. The 'accident' occurred when you took up with Philip. Now, he was very much involved. Richard supplied the young girls to him."

"Beau told me he killed Philip, he was ordered to," I said, lowering my voice.

"Philip was in trouble, there seems to be an open case file with the FBI and he might have known about that. Perhaps Richard knew that Philip would tell the FBI everything he knew, if it meant not going to prison himself, so he had to be silenced. I fear that someone who Beau trusts had set him up there. He believes he received an order, and he did, but I can't see the top of our chain of command even knowing who Philip Stanton was. I think Richard has someone on the inside and what better way than to set up someone like Beau."

"Someone like Beau?"

"Volatile, violent, unhinged, and one of my platoon's best soldier."

"I just feel Philip didn't need to die."

"Philip Stanton was a pedophile, Charlotte. Don't make any mistakes about that. He willingly took girls from Richard; we know that for fact. Ultimately, he got what he deserved," Kieran made a point to remind me of something Beau had said.

"What I meant was, why couldn't he have been arrested?" It wasn't that I was believer in the country's justice system, but it would have made a statement to the rest of the people involved. "He could have passed over information to legitimately close down the cult," I added. I didn't care about the cult getting closed down; I cared about Beau taking it on by himself.

"He was the ex-mayor, Charlotte. Do you know how many *important* people escape jail just because of who they are, or were in his case? Thousands upon thousands."

"Where is Beau?" I asked.

Kieran smiled, I wasn't going to get an answer from the look on his face.

"He told me what he does, what you did."

"Then you know I can't tell you anything about him. He's very good at what he does, Charlotte, and it's all covert. Black ops are maybe the words you know, not that we use those in real life," he said with a chuckle.

I was more than aware of the use of the word, 'we', Kieran was obviously still involved, which surprised me bearing his age.

"Anyway, enough for now. Corey will be here in a minute, and I don't want you overloaded with information he doesn't need to know."

I nodded and hoped that I wouldn't slip up.

———

I sat with Corey and Kieran for over two hours, explaining what had happened. I didn't know who was shooting at us, or who Rachel had intended to hand me over to. I assumed Paul or Richard. I asked where Paul was, and was told that he'd disappeared. The state police had visited his office and found it locked up. When they'd gained access, all his files were missing. Not that I was told directly, but it seemed Paul represented the cult whenever there was trouble, he was known to Corey. I also wanted to know what the connection between Richard and Paul was.

"We believe that Paul owed Richard money. We've audited him before and we know there was an initial set up loan given to him when he passed the bar. We were never able to track back far enough to know who gave him the money, though," Corey said.

"Kieran, what level of risk do you put Charlotte at?" Corey asked.

"We'll take care of that. No disrespect, Corey, but you've lost way more men than I ever have."

"Fair enough. Charlotte, I'm probably going to need to speak to you again. Right now, and I hate to say this, but I have nothing really to work on. I know the fire department is still sifting through the ashes. They have a body, we presume to be Rachel's, and we know exactly how the fire started. Someone poured a shitload of gasoline around the property, but we don't have any evidence of who that was. So, for now, Kieran has taken on your protection. You'd be wise to follow everything he says."

"You can't just pick up Richard and interview him?"

"No, not without just cause. Believe me, I've had that prick in my office so many times, and the slimy fucker always manages to slither out of my grasp. I'd love nothing better than to see him behind bars. You've no idea of the devastation he's caused over the years, but if I'm to keep my job, and follow the law, I need evidence."

We concluded our meeting with Corey, once again, telling me to do whatever Kieran told me to. I walked with the two men to the front yard. There came a point when it seemed I should leave, a conversation was to take place that I wasn't to be part of. Although neither of them outright said so, it was the slight glances and the clipped, cryptic sentences that had me give my goodbye and walk slowly back.

I knew it wasn't necessarily the right thing to do, but I paused on the front porch on the pretense of tying my shoelace. A silver sedan sat parked by the sidewalk and just before Corey got in, he handed Kieran what looked like a small envelope. Kieran pocketed it without even looking at it. I heard Corey mention Beau's name, and wondered if the envelope was connected. He also revealed a couple of names I'd never heard of, Gabriel and Mich.

"One of Beau's many contacts," Kieran said as he passed me. There was no fooling that old man.

The FBI paid Beau to do their dirty work? I wasn't sure that was what Kieran meant and hoped I'd misunderstood.

"Let's start your training," Kieran said.

Before a month ago, I'd never had any desire to hold a gun, let alone learn to shoot one. But then, I'd never been in this situation before. For a few hours I stood beside Kieran, and he taught me the mechanics of a handgun, none of which I would be likely to remember, how to load it, and lastly, how to shoot. It surprised me that it actually wasn't as simple as some TV shows would have you believe. Not that I'd watched much TV, but the heroine was always able to pick up a gun for the first time, not worry about whether the safety was on, or whether it was actually loaded, and fire, to wound or kill someone.

I learned the difference between the weight of a loaded gun and an unloaded one. I was given many to test, and each time the seconds I was given to answer became shorter. Kieran wanted me to get to a point where I picked up a revolver and knew instantly. Of course, there were many guns out there and he only had a limited selection. By limited, he had a gun safe similar to Beau's with a range of rifles, some automatic, and handguns.

Had the reason for me learning to shoot not been so serious, it could have been a fun session, and I was disappointed when Kieran stated that it was time to go in. I stamped my feet to gain some feeling into my freezing toes and sniffed back the snot about to run from my very cold nose. I should have bought that coat when I'd first thought of it. I also needed boots. My Converse were no match for winter.

My right palm tingled from the number of times I'd shot the gun; my left ached. Kieran had me using both hands, not that I was ambidextrous but as he said, who knew where my body would be, which hand was the closest to my weapon, when I needed it in an emergency. My shoulders ached from holding my arms aloft, and my stomach grumbled to remind me I hadn't eaten since breakfast.

Rose had been at the diner all day. She scolded Kieran for not feeding me when she returned. I laughed; I could have helped myself had I not been so busy. She had brought back some leftover chili, which she reheated and we tucked in. I imagined one of the benefits of owning the diner was the fact she never had to do a food shop.

"What happens with all this?" I asked as we ate dinner and tapped the copy of Cecelia's will.

"Beau is the executor, he gave me that copy to show you. He's met with Cecelia's lawyer and we need to set up a meeting for you."

"When is he coming back?" I asked.

I had questions for him, and as much as I didn't necessarily want to admit it, I missed him. Those few hours we shared in his basement were the most 'normal' we'd been with each other.

"I don't know," Kieran said.

"What happened to Rachel's sister? Is she in the cult?"

"Not now," Rose said.

"You got her out?" The *gang* had obviously liberated her.

Rose smiled, "We did, the last time we knew, she was in California."

"Beau seemed genuinely surprised by the message I found in that novel, which confused me since Rachel had left so suddenly. I mean, Beau didn't indicate they had problems before she ran. If she was scared of someone, worried she was about to be killed, I can't believe Beau wouldn't have picked up the vibes. I guess I should have thought a little more about that. I wonder now if that message was from her sister."

A look passed between Rose and Kieran. "You might be right," Rose said.

"What actually happened to Rachel's sister?"

"She was passed off as divine child, I think that was the trade-off for getting the start up loan Paul wanted. We tracked her down, extracted her, and sent her to a family we knew in California. We have families that help us all over the country," Kieran said.

"Beau never mentioned the sister at all, I wonder why?" I said, mainly to myself.

"I guess he didn't think you needed to know, not at the beginning. He thought you might have been part of the cult, Charlotte. You're not going to like this, but it was one of the reasons we brought you in close. It was so we could find out if his fear was true, and if it was, to see if we could help you. I guess in one way, you were involved, you just didn't realize it."

"Beau didn't like me in the beginning, I'm still not sure he actually does. I know I remind him of Rachel and now...well, he killed her to save me, and he must have loved her at one point. I imagine he hates me right now. Perhaps it would be best if I wasn't here when he returned," I said, sadly.

Despite knowing Cecelia had wanted me to have her house, I didn't believe it was fair to stick around if Beau was going to be affected by my presence. It seemed life was difficult enough for him without me being in the mix.

"You've been thrown right into the middle of all this, I can imagine that, right now, you don't even know what way is up. Maybe you need to sleep on everything you know before you make any decisions," Kieran said.

I did what he suggested and the following morning I had a clearer idea of what had happened. I'd been lied to, manipulated, and yet had found a group of people who would go out of their way to protect me. They *knew* me, they knew the kind of life I'd had and the kind of life I could have found myself in. I would be eternally grateful to them all. However, I needed to toughen up. I needed to grow up, and quickly. I might have been twenty years old, but I'd led a very isolated life. Despite my background, or rather, the years I'd been controlled by Damien, I still believed there was good in the world. Rose, Kieran, Beau, and Cecelia were it.

CHAPTER 16

A week passed before I was able to hit a target with some accuracy, and I think I'd about exhausted Kieran's patience with the gun training. I could take a revolver apart, clean it, and reassemble it in good time. I could pick it up and fire blindfolded, and I could shoot with either hand. Kieran thought it time I owned my own. He escorted me to the gun store and selected a revolver for me. Before he purchased it for me, I tested it. I liked the feel of it in my hand. It was lighter, designed for women, but with a powerful punch. The storeowner rang up the cost and I noticed a substantial discount was given. Kieran winked as he paid. A *gang* member, perhaps?

When we returned home, Rose was in the kitchen with Ellie, Kacy, and three other women I didn't know. Kieran took my gun to place in his cabinet. I was ushered to a chair and a mug of coffee was slid across the table to me.

"Welcome to our newest member," Kacy said, raising her mug to me.

"Charlotte, you've met Ellie and Kacy, of course. Let me introduce May, Hannah, and Janet. May is a school teacher, Hannah owns the general store, and Janet works in the local sheriff's office."

Janet chuckled when her job description was given over. I guessed, considering Cody was the sheriff, it was a little ironic.

"We meet weekly, each of us has different *projects* that we're working on. The girls wanted to formally meet you."

I smiled at each one. "It's great to have you here, safe," Janet said.

"It's taken me a few days to come to terms with everything but I want to help. I don't know what I can do, obviously, but I'm willing to learn," I said.

"We need some young blood, we're all getting on a bit," Hannah said.

"Well, I did laugh when Rose told me. Not that I thought you weren't capable..."

Their laughter stopped my hasty apology. "So, where are we at?" Rose said, I guessed the meeting had started.

Janet told us that Corey Lowe had taken over one of the offices in the station for a little while, that had Cody on edge. She had managed to give details of Cody's movements, it seemed all the department's vehicles had some form of tracker and she printed off the details. Cody visited one property on a regular basis; Corey was to look into what that property was and whether it needed our intervention.

"So we work with the FBI?" I asked, amazed.

"Unofficially," Kieran said, taking a seat at the table.

Hannah gave us an update on the urgency of getting Allana from the compound. She had an 'in' in as much as she delivered groceries to the compound and had developed a relationship with Rose's sister, who ran the kitchen. Allana had been in the kitchen when Hannah had been invited in for a coffee, something not normally allowed.

Allana was growing fast; Hannah felt she had no more than a couple of months before her removal was critical.

"Does Allana know about you?" I asked.

"No. We can't run the risk that she'd tell Richard if put under pressure. However, we do know that she's not a believer of their faith. Emma, my sister, has been helping her conceal her monthlies."

I took that to mean she had hit puberty and my stomach tightened in fear for her at the prospect of what that meant.

"Corey's old partner in the FBI, Mich Curtis and his friend, remember Gabriel? They're going after the cult. Corey thinks they might need our help," Kieran said to Rose.

"What do you mean, they're going after the cult," I asked.

"Gabriel's wife was a divine child, she escaped a long time ago. I remember her, Savannah was her name. The cult killed her while her child was in the house," Rose said.

"Shit!"

"Shit, indeed," Rose said. "Do we know when this is likely to happen?"

Kieran shook his head. "Mich has gone rogue. He has a cell but doesn't use it. Corey has been trying to contact him, to give him the location of the compound, and try to talk him into leaving it to the officials, but right now, he doesn't know where they are."

"Why would he ask him to leave it to the officials when he's happy to work with us, unofficially?" I asked, Kieran's statement didn't make sense.

"I'll know more when I meet Corey again, but it seems this is personal for Mich now. Corey doesn't trust that Mich won't go in there and shoot the place up, that might bring a lot of unwanted attention, and who knows if they will get out alive, if the cult might get away, or we get exposed."

"And he doesn't feel it's personal for *us*?" Rose had been involved in the cult, Kacy had been abused by the cult, I'd nearly been kidnapped into it, and I didn't know the involvement of the other women.

Kieran laughed. "You're a group of old women, except you two. I don't think he realizes exactly what we've been able to do." He beamed at the women around the table.

Janet had a blue rinse, a floral oversized dress and sensible shoes. Hannah was a typical schoolteacher, even down the tight bun at the back of her head. Ellie was about the most glamorous of the lot. Kacy must have been telepathic; she looked at me and laughed.

"I know, I thought the same!" she said.

"It's the best disguise ever," Janet added.

"But you said we *unofficially* help the FBI," I said.

"No, me and Beau *unofficially* help the FBI, Corey doesn't realize the extent of the ladies' involvement. You have to remember, any girl officially extracted has to go through the FBI for deprogramming. We don't think that actually helps. Think about it, these girls are so brainwashed, so scared and very naïve, we feel it's better they are in a family environment, with people who actually know what they went through. They are the best counselors."

I let the rest of the conversation wash over me. Here were a group of women that had either been directly affected by the cult, or volunteered to put themselves in danger for the sake of others. Kacy and her son, me, plus the girls they'd saved, had been taken into their care without a thought for their own safety and with one common goal. I admired them. I was grateful for them, and I wished I'd known them a few years back. I believed I had something to offer. It might not be muscle, not that any of the others had that either, but I had knowledge and an understanding of what it was like to be controlled by a man. I knew what it was like to live a life, albeit only a part of mine was, where someone decided everything I did.

"Guardian Angel," I said.

The conversation stopped. "There is a rose called a Guardian Angel, I remember my grandmother trying to grow it. That's what you should call yourselves."

For a moment the women were quiet.

"We'd sound like a fucking cult," Kacy said. The women around the table stared at Kacy for just a moment before bursting into laughter.

"Guardian Angels it is," Rose said.

I had no idea how these women had managed to do what they had so far. If I wasn't sitting around that table and listening to their catch-up, I would have thought I was in some kind of TV show.

It was so unrealistic that it was brilliant.

With the backup from Kieran, although I still didn't understand his role, Beau, and I guessed, Corey, it was the perfect team.

For the first time in my life, I knew I belonged somewhere.

———

A couple of days passed, I practiced with my gun, always with Kieran when he wasn't working, and until I was confident I could shoot it. Whether I'd ever be able to shoot a human being was another issue, of course. I returned to work, enjoying getting some normality back in my life, and it pleased me to be welcomed back by customers. It pleased me more to feel my tip jar at the end of each shift was a little heavier.

Kieran and I visited the lawyer, paperwork was signed, and

although I was given the key to Cecelia's house, we were a little way from me actually owning it. Beau needed to sign some papers and he was still missing. I wasn't confident to move into the house straight away, and I wasn't sure Kieran and Rose would allow it, but we did go there each day to clean and pack away Cecelia's personal possessions. I wasn't sure it was a job that Beau would be up to. Kieran arranged for all the locks to be changed and for a security system to be installed. I gave him a set a keys, and kept another spare for Beau. We also arranged for the chair to be brought back from the apartment.

I needed to get a bank account. The money I'd been left couldn't be given to me in cash, and I agreed that Kieran would become trustee. Not that I wasn't old enough to handle my own money, but if something should happen to me, I wanted the money to be used to fund the 'cause.' I was sure that Rose must use her own money to relocate the girls and help them get on their feet.

I was sitting on the deck at the back of Cecelia's, with a coffee in my hand, when a figure walked from the woods. It was midday and Kieran was in the kitchen with the security guy. I was about to shout out when I recognized him. Without speaking, he sat beside me. He looked shocking. Dark circles framed his eyes as if he hadn't slept for a while. His hair was a mess, and he hadn't shaved for days. He'd aged in the six weeks since I'd seen him last. He smelled like he'd been living rough and I tried not to wrinkle my nose. I raised my coffee mug in his direction and he took it.

"You don't look so good," I said.

"That implies I looked good before," he answered, taking a sip.

"You smell."

"I'm sure I do."

"Where have you been?" I asked.

"Working, sometimes I have to spend a lot of time outdoors, hence the stench."

"Kill anyone recently?" I wasn't sure if my joke was appropriate or not. He chuckled.

"No, surveillance only this time."

It dawned on me then. He didn't look like a bum; he looked like someone who had camped out for a week without the luxury of a shower.

"Beau..."

"Charlotte..."

We'd spoken at the same time. "You go first," I said.

He sipped the coffee and sighed. "I didn't know it was going happen, I had no idea Rachel would turn up like that. I would never have taken you there if I thought for one minute we'd have ended up in trouble. I lost focus; I fucked up, big time. I should have taken you someplace not so isolated."

"Is that an apology?" I said with a smirk, not that he could have foreseen Rachel returning, not that he could have stopped what had happened to both of us. I didn't want to let the opportunity of an apology from Beau pass me by, though.

"One as close as you're ever going to get." He matched my smirk.

"Do you think we could be friends? Not bicker anymore, maybe?" I asked.

"Mmm, that I don't know. You get on my last nerve as my dear old aunt used to say to me."

He drained the coffee cup and went to hand it to me. I kept my hands folded in my lap. He gave me a wink and a smile before placing the mug on the deck.

"I'll be back later, *friend*," he said, then rose and walked away.

"That was Beau," I said, as Kieran walked on the deck.

"I saw, thought I'd give you guys a little time alone."

"I think we have agreed to be friends. I'm not sure how long that'll last, though," I said.

Kieran laughed. He sat beside me. "How are you really feeling?" he asked.

"I don't know, to be honest. Some days I feel like it's all a dream and it's a load of fun, and then I realize it isn't and it's all quite scary. There are times when I think I'm the ideal person to join your *gang,* and then others when I feel so ill-equipped, so naïve, that I wonder how I've lived for twenty years."

"That's exactly how the girls we do manage to get out feel. That's why you're the ideal person."

"Tell me about Beau's friend, the one who got killed?"

Kieran sat beside me. "You know about his parents?" I nodded my head.

"For a little while Beau went off the rails, teenage hormones, angst and anger, the usual, because he felt abandoned. Cecelia didn't know what to do with him. She asked me if I could help, I thought a stint in the army would sort him out. He seemed excited by the thought and went through training without any problems. He made a friend, someone who didn't have any parents, and I guess they bonded over that. They were both sent off for their first tour, and that's where it all went wrong. They'd only been out in Iraq for a short while and were sent, as part of a team, to scout for IEDs, homemade bombs. Beau takes everything he does super seriously, his friend was joking around. Beau spotted something on the ground and called to his friend, who stepped straight on it. He lost both legs. Beau got to him and held him in his arms while he bled out. There was nothing he could do and no one could stop the bleeding. But there was a failure, Charlotte. It took too long for help to arrive and Beau got pissed at that. Beau, being Beau, freaked out, punched his sergeant, and was discharged. He had so much anger, and I didn't think he was someone for *normal* society, so I put him in touch with an old colleague."

"Doing what?"

"I guess the easiest way to explain is to say it's a private army, contracted not just to the government but large corporations as well. Say someone was kidnapped for ransom, an employee of a big oil company, maybe. We might go in and get them out."

"How is that a private army?" I thought the only private armies were mercenaries who were paid lots of money to start shit in other countries. I vaguely remembered learning something about Angola when I was in school.

"It's not what you think. T10 is a legitimate company. Half the guys in the war are contractors; we don't have enough soldiers to fight a long-term war. They do all manner of things, and it's mostly on the orders of the government. Beau is freelance. He chooses what jobs he wants to take on; he's a royal pain in the ass, but one of the best shooters I've ever seen. He could hit a hare's whisker at a mile away. Lately, though, he's lost focus and I don't know why.

"Maybe he's had way too much to cope with, you, Rachel, Cecelia. Maybe he's just had enough and wants to settle down for a while. It's a hard life. At any one minute he can get a call and he's off. He doesn't know when he'll be home, *if* he'll even get home. Most of the guys can't stick to that life for too long. Half of them end up in close protection security of some kind," he said.

"And the other half?"

Kieran didn't answer my question.

———————

A hulk of man, with a blond buzz cut sat in my kitchen, Kieran introduced us. It seemed that Callan was to babysit me while Kieran went back to work. He was going to shorten his shifts and give Jack more.

"I'm not sure I need babysitting."

"For now, until we know where Paul is, Callan stays here, no arguing."

Callan sat stiff backed, looking uncomfortable. "Charlotte, I won't get in your way but you do have to follow my orders," he said.

"*Follow your orders?* I'm not in the army or whatever you call yourselves, and you aren't my..." I paused when I saw the look on Kieran's face. "Whatever," I said, hating the smirks I received.

For two days Callan shadowed me around but at least I was in my own house. I missed being at Rose and Kieran's but I'd insisted on moving out. I decided to repaint some of the rooms, not to erase Cecelia but just to put a little of me into the place with her. Callan was useful that day. We visited the hardware store and he carried the paint cans and all the stuff I needed to get started in the den. He caused quite a stir among some of the locals, and I wondered if they thought he might be my boyfriend. I was happy to let them think what they wanted.

Kacy paid way more visits than was usual, considering she had to find childcare, and I wasn't sure the fully made up face, and the skimpy top, were necessary to help me paint a wall.

It was late into the evening when I finished the last of the den. I opened one of the windows to blast through some cold air and rid the room of paint fumes. I rearranged the furniture until it was exactly as Cecelia and I had envisioned all those months ago. My chair was angled towards the fireplace, and the sofa and chairs faced each other, with a small coffee table between them at the other end of the room. The desk had been moved out into one of the outbuildings, until I could decide what to do with it, and I'd found an old wooden bookcase. It would be perfect for that room. Again, Callan came in handy for shifting that. It would need a rub down, maybe a revarnish, but placed against the cream wall, it fit the room perfectly. I would fill it with books. I pulled the den's door closed and took a break for a coffee.

I was pouring the coffee when I remembered the open window.

"Shit," I said.

Callan looked up. "I left the window open, I bet it's freezing in there now."

"I'll go shut it," he said.

We didn't have many conversations; often it was just a few words, or a *command*. I had gotten used to him being around the house, though. He wasn't as obtrusive as I'd imagined he'd be, and whether we had in depth conversations or not, he was company. I hadn't realized just how lonely living on my own could be.

Perhaps it was Kieran's training but when Callan wasn't back in the time I expected him to be, and I hadn't heard the squeal of the sash as it protested at being moved, I knew something was wrong. I did what I was told to do. I pressed a silent panic button, reached for my purse and retrieved my gun. I checked it was loaded and snapped off the safety catch. I crept to the den, the door was ajar and I tried to peer through the gap. I couldn't see anything.

"Come on in, Charlotte," I heard. I recognized the voice.

I kept my gun aloft, held in both hands, and I kicked open the door. I stepped into the room, knowing I shouldn't have but Callan was in there.

Paul stood behind Callan, in his right hand he held a knife to Callan's throat, already a small trickle of blood had started to run down his chest. In his left hand he held a gun pointing directly at me. The gun was slightly tilted and his hand very gently shook. That told me Paul was right-handed. The weaker hand struggled with the weight of the handgun.

"Charlotte, for fuck's sake," Callan said, obviously pissed I'd come into the room.

Callan was twice the size of Paul, but with a knife piercing his throat, size didn't matter. I was pissed that he was pissed.

"This is rather cozy, isn't it?" Paul said.

"I met your daughter, but I guess you already know that," I said. He shrugged his shoulders as if he didn't care.

"And I put a bullet straight through her temple, Paul. It made a satisfying sound as her brain exploded all over the wall," I heard.

Beau stepped up behind me. He wrapped his arms around me, extending his hands until they covered mine. We were both holding the gun. Paul became clearly nervous.

"You're hiding behind Charlotte? Not wanting to protect her now, are you? Maybe those couple of bullets have you scared," Paul nodded toward me.

"No, Paul, this has to be her first kill."

I heard the words; I felt his finger gently push down on my trigger one, and I felt the slight recoil as the bullet was ejected from the barrel at a speed I couldn't watch. I saw red splatter on my newly painted wall, and I was immediately taken right back to the beginning. It arced up in a rainbow shape. I watched Beau take the few strides necessary to punch Callan straight in the face; he fell like a sack of spuds.

All that happened in less than half a minute, I guessed.

I wasn't prepared. I dropped the gun and I opened my mouth and screamed. Beau was in front of me; he placed his palms on my cheeks.

"Shush, it's okay," he whispered a few times.

"You made me kill him," I shouted.

"You walked in here with a loaded gun, primed and ready. What did you think was going to happen? Were you going to politely ask him to leave?"

As Beau finished his sentence, Kieran walked into the room and Callan pulled himself up from the floor. His nose looked broken and blood ran down to his lip.

"You made me," I said.

"Yes, I made you. The first is the worst, it's over with now."

I stared into his eyes, there was no emotion there and I was stunned at just how easy it was for him. He was numb, I could tell that then.

Beau wrapped an arm around my shoulder as I started to shake. He turned his head to Callan. "Clean this up," he growled.

He led me from the room, I wanted to talk to Kieran but I didn't get the opportunity. Beau walked me up the stairs to my bedroom, he pushed open the door with his foot, and it was as I sat on the edge of the bed that I started to cry.

"I killed him," I whispered.

"*We* did. I know you killed Damien but to look someone in the eye and pull a trigger, plan their demise, is the hardest thing you can do. You've done it now, the next time won't be as hard."

"What next time? Look in the mirror, Beau, your eyes are dead, you're immune. I don't want to become immune," I said.

Beau sat beside me, he wrapped his arms around me and I sobbed into his chest. I felt him rest his chin on top of my head. His arms tightened around me the harder I cried.

"It's going to be okay, Charlotte, I promise you," he whispered.

"I don't think I'll ever be okay."

"You will. You'll get over this."

I looked up at him. "Did you?"

He stroked some hair from my face and gently shook his head.

We were two damaged people, thrown into worlds that we had to fight to survive in. We'd seen, and done, some terrible things, separately, and together. A bond had formed between us in that moment. One that would be tested over time, I had no doubt.

"We're the same, Charlotte. One day we might figure out all the shit and get our happily ever afters. For now, we just have to do what we do. But you're not alone anymore. Will you make me mad sometimes? Sure. And I'll make you so pissed as well. Just focus on the end game, Charlotte. One day, we'll get there and then we can be free of all this."

CHAPTER 17

The state police interviewed me. Our stories were tight, it was self-defence and no charges were brought against any of us. Corey visited a couple of times and Beau disappeared again. It was decided that I'd take a break from the *gang*, not that I'd actually gotten started with them. I was happy about that. I wanted to reground myself, work at the diner, and decorate my house. Christmas was fast approaching and for the first time in years, I started to get excited. I was going to spend the holiday with Rose and Kieran, and I secretly wished Beau would come home.

There was a lot left unsaid between us. I'd felt a connection, and was sure he had, too. We would never be more than friends, good friends, I wanted for us to be *best friends*. We knew secrets about each other, which in itself would bond us for life.

Slowly life returned to 'normal' and I'd always chuckle at that thought. There would never be a normal in the traditional sense. I'd killed two men, I'd witnessed things I never should have, and I knew things that could be dangerous to me. I was living in a world that had jumped straight out of the pages of a novel. Maybe, one day, I'd write that novel.

Kacy and I had our first night out together. Although we only spent the evening at the diner, neither of us were confident to go to a bar, it was fun to sit and chat. She told me of her time in the cult, without being overly graphic. It was enough to break my heart. I envied her ability to live her life; I was in awe of the fact that she had kept her child.

"Do you think you and Beau would ever get it on?" she asked.

"No. We're friends, neither of us have the ability to form a relationship. I can't imagine ever having sex with anyone, Kacy. I just don't feel that way about men. Who knows, maybe one day in the future, things will change, I'll change, but for now, my body is my own for the first time in years, and I intend to hang on to it."

"I can understand that. I want company; do you know what I mean? I'd like a father for my child, does that make me selfish?"

"No, not at all. I mean, why shouldn't you have a family?"

Rose joined us for coffee after we'd eaten our meal. "How are my two favorite girls?"

"I think we're all good," Kacy said.

"I think we're getting there," I replied, laughing.

"Tomorrow we're all going Christmas shopping. I'm so far behind this year," Rose said.

There were two sides to Rose. The one that sat in front of me getting excited about the holiday, planning the menu and worrying about gifts, and the Rose that had spent her life living right on the edge in a dangerous world totally disguised by her *old woman* act. I started to laugh and it felt really good.

The following day, wrapped just in a towel after my shower I heard the front door open and close. I froze on the landing until I saw him.

"Will you fucking knock? You can't just walk in here, this is my house," I told Beau.

He chuckled. "I seem to recall there is the matter of some paperwork until it is truly yours."

"Not the point, I have an arrangement with the owner. Knock next time."

"Haven't had your coffee, I take it?"

"I'm not grumpy because I haven't had coffee. I'm grumpy because I'm half-naked and you just walked into my house."

"Do you want me to leave? Go out and then knock?" He stood with his hands on his hips.

"No, I want you to go make coffee while I get dressed." I stomped away to the sound of his laughter.

I took my time to dress and then made my way down the stairs. Beau stood in the kitchen holding two cups of coffee, he handed me one.

"Drink that, and then get your shoes on."

"Why?"

"Because I asked you to."

"And you're my boss?"

"Charlotte..."

I raised my eyebrows in challenge. "Please, can you get your shoes on? I have something I'd like to show you," he said.

"That's better. See, it's not actually hard to be nice." I drank my coffee and found my sneakers.

I was sitting on the first step of the stairs, tying my laces, when he reappeared. I took my time, he sighed.

Beau opened the passenger door of the truck and I climbed in.

He walked around the front of the vehicle, trailing a hand over the hood as if he were caressing it.

"Checking me out, were you?" he said, when he joined me.

"Yeah, of course," I mocked.

We drove out of town and it was as we came to a gap in the woods that I realized where we were.

"Hold on," he said, as we bumped over the ground and weaved our way through the trees.

My heart started to race a little at the thought he was taking me back to his house, a place that had caused me such fear. As we cleared the trees, a new wooden cabin rose from the ashes of the old house. Although smaller, it was perfect.

Beau brought the truck to a stop and we climbed out. He smiled as he opened the door and let me walk in first.

"It's beautiful," I said, looking around the open plan hall, living room, and kitchen at the end.

Something caught my eye. Sitting on top of his dining table was what looked like a piece of metal. I walked toward it. At first I didn't want to pick it up.

"Hold it, it's part of your past, Charlotte."

I picked up my old money tin. It was charred, dented, the only thing that I owned that had survived.

"It doesn't feel like it belongs to me now, does that make sense?"

"It does. You're not that person anymore."

I placed the tin back on the table. "How do you feel, being here?" I was conscious that Rachel had been in this house.

"What was here is gone, along with all the memories. This is a fresh start for me. I'm selling the townhouse and the apartment. I'll live here. I like the peace and the quiet."

"I can't visit you here," I said, quietly.

"I'll always be wherever you need me to be, Charlotte. And maybe you should learn to drive. It has two bedrooms, you can take one and stay over whenever you want."

"Am I allowed just to walk in whenever I want, regardless of what you're doing?"

He threw a set of keys. "Yes. Because that's what friends do."

"What if you have *company*? I don't want to walk in on that."

"Then we'll have a code. I'll tie something to the front door as a warning," he said, laughing.

He walked toward me, stopping just a foot away. "You'll be the only woman here, Charlotte. I have no desire to bring anyone else to my home. This is my sanctuary. Piss me off, and I'll quickly kick you out, of course."

For a moment, he stared at me without speaking. "If you bring a guy back here, that will guarantee a fight, you know that, right?" he added.

"A fist fight only though. You can't go around shooting people for no reason. And you'll ruin this nice wooden floor."

"It wouldn't be for no reason."

"Beau..." I needed to defuse the situation.

He smiled at me. "I know. I mean it, though; it's just you and me, at least here. What you do when I'm not around is your business, but I'll always protect you."

I placed my arms around his waist and he held me to his chest. It was comfortable to be in his arms.

"I'm not capable of a relationship," I said.

"Not yet, but one day. Now, enough mush for today. I want to show you something."

We headed back to the truck and he drove toward Whiteling, passing it, and carrying on for a few miles. He hummed along to a tune on the radio and I watched the scenery pass by. He came to a lane and slowed. Although he didn't turn into the lane, he stared up toward what looked like a collection of wooden barns, with a chain link fence surrounding it.

"Open the glove box," he said.

I did, and pulled out a pair of binoculars, the only item in the glove box. He drove a little way up the road until he turned off and onto what he told me was a farmers' route. It was another five or ten minutes before he came to a stop and turned off the truck. I waited until he'd opened the passenger door for me. He took my hand and led me through a small copse of trees. We came to a small ditch that looked man-made.

"Lie down here," he said and then took the binoculars from me. He scanned the compound until eventually handing them back to me. I raised them to my eyes.

He moved my head slightly, angling me in the direction he wanted. At first the image was blurry. I fiddled with the dials until a young girl came into focus. She was standing in just a white floral dress, bare feet, despite the weather, and had her face raised to the weak winter sun. Long blonde hair flowed to her waist, waving gently in the breeze. To call her hair blonde was probably wrong; it was nearly white.

I doubted she knew we were there, but she seemed to lower her chin and turn toward me. I zoomed in a little more, concentrating on her face. She was breathtaking, just as Rose said she would be.

"Allana?" I whispered.

"Yes. My next project."

"She's beautiful," I said.

"The last divine child."

"When do you go for her?" I asked.

"Soon. I have a plan, I just need to do it before two others fuck it all up."

"Mich and Gabriel?"

I lowered the binoculars and looked at him. "Where did you hear those names?" he asked.

"I overheard Corey and Kieran talking."

"Yes, I need to extract her before Mich and Gabriel arrive and turn this into a fucking shoot out."

"Are they after her, too?"

"No. I don't think they've even found this place just yet. They're getting close though, Corey tracks them as much as he can."

He shifted back slightly; I followed, trying to rub the dirt from the front of my sweatshirt. In a crouch, we made our way back to the truck.

"This is where you'd been, wasn't it? That day when you walked through the woods to take my coffee, you'd been here?"

"Yes. Surveillance, I told you."

"How easy is it going to be, to rescue her?"

"Not easy at all. Probably our biggest challenge to date and will come with all sorts of repercussions."

"Why are you contemplating it, then?"

"Because Allana needs us. Because we need to rid our world of this cult once and for all, and it won't be the fucking authorities who do that."

"I don't know that I want to know too much, I can't think about you being in danger," I said, as I climbed back in the truck.

"Worried about me? That's very sweet of you, Charlotte," he said, smirking.

"You have to sign the house over to me, so I'd rather you didn't get yourself killed before you did that."

He laughed, turned on the truck, placed one arm on the back of my seat while he looked through the rear window, and reversed, at a speed higher than I thought necessary, through the fucking woods.

He laughed, I screamed, especially when he pulled his dumb trick of pulling on the brake and spinning the truck to face the right way.

"You fucking jerk," I shouted, righting myself in my seat.

"Yep. Buckle up, sweetheart, we're about to go on one hell of a ride."

I screamed, in delight that time, as we went off-road through the woods, crossed the road, and did the same on the other side. He cranked up the music and drove us through the woodland, all the way back to my house. I knew then how he was able to just appear from the line of trees each time he had.

He stopped the truck outside my back door. I cursed at the tire tracks across the lawn area.

"You better repair that," I said, opening the passenger door.

"Of course. Used to tear up those fields all the time, can't understand why I didn't give Cecelia a heart attack years ago."

"Do you want a coffee?"

"No, things to do, places to go."

"When will you be back?"

"A few days."

"You're going after her sooner than you meant, aren't you?"

He gave me a small smile. "Maybe."

"Beau…"

"I'll take care, don't worry. You need me. And I need you, too, Charlotte."

I climbed from the truck and knew he wasn't jerking me around with a snarky comment; he was being honest. I did need him, and he needed me. I watched as he reversed the truck, throwing up clods of earth as he did. I shouted an obscenity; he extended his arm through the open window and gave me the bird.

I walked up to the porch, opened the door and disarmed the alarm system. I grabbed a coffee from the pot, although only lukewarm, and returned to survey the mess in my yard.

I sat on the edge of the porch, letting my feet dangle over the edge and sent up a silent prayer to keep Beau safe.

I loved him. Not in a sexual way, but in a best friend's way. I wanted him to come home and annoy me, give me the bird, or boss me around. I couldn't imagine my life without him anymore.

I sipped the coffee, sighed, and then I smiled. I had a home, I had money in the bank, and I had Beau. I was looking forward to my life, with all its drama, because I knew I had the one thing I hadn't had in years. I had a family. That thought made a decision for me.

"Kieran, I need a lift somewhere," I said, when he answered my call.

He arrived within the half-hour and I gave him an address. At first he stood by the side of his car and shook his head.

"I really need to do this, closure," I said.

With a scowl, he climbed into the car. I thought I heard him mumble that Beau would be furious with us; I didn't care. I was sure I'd make Beau furious many times in the years to come, might as well start then.

It took an hour to get to my grandmother's house, to my house. Kieran was reluctant to let me leave the car until I saw a young girl with a child on her hip leave the front door.

"Do you live here?" I asked as I climbed from the car.

"Yes," she was hesitant, clutching her child closer to her and looking around as if for help.

"How long have you lived here?"

"I..."

"It's okay. This is my house, it was left to me when my grandmother died."

"Are you related to Damien?"

"I am, I'm his cousin. And you are?"

She relaxed a little but a tear fell down one cheek. "I know who you are now. I've never met you, but you did us both a favor, can I thank you for that?"

"Who are you?" I asked again.

She placed her daughter on the ground and it was when the child looked at me that I knew.

"My name is Carly, this is my daughter."

"Damien's daughter?"

The look of disgust that crossed her face had my heart break for her.

"My daughter, although he had a part in that," she spat.

"Did he rape you, Carly?"

She didn't answer; she didn't need to. She slumped into a chair on the grass in the front yard. I sat on the ground in front of her.

"So you like living here?" I asked.

The house was outside of Whiteling, although not the best neighborhood, it wasn't the worst. It needed some repair but the lawn was mowed, a range of children's toys were scattered around.

"I do. My mom is just around the corner. I'm back in school and she helps with childcare."

"Are you safe here? I was thrown out of this house by some nasty individuals."

She nodded her head. "There's just me here. My brother might have been one of those *nasty individuals,* but he's gone now. He won't get out of prison, not until he's in a wooden box. I moved in just before he got arrested. I've done the place up. I thought Damien owned it and...I guessed he owed me."

"He did, Carly, he still does."

I reached out my hand to her daughter, who shyly took it. She had her thumb in her mouth, and I prayed that she hadn't inherited any part of her father's nature.

"I think my grandmother would rather you had this house. I'll get what paperwork I can, and then I'll just transfer it to you, I guess."

I knew Paul had managed to find some paperwork on the will and the house; he wouldn't have had originals, so all I had to do was to start with the courthouse.

"You don't have to do that. I mean, I'd hate to move but if I have to..."

I shook my head. "I want to help you, Carly. I want to help your daughter. I do want you to promise me one thing, though. You stay in school, better your life and when you can, sell this house and move on to somewhere better for your child."

I didn't know how old she was, younger than me, I thought.

"I'll come back in a week or so. Let me sort the paperwork out. Maybe I can meet your mom and explain what I'm doing."

She nodded and I watched her smile. "No one has ever done

anything for me," she said.

"Then I'd like to be the first. I can imagine what you've been through and right now, I'm in a position to help."

"What is your name?" she asked.

"Charlotte, I'm pleased to meet you," I said, holding out my hand. She shook it.

I rose, wincing at the creak in my knees. "I'll be back in a week."

Carly picked up her daughter and held her on her hip again. Both waved as I climbed into the car and Kieran turned the car around. They continued to wave until we rounded the corner and were out of sight.

"What was that all about?" Kieran asked.

"I just started my initiation into the *Guardian Angels*," I said.

He frowned at me. "She was raped by my cousin, she has a child by him, so I gave her my house."

Kieran smiled broadly at me. I smiled back at him. "How did that make you feel?" he asked.

"Amazing, empowered, like the past four years of my life finally has a purpose. And I have blood family, Kieran."

I laughed and rested my head back on the seat. Yes, the four years of hell I'd been through, although I couldn't say had been worth it, but all the hurt and pain melted away in that moment. I'd do good; I'd use my experience, initially, to help Carly, and girls like Carly, who were caught up in Damien's life. I was sure there would be others.

"Look at you. Pull down that visor and take a look at that smile," Kieran said. I didn't want to pull down the visor and look at myself, but I did.

The woman looking back was a far cry from the one I'd seen in the mirror some months ago. In a week it would be Christmas, then it would be a new year. I intended to start my new year that very day.

"Stop by the courthouse, let's get my *crusades* started," I said.

The End

OTHER BOOKS BY TRACIE PODGER

Harlot accompanies Gabriel and A Deadly Sin. Although standalones, you may enjoy meeting some of the characters mentioned in this book. You can find both Gabriel and A Deadly Sin on Amazon and in KindleUnlimited.

Gabriel – http://mybook.to/GabrielbyTraciePodger
A Deadly Sin – http://mybook.to/ADeadlySin

How about a free novella?

Evelyn is an important character in the Fallen Angel series and she has her own novella!
Would you like a free copy? Sign up for my newsletter and you'll be able to download a copy...

http://eepurl.com/clbNTP

ABOUT THE AUTHOR

Tracie Podger currently lives in Kent, UK with her husband and a rather obnoxious cat called George. She's a Padi Scuba Diving Instructor with a passion for writing. Tracie has been fortunate to have dived some of the wonderful oceans of the world where she can indulge in another hobby, underwater photography. She likes getting up close and personal with sharks.

Tracie likes to write in different genres. Her Fallen Angel series and its accompanying books are mafia romance and full of suspense. A Virtual Affair is contemporary romance, and Gabriel, A Deadly Sin, and Harlot are thriller/suspense. The Facilitator is erotic romance.

Available from Amazon, iBooks, Kobo & Nook

Fallen Angel, Part 1
Fallen Angel, Part 2
Fallen Angel, Part 3
Fallen Angel, Part 4

Made in the USA
Columbia, SC
23 September 2017